To Frank, Inspired by me time at a law firm . . . Enjoy! Susan

LUCKY CHANGE

SUSAN LAW CORPANY

Susan Law Corpany

BONNEVILLE
SPRINGVILLE, UTAH

The views expressed within this work are the sole responsibility of the author and do not necessarily reflect the position of Cedar Fort, Inc., or any other entity.

This is a work of fiction. The characters, names, incidents, places, and dialogue are products of the author's imagination, and are not to be construed as real.

ISBN 13: 978-1-59955-392-4

Published by Bonneville Books, an imprint of Cedar Fort, Inc., 2373 W. 700 S., Springville, UT 84663
Distributed by Cedar Fort, Inc., www.cedarfort.com

LIBRARY OF CONGRESS CATALOGING-IN-PUBLICATION DATA

Corpany, Susan Law.
  Lucky change / Susan Law Corpany.
    p. cm.
  Summary: An unpopular and unrefined single mother wins the lottery and helps the people who were unkind to her.
  ISBN 978-1-59955-392-4
  1. Lottery winners--Fiction. 2. Mormon women--Fiction. 3. Domestic fiction, American. I. Title.

PS3603.O77L83 2010
813'.6--dc22

                              2010012358

Cover design by Danie Romrell
Cover design © 2010 by Lyle Mortimer
Edited by Kimiko Christensen Hammari
Typeset by Kelley Konzak

Printed in the United States of America

10 9 8 7 6 5 4 3 2 1

Printed on acid-free paper

To SJQ, HCL, and JSJ of RQ&N

and

To my granddaughters, Ellie and Lucy

Other books by Susan Law Corpany

Brotherly Love
Unfinished Business
Push On
Are We There Yet?

ACKNOWLEDGMENTS

● ●

First, there are always people you remember you wanted to thank and left out, so _____ (insert your name here), thank you so much for any or all of the following: proofreading, serving as inspiration for a character, listening to me talk endlessly about my book, buying my book, reading my book, or whatever else you did. Remember that I might have forgotten you, but I thanked you first. Thanks to everyone at Cedar Fort who helped bring this book to life, including Jennifer Fielding and especially my dedicated editors, Kimiko Christensen Hammari and Kelley Konzak.

Thanks to my family of origin and extended family for their encouragement and support. I'd name names, but I come from a big Mormon family, and I'd run out of room.

Thanks to my advance readers and faithful naggers. Thanks to the lady on the airplane who gave me the recipe for Persimmon Pie and let me pick her brain about North Carolina.

Much gratitude goes to Kerry Lynn Blair for her superlative editing help and encouragement, both given in generous measure. Above and beyond the call of duty, she even tracked down a picture of Karen's ratty secondhand sofa.

My kids have each contributed in their own way. Christopher always told me this was his favorite. Shawn made me hot dog omelets when I was too busy to take a break. Aaron was the first of my stepchildren to read one of my novels, and I've never told him how much that meant to me. Thanks to both Scott and Becky for their read-throughs and their willingness to be brutally honest with me. Rob, thanks for not inserting any fake pages about zombies this time when I was about to go to press.

Besides my husband's unfailing encouragement and belief in me, his eagle-eye editing has been priceless. Sometimes I think he knows my characters better than I do. The combination of his insights about people, his professorial and encyclopedic knowledge of everything, and his willingness to tell me what I might not want to hear—not to mention his skill at finding run-on sentences like this one—always helps me turn out a better product. Thom, words fail me, even though I've got that gigantonormous dictionary you gave me.

Last, thanks to my former boss Randy for giving me the idea for this book because of his cheap (and yet potentially rewarding) way of giving the members of his sales team a bonus.

DON'T QUIT YOUR DAY JOB

O n the way out the door after his last appointment, the sign on Bishop Rex Parley's office wall caught his eye:

> Work for the Lord. The pay is not great,
> but the retirement benefits are out of this world.

He noticed a recently scrawled addition: *But don't quit your day job.*

He smiled, recognizing his first counselor's chicken scratch handwriting—not to mention Greg's warped sense of humor. He flipped the light off and closed the door. Muffled voices from a nearby room told him that Brother Greg Andrews was still meeting with someone.

I wonder how many pro bono bishop hours I've logged this week, he thought. Catching himself, Rex spoke heavenward, "Sorry! Thinking like a lawyer again."

Thoughts of his day job brought to mind the many tasks that awaited him the next day. Besides his duties as a Mormon bishop, he had his thriving estate planning practice, and he was managing partner at Frost, Bringhurst & McLelland, one of the largest law firms in the Salt Lake Valley.

Tomorrow, widowed Edna Endsley would bring in shoeboxes of disorganized documents, expecting him to pull order from chaos. His ward members expected him to have the answers to their varied challenges, large and small. His wife and children relied on him for support and guidance. It all weighed rather heavily on his shoulders.

He was jarred out of his thoughts by a tapping on the side door to the building. He opened the door to a breathless Karen Donaldson. "Bishop!"

she exclaimed. "You're still here! We need to talk!" She stomped the snow off her feet and entered the building. "Happy Groundhog's Day! I guess winter ain't over yet, huh?"

Rex led the way down the hall, unlocked his office, and turned on the light. Karen unbuttoned her coat and hung it haphazardly across two or three hooks on the wall. She followed the bishop to his office and plopped her ample backside onto a chair across from the desk. He ignored his grumbling stomach and offered a kindly bishop's smile.

"What brings you out so late, Karen?"

"Just got off my shift at the grocery store and hurried right over." She pointed proudly to a row of pins on her red cotton vest. "I've been voted 'Most Friendly Cashier' three months in a row!" Her broad smile revealed teeth that could have put an orthodontist's children through college.

"Is everybody okay?" the bishop prodded, trying to hide his impatience.

"Pretty much." She fidgeted with her pins and then tore off a piece of broken fingernail, chewing straight the ragged edge. "Austin's workin' in Wyoming. He waits tables this time of year and does river raftin' in the summer. Delia's got her own place, but she's still not the most responsible single mom in the world." She spat out a small piece of fingernail. "At least I started out married." She leaned forward. "But my kids ain't why I'm here."

"Problem with your calling?"

"Nope. I love gettin' the Primary kids to sing!" Karen looked down, avoiding eye contact. "I have a confession to make. It's bound to be obvious sooner or later." She continued. "I only gave in because the guy flirted with me. I didn't think nothin' would come of weakenin' just one time. What are the odds? One in a kazillion?"

Bishop Parley's stomach dropped and his mind raced. Sister Donaldson had committed moral transgression and was pregnant! He imagined that someone as homely as Karen would be vulnerable to any male attention she might receive. She'd married young and divorced shortly thereafter, raising her two closely spaced children alone. They were now twenty-something, so that would make Karen forty-something. Pregnancy was possible, if unlikely. He ran a hand over his eyes. *Oh, Karen, anyone but you!*

"I told him it was against my religion, but he said one time wouldn't matter." Karen brushed a strand of drab brownish-gray hair from her cheek. "Ya know, Bishop, I ain't no spring chicken. There ain't been much attention in all them years since Ray left. I don't get flirted with very often. I let him talk me into it because I was enjoyin' the attention."

It wasn't the first time Rex had wished he could go AWOL from God's army. He wondered if he should say something now or let her continue to beat around the bush until she finally got to the actual confession.

He let out his breath in a long sigh of disappointment. Apparently unaware of the torment she was causing him, Karen concluded, "So I bought one."

Confused, he asked, "One *what*?"

"I bought a lottery ticket."

"You bought a lottery ticket?"

When she nodded, he let out a sigh of relief. "Karen, do you have any idea what I thought you were confessing?" Looking at her guileless face, he answered his own question.

"It was at a store up in Idaho," she explained. "When I finally got to the register to pay for my gas, I asked the cashier why the line was so long. He said it was because the prize for the lotto was really high on account of nobody winnin' in a long time. He asked me if I wanted a ticket. I told him I didn't gamble, but then he said, 'Honey, you stood in this long line. You oughta get at least one. The guy before you bought thirty.' That's when I weakened, Bishop, because he called me 'honey.' "

Rex regained his composure. "Karen, the Church counsels against gambling because it fosters an idea of getting something for nothing."

"Like when I saw the furniture truck unloading new sofas at the Arlettis'?"

"Hoping for a secondhand sofa is a different matter."

"Art and Olive was good to us. Maybe someday I can do something nice for them."

"Perhaps." He continued, "Now as I was saying, you've made an honest living at Smith's. Honest labor is acceptable to the Lord, whether we work with our minds or with our hands, although the world compensates them differently."

"Ya think?"

"It's unfortunate that Delia and Austin's father never helped out financially. How old were they when you divorced?"

"Dee was two, and Austin was almost a year old. Now she's twenty-three and Austin's almost twenty-two. Mandee, she just turned six. You wasn't bishop then, but you probably remember that Dee was only seventeen when she had her."

"So, you went over twenty years with no financial support?"

"If you're countin'."

"You've done a remarkable job of surviving financially, Karen."

"People in this ward helped a lot with that." She hesitated. "Speakin' of survivin' financially, there's one more thing, Bishop, about the lottery ticket." Karen withdrew an envelope from her purse. "I won."

He stared at her blankly.

"I won the lottery," she repeated and pushed the envelope across the desk. "Here ya go."

Rex opened the envelope and stared at the personal check made out to the Winder 24th Ward. "Heaven help us, Sister Donaldson! This would cover the annual ward budget through the Second Coming!" He pushed back his chair as if to distance himself from the whole situation, the ramifications of which he could only begin to imagine. "I can't accept this. Church policy states . . ." Normally calm, he became agitated. "For crying out loud, Karen, do you have any idea how much money this is? You can't donate your entire lottery winnings to the Church!"

"No, that's just my tithing."

"*Tithing?* You mean this is only ten percent of what you won?"

"Yup. I won big. I didn't break the record, though. The guy at the store told me a guy once won 285 million." Karen continued. "Anyways, they always tell ya to pay your tithing first."

"I'll need to check with President Pearson, but I'm reasonably sure the Church doesn't accept tithing on money won by gambling." He tried to gather his thoughts. "Is all the money in your checking account? When did this happen? I wish you'd come to me immediately." How, he wondered, had he missed the publicity?

"I did come here first. I ain't got the money yet. That's why I postdated the tithing check."

"I missed that detail, Karen, considering the amount."

"They gotta verify everything, and then they wanna do a news story and . . ."

The attorney in Rex took control. "Okay, for starters, don't write out any more checks for millions of dollars until you actually have the money. Do they pay in a lump sum or in incremental payments?"

"Huh?"

"Do you get the money all at once, or do they give you some each year?"

"I get to choose." She shrugged. "They sent me some official forms to fill out. I hope you can help me figure 'em out. I have to prove I've got the winning ticket before they do the news story."

"Good. No news story yet. Thank heaven for small favors. Where is the ticket, Karen? I don't suppose you have a safe-deposit box."

"I ain't never needed a safe-deposit box."

"The ticket?"

"In muh shoe."

Rex Parley's kindly bishop's smile froze, and the words came out in slow motion. "In. Your. Shoe." There was Karen Donaldson, of all people, sitting across from him with a ticket worth $230 million in her shoe. He didn't know if he should laugh or cry.

"But Bishop, if I can't pay my tithing, how am I gonna go to the temple?"

"This won't keep you from attending the temple," he assured her. "Whatever you do with the money to generate income, you can pay tithing on that increase."

"Ya mean like start a business?" Karen asked. "I wanna find ways to help people."

"Perhaps you'd like to have a charitable foundation?"

"It's always a good idea to make charity your foundation. The scriptures say if you ain't got charity, nothin' else matters."

Rex smiled at her misunderstanding. "A charitable organization is often called a *foundation.*"

"Oh. Then let's start one of them."

"Immediate concerns first," he said. "This is more in the realm of my duties as an attorney than as a bishop. Call my office tomorrow morning, and my secretary, Camille, will schedule an appointment."

"Okay, do ya got a card?"

"I'll give you the number. We'll go over the forms you mentioned, consider the ramifications of your different options, and explore the taxation issues. The Church may not want any of this money, but I assure you, Uncle Sam does." Kindly, he added, "I'll do my best to help you, Karen, and we'll try to keep the publicity under control. Fortunately, since nothing's official yet, we have a little time. Nobody else knows about this, do they?"

"Austin was home for the weekend when the winnin' numbers was on the news. I told him I won. He said I probably wrote it down wrong, but I double-checked it a bunch of times before I called the lotto people. He went back to Jackson Hole right after that."

"Perhaps Austin still thinks you misread the numbers. In any case, ask him not to say anything to anyone. When we meet tomorrow, bring all the papers you've received." She nodded. "And, Karen, when we're at the office, if you would, please call me Mr. Parley."

"Okay."

"And, um, be sure to wear that same pair of shoes. We'll put the ticket in the office vault for safekeeping."

Before she could rise, the bishop added, "Perhaps we could have a word of prayer?"

He bowed his head as his thoughts intruded. *And that word should be "Help!"*

Rex stood shivering in the parking lot with his counselor, watching Karen drive off in the beat-up, secondhand orange Volkswagen she called the "Rusty Pumpkin." *What will Cinderella turn her pumpkin into by next month?* He wondered. *A BMW? A sports car? A Hummer? How will Karen handle her newfound wealth?*

He turned to Greg. "Do you like roller coasters?"

"Sure. Can't wait for summer and Stake Lagoon Day."

"Being a bishop is like riding a roller coaster—both exhilarating and terrifying."

Greg looked at him questioningly, knowing that something was on Bishop Parley's mind. Rex reached for the icy door handle of his car. "And I thought all I had to look forward to tomorrow was Mrs. Endsley and her shoeboxes."

ANN O. NYMOUS

It was the third time Ted Simon had come by her desk and made an off-color remark when no one else was around. Camille Decker felt powerless at home, and now she felt powerless at work. She knew a complaint without any proof would not hold water in a law firm unless there were other similar complaints. She struggled to get her emotions under control, wondering if anyone else besides her was having troubles with Ted.

Camille blew her nose and looked up, embarrassed to find someone standing by her desk.

"Are you Camille?" Karen asked. "You okay?"

"Sorry." Camille smiled weakly. "We just moved here from Georgia. My allergies are going crazy. You must be Mrs. Donaldson. Mr. Parley is expecting you."

"It ain't spring yet. You allergic to cats? I don't wanna make ya worse."

Camille shook her head and forced another smile that didn't quite make it to her blue eyes. She rose. "You'll be meeting in a conference room. Follow me."

"How do you like Utah so far?" Karen asked, following Mr. Parley's secretary down the hall.

Camille smiled. "Salt Lake has been a bit of a culture shock. My husband's company transferred him."

"Us Mormons ain't so weird once you get used to us," Karen assured her. "And a move can be a good thing. Got any kids?"

Camille wasn't used to people asking that, but it seemed in this land of large families, it wasn't an uncommon question. "A two-year-old daughter, Jordan."

"Pretty name. Is she blonde like her mama?"

Camille smiled and motioned the overly friendly lady through an open door. "Have a seat. Mr. Parley will be right in."

• • •

Karen was soon joined by her bishop and a tall, distinguished-looking man with glasses and graying hair.

"Karen," Rex said, "this is Barry Luskin. My hope is that you will let him help you deal with your newfound wealth."

Barry clasped Karen's outstretched hand between his hands, holding it a moment or two longer than was customary. "Good to meet you, Karen," he said warmly. "Rex has told me a lot of good things about you."

"Barry is one of our best litigators," Rex said, "but he's ready for something a little less stressful."

Rex sat at the head of the table, and Barry took the chair across from Karen. "Let's say I've been reordering my priorities. When Rex brought up your situation, we thought it might be a good fit." Clearly hesitant to share the details of his private life, he added, "My wife passed away recently. I overcompensated for the loss by throwing myself into work, to the detriment of my health. I'm recovering from a massive heart attack. I mean to take it as a wake-up call that my grandchildren still need a grandfather."

Karen nodded, uncharacteristically at a loss for words.

Rex filled the silence. "We'll be working for you, Karen. It's important that you're comfortable with your legal representation. I brought Barry in so you could get acquainted."

"If you recommend him, Bishop, that's good enough for me."

Rex nodded and continued. "Barry's experience is a good match for your unique circumstances. He'll watch out for your interests. He has a reputation for being a pit bull with a big heart. He makes things happen. When people tell him something can't be done, he tells them to get out of his way and watch him do it. If he can't move a mountain, he'll tunnel through it."

Karen grinned. "Let's fire up the bulldozer!"

"I'm looking forward to working with you, Karen," Barry said. "First, let's go over the papers you brought in. Rex suggests we minimize publicity by having the firm accept the check on your behalf. You can then remain anonymous."

Karen was disappointed. "I don't get to be on television holding a gigantonormous check?"

"Karen," Rex said, "you'd be swarmed by reporters, by opportunists and charlatans who . . ."

"By *what*?"

"People who want money," Barry said patiently. "Dishonest people, people who would want you to invest in their ideas or companies, even friends and relatives with requests for financial help. Job one is for us to protect you from *all* of them. We'll set up the foundation so you can donate to organizations or persons of your choice while minimizing tax liabilities."

Karen understood just enough of it all to manage a nod.

Barry continued. "Rex suggests we set up two accounts. One will hold a lesser amount of money from which you can withdraw funds, much as you would from a personal checking account. The other account will be less fluid, funded primarily by investments, and it will contain the lion's share of the money."

"I trust Bishop Parley to . . ." Catching his eye, Karen cut herself off. "I mean, *Mr. Parley*. Anything he thinks is a good idea is fine by me."

"The checks from the larger account will require two signatures—yours and mine or Mr. Parley's," Barry continued. "That way, if someone comes to you for a significant amount, you can tell them honestly that you have to run it by your attorneys first. It's built-in protection that lets you use us as scapegoats when you have to turn down family or friends."

Again she nodded her agreement.

Barry explained, "You know those insect baits you put out to get rid of ants?"

"Yeah."

"This will operate the same way. If you have a relative who makes an unreasonable request and you turn them down, our hope is that they will take that news back to the rest of the family and discourage others from asking. If you say yes, that news will also spread and there will be no end to the requests you will get."

Barry looked at her over the top of his reading glasses. "Rex says you are bighearted, Karen, so as hard as this will be, you're going to have to turn down some of the people who want things from you."

Rex added, "And you can blame it on us."

"I sense you are a little overwhelmed. We'll deal with things individually as they come up," Barry suggested. "Eventually, word will spread about your good fortune, and you'll have to face the consequences. In the meantime, that ticket needs to be someplace safer than your shoe."

"Ya think?" Karen smiled broadly as she handed over the file folder containing a stack of papers. "Everything they sent me is in here." She hesitated. "You want me to air the ticket out a little before I hand it over?"

"Just give it to Barry," Rex said. "He'll take it to the office safe."

Karen slipped off her worn brown shoe and retrieved the limp and somewhat damp slip of paper. *Lucky Duck* was emblazoned in yellow and black across the top.

Barry gingerly took the rather aromatic ticket from Karen and slipped it into the file folder. "I'll be back shortly."

"Thanks, Barry." Rex turned to Karen. "We need to talk about Austin and Delia. It would be easy for you to give them each several million dollars, but I don't think that would be wise. While you might want to provide opportunities for them, like further schooling, you can blame denial of requests from them on us as well."

"Nobody gave me no ten million dollars when I was their age," Karen said.

"Then we're in agreement on that point." Rex nodded. "Now, you need to understand the pros and cons of lump-sum settlements versus annuities—money paid in annual payments over a period of twenty or thirty years." Before Karen could tell him to decide for her, he said, "I know you want to acquiesce to our knowledge and experience, but you're flying this plane, Karen. It is ultimately your decision to make."

Karen's head felt like it might explode. "Okay, but I don't have to decide that right now, do I?"

"No, but soon. We'll need to get started with some estate planning, as well, and we need to talk about our compensation. Do you know what a retainer is?"

"Look at these crooked teeth, Bishop. Does it look like I know what a retainer is?"

Rex chuckled. "A retainer is what you pay to have an attorney work for you on a full-time basis."

This was one thing Karen didn't have to think over. "Oh, I want as much help as I can get!"

Soon Barry joined them again. "All squared away for safekeeping," he told Karen. "So, have you thought of a name for your charitable foundation? Perhaps your own name—the Karen Donaldson Foundation?"

"I don't know," Rex said. "It's probably not judicious to have her name attached. The fewer ties back to her, the better."

"Anonymous would be best," Barry agreed.

"Is that what they're gonna write on the gigantonormous check?" Karen asked.

Rex turned his attention from Barry to Karen. "I'm sorry, what?"

"Ann O. Nymous." She chuckled. "Get it?"

While Rex wondered what was about to be unleashed on the world, Barry responded, "Clever, Karen, but no. We'll have them make it out in the name of the firm because that clearly shows there are lawyers already involved."

"What it says on the check won't have any bearing on how the money is paid out to you," Rex added. "Those big checks are for show. They're non-negotiable."

"So are some of the words you guys use," Karen complained.

"He means you can't cash the big check," Barry explained. "Are we too *erudite* for you, Mrs. Donaldson?"

"I'll let you know soon as I look it up." She turned to Rex. "I like him, even if he's kinda full of himself sometimes." She looked at Barry. "I *know* ya can't cash the big cardboard checks 'cause the bank teller couldn't fit it in that little compartment in the drawer. And I like Ann O. Nymous! I think I'll get some business cards made up."

She glanced at the clock, put her shoe back on her foot, and rose. "Gotta get to work. You'll let me know when I'm gonna get the money, right? I gotta give notice at the grocery store."

③

. . . .

SPRING CLEANING

Olive Arletti had spent the afternoon setting up for the March Relief Society meeting, draping tables with yellow and lavender tablecloths and adorning the room with wicker baskets of spring flowers. As always, Sister Donaldson's entrance was a jarring note in an otherwise beautiful symphony.

Karen's slovenly appearance interrupted Olive's admiration of her handiwork. When she plopped down in her faded gray sweatpants onto the nearest chair, Olive was reminded of a saying she'd seen on her sister's fridge: "Some stretch clothes have no other choice."

Worse, Karen still wore her work clothes—a red cashier's vest from Smith's Food King—over a faded green top. "Hiya, Sister Arletti."

Olive's smile froze. "Karen. You never miss a meeting."

"Come straight from work."

"I see that. You're early. You still have time to go home and change if you'd like."

"Oh, I'm here now," Karen said. "And I got my green on so I won't get pinched for St. Paddy's Day." Olive didn't respond, but Karen continued, "D'ya know I was voted 'Most Friendly Cashier' three months in a row?" Karen pointed proudly to the pins on her vest. Then she looked around the room. "So, ya need any help?"

I've been here decorating since three o'clock. Does it look like I need help? "Thank you, no, Karen. Everything is fine," she said.

Bishop Parley walked into the room. "Olive, I just got a call from Sister Barnes. She's had a family emergency and has to leave immediately for Logan. She apologized profusely and says she hopes you can find someone else to teach the lesson on spring cleaning."

Karen piped up, "Hey, I got some ideas on spring cleanin'. The Good Lord's lookin' out for you, huh?"

"Undoubtedly."

Karen either missed or ignored the sarcasm. "I got time to throw together a lesson. I'm off to the little girls' room, but I'll be right back and start writin' some stuff down."

"I think it would be great for Karen to teach tonight," Bishop Parley said. "She wants a chance to do something for you, Olive. You've mentioned that she always comments a lot during the lessons."

"Have I?" Olive placed her hand at the base of her throat in feigned surprise. *You well know I've threatened to quit if she heckles another of my teachers.*

"She could share some of her unique views."

Olive felt her blood pressure rise as negative emotions surged. *Bishop, you can't do this to me. Not tonight.*

She fussed over the nearest centerpiece, avoiding eye contact with Bishop Parley. "We'll be fine if we skip the lesson and just enjoy dinner and the entertainment. I tend to overplan for the Relief Society birthday celebration."

"Karen wants to be part of this sisterhood."

Olive lowered her voice as Karen came back into the cultural hall. "Rex, pardon me for saying this, but no matter how much she may want to, she'll never fit in." *Just look at her—she even clashes with the decorations.*

"We need Karen in our ward," Rex said. "She is a wonderful example of many things."

Olive was emphatic. "Spring cleaning is not one of them!"

"Look how willing she is to serve." His tone deepened. "I'd like you to let her teach the class."

Their long-time friendship aside, Olive knew he was speaking as her bishop. She sighed. "Very well then, but I bear no responsibility for the outcome." *And I may never forgive you, Rex.*

●　●　●

After the opening hymn and prayer, Olive announced, "First, we'll have our Homemakers' Hints with Sister Potter. Today's topic is reading warning labels."

Louise Potter approached the podium, a basket of products in tow, prepared to shed light on yet another important facet of homemaking. "I want to remind you of the importance of reading labels on food products, electronics, and pharmaceuticals," she said, picking up one of the products. "For example, this cold medicine has a drug interaction warning for monoamine oxidase and cautions that certain drugs should not be taken if you are breast-feeding."

Next, Louise held up a portable DVD player. "Listen to this." She read from a label attached to the cord: "'Warning: This product contains chemicals, including lead, known to the State of California to cause cancer and birth defects or other reproductive harm.'"

Karen piped up. "Good thing we ain't in California!"

Sister Potter waited for the laughter to die down. Somewhat flustered, she continued. "Labels contain much information, from ingredients and uses to side effects and warnings. Please, sisters, read your labels."

Olive returned to the portable wooden podium. "Thank you, Louise, for keeping us informed." She saw Bishop Parley slip in and take a seat at one of the back tables, next to the Relief Society president, Marion Pentelute. He could tell Olive was having a difficult time announcing Karen's part on the program.

"Sister Barnes had a family emergency," Olive said with a tone suggesting great empathy for the trials of Emily Barnes, when in reality it was she who felt as if on the receiving end of a great hardship. "So, in her *unscheduled* absence, we have a last-minute replacement who *volunteered* to, uh, share a few *thoughts* on spring cleaning." She cleared her throat and forced herself to continue. "Sister Donaldson."

These sisters were too well bred to laugh out loud, but Olive felt validated by the many amused smiles and raised eyebrows. Surely they realized this wasn't her idea.

Karen approached the podium, with hastily scribbled notes in hand. "After a long winter of being cooped up, my mom always made us help with spring cleaning."

Olive had vowed to interject substance wherever possible. "I have certain chores I do quarterly and semiannually, as well," she said.

"We ain't all that dedicated," Karen responded cheerfully, "but go for it if that's what floats your boat." She continued. "I saw this book one time called *Clean Your House and Everything in It*. Don't it make ya tired just thinkin' about it? I think writin' books like that is a great idea, though. If you sell enough of them, you can hire a cleanin' lady to do the sweepin' and dustin'. I have to admit," Karen continued, "I never could see a reason for dustin'. You stir it up in the air and wait for it to settle back down. Seems to me you could spend your whole life just dustin'. Me, I have a rule that if the kids write their names in the dust on the furniture, they ain't allowed to put the year."

Amid the laughter, Karen consulted her notes. "You should turn over your mattresses so all them dust mites Olive tells us about will be on the wrong side and they'll suffocate."

Olive interjected, "Just because we can't see something doesn't mean it can't be harmful."

Karen shrugged. "I gotta confess, I can't keep up with the dirt I can see, much less all that invisible stuff."

More laughter only encouraged Karen, to Olive's dismay. Even no-nonsense Sister Pentelute was laughing. "After Halloween, you don't need the cobwebs on the ceiling no more. I only worry about the ones in the bedroom 'cause that's the only room where I'm layin' down lookin' at the ceiling."

She continued. "Here's a tip for you single sisters. If ya trade off which side of the bed ya sleep on, it takes twice as long for your sheets to get dirty."

She grinned. "For window cleanin', my best advice is to wait 'til your husband kicks off and get the Cub Scouts to come clean 'em as a service project." She forged on, enjoying the giggles, ignoring the gasps.

The more Karen shared, the quicker the sisters were to laugh, but their enjoyment of the lesson was lost on Olive.

"My rule for cleaning out closets is that if somebody's life's in danger when you open it, it's time to shovel it out. Sort through everything and take what you don't want down to the Deseret Industries."

Sister Cooper raised her hand. "If you've lost weight, donate your fat clothes."

"Nope," Karen argued. "I say hang onto them. It's fun to buy new clothes when you've lost a few pounds, but it ain't no fun when you gain it back. I'd rather pull something outta the back of the closet after the holidays than try to stuff the back forty into a new pair of jeans under fluorescent lights in some dinky dressing room." She glanced at one of the more substantial women in the ward. "You know what I mean, Colleen?"

Olive gasped, but Karen kept on, undaunted. "Speakin' of the D.I., I was shoppin' there one day and noticed people lookin' at me and kind of snickerin'. Turns out I was standin' under a sign in the furniture department that said 'Large, As Is.' If I ever sign up with one of them websites for LDS singles, at least I know where to go to pose for a picture, huh?"

Karen joined in the laughter—Colleen Cox laughing loudest of all—but Olive's face was grim. Obesity was no laughing matter. It contributed to heart disease, diabetes, strokes . . . *Oh my goodness,* she thought suddenly, *I wonder if the sisters know the warning signs of a stroke! This could be on my head if I haven't taught them.*

"Anyways," Karen said, "back to the lesson. You wanna get your floors lookin' good. What I do is take some of them Swiffer cloths, but instead of buyin' the mop, I just put 'em on my feet and tuck 'em into my tenny runners, and while I fix dinner, the floor gets cleaned."

Rebecca Paskett spoke up. "Wow! That's a great idea!"

Karen beamed. "Of course, my best suggestion is to just skip it all and get a cleanin' lady. That's my plan because . . ."

Olive noted that she cut herself off at a vigorous shake of the bishop's head. She looked suspiciously from one to the other.

". . . because I just ain't that good at it myself," Karen concluded. "Anyways, I hope some of this was helpful."

Olive started to rise. To her dismay, Karen was not yet finished.

"Sister Arletti is always quotin' us that scripture about cleanliness bein' next to godliness. I'm confused about that, I admit. I always figured it meant bein' clean on the inside, 'cause that's what makes me feel closest to God. I just can't picture Him sendin' angels down to check for dust bunnies under my bed before He lets me through the pearly gates."

This time, a deep male voice led the laughter. Olive shot Bishop Parley a "don't encourage her" glance.

"In closing, I wanna tell Olive I'm grateful she let me fill in. Let's keep Sister Barnes's family in our prayers, and I wish the Relief Society a happy birthday!"

Later, in the kitchen, Olive unloaded to Pat Thompson. "I had a perfectly elegant evening planned before Karen came along to set the stage. Now everything is ruined, completely ruined!" She wiped her hands on her crisp linen apron.

"Calm down, Olive. Everybody's having a great time!"

"Even my medley of fruit cobblers won't be well received now. Thanks to Karen, with each bite every sister in the room will imagine the contours of her derriere under fluorescent lighting. And poor Colleen! I was mortified when Karen singled her out. That woman has absolutely no boundaries!"

"After Colleen got over the shock, she laughed as hard as everyone else," Sister Thompson observed.

"Well, I wasn't laughing," Olive intoned dramatically. "I can't believe you're defending her!"

"Olive, don't you see? Karen is without guile. If it had been anybody else, it could have been meant to hurt Colleen's feelings, but being a little on the heavy side is a point of fellowship Karen feels they share. Colleen realized that and laughed it off."

Pat placed the last of the dessert plates on the tray. "Karen keeps us from becoming a bunch of stuffy Stepford Sisters, goose-stepping our way to the celestial kingdom. I loved what she said about the dust bunnies."

Olive threw up her hands in disgust. "I should have known you were the wrong person to talk to. After all, you've rented your basement apartment to her all these years, despite her slovenly ways."

• • •

On his way out of the meeting, Bishop Parley caught Karen's eye and motioned her over to a corner of the cultural hall. "I enjoyed your comments tonight, Karen. But it probably isn't a good idea for people in the ward to know about this whole lotto-winnings thing just yet."

"I caught the drift when I saw ya shakin' your head," Karen replied. "I just figured the cat's gonna be outta the bag soon anyways. After all, I've given notice at Smith's."

"What did you tell them?"

"I told them I struck it rich and was gonna sit around the rest of my life eatin' Mrs. Fields cookie dough. Everybody just laughed. Nobody believed me, even though I had a whole shopping cart full."

"So, you deceived by telling the truth. Very clever, Karen."

"It was, wasn't it? Other than that, I ain't told nobody nothing. But I thought it'd be okay to share my good fortune with the sisters."

"The more people you tell, and the more people they tell, the more people will want to share in your good fortune—literally," the bishop said. "Frankly, I'm surprised we've managed to keep it under wraps this long."

"But if I start buyin' stuff, won't people think I held up a 7-Eleven or something? Besides, I thought my sisters . . ."

"Karen, no one spreads news faster than Relief Society sisters."

"I reckon you're right about that." She nodded her head.

"Also, Barry asked me to let you know that the checks have come in and the money is in the accounts. Any chance you could come by the office tomorrow afternoon?"

"Can we do it in the morning?" Karen asked. "I pick Mandee up from school in the afternoons when Dee works."

"Check with Camille and see what time we can squeeze you in. We want to give you the checkbooks."

"Good deal! And I wanna talk to you about a business idea me and Austin been talking about."

"That'll be fine. Set it up with Camille. And remember, it's 'Mr. Parley' at the office."

"Sure thing, Bishop!"

HAND-ME-DOWNS

Dee took the brochure off her lap and set it on the table. "Imagine me driving this around town."

"I told you I was gonna get my car tuned up so you'll have reliable transportation," Karen replied. "*Reliable* ain't what comes to mind when I look at that, Dee."

"You got all that money, and you still expect me to drive the Rusty Pumpkin?"

"Nobody bought me a new car when I was twenty-three," Karen said. "We ain't puttin' on the dog just because I got some money." She reached down and petted the chocolate cocker spaniel at her feet waiting for a morsel to fall from the dinner table. "Nothing personal, Boomer." She handed off a piece of chicken to the waiting dog. "I ain't buyin' you some fancy-schmancy car to go drivin' around pickin' up guys."

"You're buying yourself a new car," Dee said accusingly.

"Yup, my very first brand-spankin'-new car. It'll be ready next week." Karen stood up and jingled her car keys. "I'm headed to the grocery store. We're outta milk. Since I finally ain't the only person on the planet without a cell phone, call me if you need something. Call me anyhow, so I can learn how to use the thing."

• • •

Austin, who was home for the weekend, looked at his sister across the table. "Dee, ya might as well just take Mandee and go back to your apartment. Mom's not gonna buy you that car."

"You've got a nice truck."

"I bought it myself, used."

"She's helping you start a business, so I think she should buy me a car."

"Mom knows that if she helps me start a business, I'll work hard. She knows that if she buys you a car, you'll just party in style."

Dee relocated to the nearby duct-tape-patched sofa and gazed wistfully at the brochure. "I could picture myself driving past Alison Arletti and her little henchwoman, Heidi Marchand."

Austin's expression softened, and he joined Dee on the threadbare tan couch. Another member of their menagerie of pets, a big tabby they called Mr. Magoo, was soon cradled in his lap. "I wouldn't mind showing up a few people myself." The floodgates opened, and feelings Austin had kept inside for years began to spill out. "Alison's mother was worse. I never thought the day would come when the tables would turn, but here it is."

"The Donaldsons now have more money than the rest of them combined!" Delia proclaimed triumphantly.

"It wouldn't have been so bad if Sister Arletti hadn't been so obvious about the hand-me-downs," Austin said. "Whenever she passed something along, she always had to say something about it, usually at church."

"How do you think I felt, getting Alison's old clothes and having her comment on them? And Mom wonders why I stopped going to church. The kids all made fun of me, and Alison was the ringleader."

"Maybe Sister Arletti meant well," Austin said, "but she just didn't know how much she embarrassed me." He stood for an impromptu impression of Olive Arletti. "'Looks like you've got room to grow in this jacket, young man.'" He frowned. "I remember once when I was talking to Adrienne and suddenly there was Sister Arletti, pulling on the waist of my pants and going, 'The length is good, but it looks like you're a mite slimmer than my Jeffrey.'"

"Adrienne Thompson," Dee said, "the girl of your dreams. Where is she these days?"

"Going to school in Provo." He plopped back down on the couch.

"You and Adrienne had that *Upstairs, Downstairs* thing going."

"I had that *Upstairs, Downstairs* thing going with a lot of people," he admitted. "When new friends dropped me off, I'd wait around before I went inside, hoping they'd think we lived in the big house upstairs."

"At least the other kids accepted you." Dee sighed. "Why did *you* get the straight teeth and blond hair? If I didn't know better, I'd think after I was born, Mom cheated on Ray with some movie star. What did I get out of the gene pool? Besides this dishwater-brown hair, I'm skinny and flat-chested. And, from the few pictures I've seen of Ray, I got the Donaldson overbite. You think that's fair?"

"I tried to get the other kids to invite you places, Dee, but I admit that most of the time, I was just a normal teenager, off in my own universe. Do you know how it felt watching Adri's prom date pick her up? I didn't ask her to senior prom because I couldn't afford to rent a tux."

"You've gotta admit, the Thompsons were always nice to us." She pulled at the fringe of the afghan on the back of the sofa. "She wouldn't have cared, Austin. She liked you for you. Remember the time you two got busted for bear hugging at the church dance?"

"Like it matters now." He turned away. "I don't think I'd bring up the dancing, if I were you. Wasn't that about the time you found out you were pregnant? That helped a lot, by the way. I was finally getting closer to Adri, and the next thing I know, our family has a whole new embarrassment."

"I'm so sorry if my problems affected your love life," Dee said with mock sympathy. "I'm the one who had to go through it all alone."

"You weren't alone. You had me and Mom."

"I *felt* alone. Mom was trying to convince me to place the baby for adoption. You were too busy spying on Adrienne and Brad from your bedroom window. What could you see from the basement, anyway? Were you trying to figure out from their feet whether or not they were kissing good night?"

"It's not my fault your loser boyfriend ditched you when he found out," Austin said defensively. "Or are you still under the impression that he enlisted out of a sense of patriotism? He dumped you for the Army just like good old Ray up and left Mom."

"Not quite. Ray stuck it out for a couple of years at least."

Austin clenched his jaw. No matter how often he told himself it was pointless, he felt rage toward his father—a man of whom he had no memory, a man who had disappeared shortly before his first birthday. Austin had always believed that if Ray had stayed around, everything would have been better. When things were tough, when money was tight, when kids were unkind—Austin had always been able to trace the cause and effect directly back to the father he had never known.

He scowled. "Someday, I'd like a chance to tell the man about the fathers and sons' outing every year where they auctioned me off to the lowest bidder. The year I went with Brother Nichols and his sons was the first time I didn't feel like a charity case." He turned his head to hide tears that still came unbidden so many years later. "He treated me like I was one of his own kids, even yelled at me for throwing a can of pork and beans into the fire to see if it would explode."

Dee leaned over to touch his arm. "I'm sorry, Austin. I didn't know."

When he spoke again, it was barely above a whisper. "After that campout, I used to pretend Brother Nichols was my dad. I cried when they moved away. I was fifteen."

Delia scooted over and gave her younger brother a hug. "I was jealous of you, Austin. The kids at church and school liked you. The kids I hung out with at Olympus thought it was funny when they found out I had a brother on the seminary council."

"And my seminary friends were impressed to learn that my sister was out smoking behind the football field. Most of the kids at school didn't even know we were related."

"Was that your doing or mine?" Delia laughed and moved back to her own side of the sofa. "You hung in with the Church through it all. I was actually kind of looking forward to having a missionary brother. Maybe I was hoping you'd make me want to give it another shot. What happened, anyway?"

Austin hesitated before answering. "Some of it was the money. Mom told me that even though I'd only saved part of what I needed, the Lord would provide. The bishop said the rest could come from the ward mission fund, so I was getting ready to turn in my papers . . ."

"Then you suddenly disappeared to Jackson Hole," Dee interrupted. "There was talk about another Donaldson family scandal, you know."

"*What*?"

"Nobody really believed it," she said with a wave of her hand. "I mean, they might have believed it of a Donaldson, but never of Adrienne."

"Don't tell me stuff like this, Dee, or I'll . . ."

"Calm down, Austin. I only heard it once. Like I said, nobody believed it. But if you're looking for someone to beat up, Alison Arletti would be a good place to start."

"Adri would never have . . ."

Dee's eyes widened. "Wow! You're sure quick to jump to Adrienne's defense. You're still in love with her, aren't you?"

Austin looked annoyed. "Real life isn't like one of those dumb romances you read, with the half-naked woman on the cover in the clutches of the muscle-bound hero."

Dee shrugged. "Sometimes there's another man in the background—the nice guy who gets the girl."

"I may have been the nice guy in the background—make that the basement—but Adrienne has moved on. She's at BYU. End of story."

Dee let it go only to return to her original question. "You still haven't told me what really happened to your mission plans."

"Sister Arletti."

"You had an *affair* with Sister Arletti?"

"Very funny!"

"Sorry! I couldn't resist."

Figuring the story might be the only way to shut her up, Austin continued. "I was talking to Adrienne and Brad Cooper one night. Adri had told us both that she'd never get serious with any guy until he was back from his mission. Brad had just received his call, so I was looking forward to some exclusive time with Adri after he left."

"Good plan, except for the part about him getting home before you."

"That hardly matters now," he said. "Anyway, you know how cocky Brad was. He asked how I planned to pay for my mission, just to embarrass me." His eyes traveled over the shabbily furnished basement apartment. "I'm sure when Mom got the chance to rent here she thought it was an opportunity to provide a good environment for us, but she probably never thought about how we'd always be looked down on."

"No, probably not."

"So I said, 'I've saved up some money,' and then Brad said, 'I heard the Arlettis told the bishop they'd donate every month to help pay for your mission.'" He leaned back and stared up at the ceiling. "It was like an instant replay of Sister Arletti pulling on the waist of my pants to see if they fit. I wasn't going on a hand-me-down mission. I told Mom I'd go when I could pay for it all myself."

"Then you headed up to Jackson?"

"Yeah. I really did intend to work hard and save up, but I always missed church because weekends are the busiest time to run the river. Then I bought the truck and stopped paying tithing. It all kind of mushroomed from there."

"So tell me about your new business."

"I'm not going back to Snake River Adventures. I'm starting my own river rafting business. I found a great location. That's why I'm down here this weekend. Me and Mom's attorney are going up this week to lease it. I learned a lot from working for Chad. I think I can make a go of this."

Dee coaxed Mr. Magoo into her lap and stroked his soft fur. He was soon joined by Colonel Mustard, a yellow ball of fur Karen had found as a kitten outside the grocery store. Sitting at Dee's feet, Butterball, their tan cocker spaniel, made a bid for attention, turning her head and looking up at Dee with large pleading eyes.

"I'm sorry, Austin. I was being selfish about the car. I hope things work out for you." She reached down and patted Butterball. "Life would have been so much easier if I'd been born a dog."

"For everybody, Dee," Austin teased. Then he sobered. "I honestly don't know how Mom's put up with being the ward charity case all these years. I'm glad she's finally got the chance to show them all up!"

UNDERCOVER ANGEL

Karen approached Camille's desk, which was in a small enclosed area across from Bishop Parley's office. "Hi, Camille! I dropped bread crumbs this time so I can find my way back to the receptionist. Ya wanna let Bishop—" She caught herself. "I mean, Mr. Parley—know I'm here?" Karen looked in the direction of the closed door.

"You'll learn your way around soon." Camille smiled. "Mrs. Donaldson, can I ask you a question?"

"Call me Karen. I ain't the formal type."

"Somebody here from your church met with Mr. Parley earlier this week. Elder somebody. I forgot his last name. Isn't Elder what they call your missionaries?"

"Did he have on a white shirt and tie?"

"He wore a suit."

"Musta been one of the elders, all right."

"He wrote something that was in a magazine from your church. Barbara showed me the next day, so I'd know who he was."

"One of our missionaries got sumpthin' in the *Ensign?* Whaddya know!"

Camille was still confused. "But everybody acted as if he were somebody important."

"Oh yeah," Karen said. "We love the elders and the sisters. I feed 'em every chance I get and honk if I see 'em on the street. He probably left his bike parked out front."

"He was older," Camille said. "I thought your missionaries were young."

25

"Nope. They send out senior missionaries too."

Camille pondered this information. "So some of the *elders* really are *elderly?* Well, everybody wanted to shake his hand. You all must really love and respect your missionaries."

• • •

Camille had noticed the camaraderie among the Mormons in the office. She had never belonged to any organization that offered the sense of identity this church seemed to. It was as if they had some sort of radar to identify fellow members on sight—like an alien race on a sci-fi show.

The women dressed alike, as if they had their own department store that sold loose-fitting dresses and conservative skirts and blouses. She had begun to dress more like them herself, partly to fit in—always wise in a business setting—but mostly because of Ted.

• • •

Karen sat across the desk from Rex Parley. "Good to see you, Karen," he said. "As you know, Barry is out today, so he gave me the Foundation's checkbooks to pass along." *Talk about a diverse clientele. A General Authority on Tuesday, Karen today.*

"Barry okay?"

"Just a routine checkup. If he has to be out now and then, I'll be here to cover for him."

Karen put the checkbooks in her bag and held it up for the bishop's approval. "Got myself a new briefcase thingy. It's genuine leather. Do ya like the name of my foundation?"

"Very nice portfolio, Karen. I'm sure it will come in handy. And I'm sure the Undercover Angel Foundation will do lots of good in the world."

"You know it! And didja know I picked up my new SUV today? It's bright yellow with black trim—easy to find in the Walmart parking lot. I'm gonna call it the "Lucky Duck." Dee's car died, so I gave her a choice between the Rusty Pumpkin and a bus pass."

Rex nodded his approval. "You needed a more reliable vehicle. I don't suppose the price of gas is an issue for you anymore."

"Ya think?"

"It's good you didn't buy Dee a new car."

"I'm tryin' to follow your advice."

Rex moved aside a stack of papers. "Barry mentioned that you've put him on retainer."

"Yup! He's already helped Austin a ton—gonna have him up and runnin' by summer—and he's done a lot of research on the dog park I wanna build. We already bought some land, and we're gonna fly to Texas to visit a place called Fort Woof to get ideas. First class."

"I'm sure it is."

Karen laughed. "I mean we're flyin' first class. My first plane ride, and I get to go first class."

"I hope it's enjoyable." Rex had learned with Karen that he had to stay on topic and move her along. "Now, I'll include the short briefings you have with me under Barry's retainer, Karen, but remember that he's your man. I'll have a draft soon of your estate planning. That will be billed separately, you understand."

"For the first time in my life, I ain't worried about bills," Karen declared. "I know you'll treat me fair." She switched gears. "You know how the scriptures say to tell yourself, 'I don't give because I don't have, but if I had I would give'? I don't hafta say that to myself no more."

"No, you surely don't."

"Maybe winnin' this money ain't a blessing exactly—the Lord probably ain't the one in charge of the lotto—but I can still use it to do good. I got some business ideas too."

"It's not easy to run a business," Rex warned. "Most small businesses fail within the first three years. On the other hand, the major reason is undercapitalization."

"Huh?"

"Undercapitalization means not having enough money."

"I figgered you wasn't talking about punctuation."

Rex smiled. "One key to a successful business is to find a need and fill it."

"Like my dog park!" Karen told him. "Even with everything Toni Cironni is goin' through with her daughter so sick, she's been givin' little Mandee piano lessons for free. She even lets her practice over there after school, since we ain't got a piano. I wanna do nice things like that for folks."

"The charitable foundation should facilitate those desires. Just remember that all your 'gigantonormous' checks have to be cosigned by me or Barry. Pick out a few causes and . . ."

"I wanna help people, not just give to organizations."

"Your intent is good, Karen," the bishop said, "and far be it from me to dampen your enthusiasm and desire to help people, but if you start just randomly giving away money, you'll have people following you everywhere you go wanting a handout, not to mention that there could be questionable suitors and marriage proposals."

"Marriage proposals? *D'ya think?*"

"Karen, this is the kind of thing we're trying to protect you from." He picked up his granite paperweight and set it atop the stack of documents. "Now let me tell you briefly how we're structuring the Foundation to minimize your tax liabilities." As Rex explained, he watched Karen's eyes glaze over. "And you need to document everything you do."

Their conversation was interrupted by insistent rapping on the door. "Excuse me, Karen. Only one man knocks like that."

Rex opened the door to C. Morris McLelland, the only living founding father of the firm, who was well into his eighties. "Mr. McLelland, what can I do for you?"

"Did you change offices again, Parley?"

Rex smiled patiently. "After the expansion several years ago, yes."

"Well, stay put from now on! I see you've got someone with you. I'm on my way out. I seem to have misplaced the minutes from the latest executive committee meeting."

Rex gestured to the vacant chair next to Karen. "Come in and sit down, and I'll print out another copy for you."

Mr. McLelland lowered himself slowly into the chair, leaning his cane against the side of Mr. Parley's desk.

"Mr. McLelland, I'd like you to meet a new client of ours. Mrs. Donaldson is the lady you've heard about who recently had a lucky change of fortune."

Karen reached over for a handshake, pumping his hand vigorously. "So, you're the head honcho?"

"I haven't done much honchoing lately. I'm 'head' as in figurehead." He motioned toward Mr. Parley. "Here's your honcho."

Rex retrieved the papers coming off the printer and handed them to Mr. McLelland, who rose slowly from the chair and retrieved his cane from its resting place. "I'll be skedaddling then. Mrs. Donaldson, welcome to the firm, and thank you for your business. If these young bucks don't treat you right, my office is in the opposite corner . . ." He looked pointedly over his spectacles at Rex. ". . . where it's *always* been."

Rex closed the door after Mr. McLelland departed. "Well, now you've met Mr. McLelland." He sat back down. "Where were we, Karen? I think we were talking about taxes."

"How about you and Barry handle the taxes, and I'll start looking for people to help?"

"Karen, I don't want to oversimplify this. It's important that you understand how your money is handled. You need to look over all the financial statements we'll send you and . . ." His words trailed off. He somehow knew it would never happen.

He looked across the desk at Sister Donaldson, anxious to go out into the world to share her good fortune. He sighed. *I'm not sure she even grasps the parts she bothers to pay attention to. Thank goodness she has Barry. Not only can I trust him to deal fairly with Karen, but I can trust him to deal with her, period.*

He rose with a final affectionate smile. "Let's meet again in a couple of weeks to go over the estate planning."

"Yup, I guess now that I'm rich, I oughta have a will."

"Actually, Karen, the most important reason for having a will, and one that many parents are unaware of, is to name a guardian for minor children. That is a moot issue for you now, but you should discuss it with Dee."

"Thanks, Bishop! I'll do that." She stood up to leave.

"It's 'Mr. Parley' here at the office," he reminded her.

"Sorry! I keep forgetting." When she reached the door, she turned. "You think it's okay if I buy a piano for Mandee so she can practice at my house? I always wanted to learn to play the piano. Mom always said I had a pretty singing voice, and I always wanted to learn to play an instrument. Maybe me and Mandee can learn together."

"It's your money, Karen," Rex said. "You don't have to ask permission for minor expenditures."

"I just ain't never thought of buyin' a piano as a *minor* expenditure." She stepped out into the hallway and almost bumped into the attorney approaching Rex's office. "Oops, sorry," she apologized.

After crossing the hall and making her next appointment with Camille, Karen poked her head in Mr. Parley's office on the way out. "See ya, Bish . . . " Karen tried to correct herself and it came out "Bishter Parley." Rex could only shake his head, an amused smile teasing about his lips. "That's one old dog who doesn't learn new tricks easily," he remarked to the attorney seated across from his desk.

Ben Gardner laughed. "Doing a little pro bono, Bishop?"

"Actually, that is our wealthiest client."

"Holy moly! That's the lotto lady? Does she have any idea how much she's worth?"

"I can't exactly illustrate it by counting out a couple of bags of pinto beans."

"I doubt anybody in her circumstances could stay grounded," Ben replied. "In a few months she'll be wearing jewelry and furs and riding around in a limo."

"I don't think so."

Ben raised an eyebrow. "What would you like to wager on that conviction, Rex?"

"You know I don't gamble, Ben." He sighed deeply. "Gambling is the reason we're dealing with all of this in the first place."

"Then let's wait a while and discuss our observations over dinner. It will become clear who should pick up the check."

6

· ·

OFF TO JOIN
THE CIRCUS

In early April, Karen again sat across the large mahogany desk from Rex Parley, looking over her estate planning documents. "I wanna buy a house, Bishop."

"Good idea," he said slowly. "You've rented for many years. Buying a home of your own is a good investment and probably something you've always wanted to do."

"I wanna buy the Cironnis' house."

Rex raised an eyebrow. Ward members Toni and Alex Cironni had recently been forced by medical bills to put their expensive home on the market. He couldn't help reflecting back on the conversation he'd had with Ben. Karen buying the most ostentatious home in the neighborhood was not a good sign.

"It's huge, I know," she continued, "but I can afford it. Right?"

"Yes, you can."

"I don't need that much room," she admitted. "I know they already sold their restaurant because Corina's been so sick with her cancer. I was in the stall in the restroom at church when Toni was talking to Sister Thompson. I pulled my feet up so they didn't know I was in there. The Thompsons are leaving because he was called to be a mission president in Colorado for three years."

"Yes, I know."

"Sister Thompson said that if they find a buyer, Alex and Toni could rent their house while they were gone—to help them get back on their feet. The Thompsons are always lookin' out for everybody, ain't they?"

The bishop nodded.

"Toni told her that her real estate guy told them the house would be a slow sell unless they brought the price way down."

The bishop was still trying not to chuckle over the thought of Karen eavesdropping from stall two. "Yes, they overbuilt, which means they built a custom house that is larger and nicer than the others in the neighborhood."

Karen nodded. "Don't need a real estate guy to tell ya that. Ya just gotta drive by and look." She pulled out a sales sheet with information about the massive house with the custom stonework and laid it on the desk in front of her. "Toni said they'd been praying for a buyer. I ain't never been the answer to nobody's prayers, Bishop. At least not that I know of."

Rex didn't know what to think. On the one hand, it would almost kill Toni to see Karen living in her beautiful house while she rented from the Thompsons. On the other hand, finding a buyer so fast would be a blessing for the struggling family. He wondered if he'd have misgivings if it was anybody but Karen who wanted to buy the Cironnis' impressive home.

"Get Barry to help you," he said at last. "You'll want to begin the bargaining process by offering an amount lower than the asking price. Eventually, you settle on a figure somewhere in the middle."

"I'll pay whatever they're askin'," Karen said immediately. "I don't need the difference as bad as they do. Will you tell them they have a cash buyer? That way they can make plans."

The bishop nodded, wishing he knew how to handle this one.

After Karen left, Rex rested his forehead on the palms of his hands. The situation with Karen was becoming every bit the nightmare he'd imagined. First there had been the media circus. Barry had leaked so many stories nobody knew what was true. One story was that Karen was a front for the real winner and had been given a small cut to act as decoy. Another was that Karen was the true lottery winner and already engaged to her attorney. Those were Rex's personal favorites, but there were several more. Barry may have missed his true calling as a tabloid reporter.

The ward wouldn't be as easy to fool, of course. Whisperings were already going around. Everyone was dying to know the truth. Rex knew the rumors would all be confirmed when Karen took possession of the Cironni home. The ward members, certain ones in particular, he imagined, would have a field day with this latest development.

Despite the name she had chosen for the Foundation, Karen's idea of keeping a low profile was a bright yellow SUV and, if she'd had her way, personalized license plates proclaiming her a LKYDCK. Barry had pulled the plug on that idea.

Oh, Karen, he groaned inwardly. *Why did you have to buy that stupid lottery ticket?*

• • •

At home that evening, Rex collapsed into his recliner.

His wife, Lydia, began to rub his shoulders. "Rex, I have always been used to the confidentiality of your clients, but now that you're the bishop, there are so many more confidences you have to keep. I can see the weight on your shoulders, but I feel powerless to do anything about it."

He sighed deeply. "Oh, I suppose I can tell you this, as long as I don't mention any names. There's a little, well, intrigue going on at the office. One of our attorneys has been accused of making off-color remarks to a secretary." He leaned forward so she could work on his shoulders. "These days, you're better off not complimenting a woman in the workplace on a new dress or hairstyle, but this situation is potentially more serious than social small talk."

"Ted Simon."

He sighed. "This is why I don't tell you anything, Lydia. What makes you think it's Ted?"

"Something he said to me a couple of years ago," she replied, "when I was twelve-and-a-half months pregnant with our caboose, about you and I trying single-handedly to replenish the earth. It wasn't so much what he said as how he said it and the way he looked me up and down when he said it. It gave me the creeps."

"Why didn't you tell me about this?"

"There were other things on my mind, as I recall, like giving birth."

Rex turned in the chair, the massage forgotten. "What did you do?"

"I looked him straight in the eye and said, 'Ted, you're supposed to be such a smart man. Do you think it's wise to make a comment like that to the wife of the managing partner?' " She rolled her eyes. "He backed right off, mumbling something about me not having a sense of humor."

"I wish you'd told me about this at the time."

"I was going to, honey. It got lost in the shuffle when I went into labor that night. It resurfaced now because it needed to." She paused. "Is it Camille he's bothering? She seemed upset about something the last time I dropped by the office." She stopped herself. "I know you can't say anything. She did seem upset, though. Maybe I'll stop by and take her to lunch sometime. Don't worry. You know I won't bring up anything about this. She just seems like she needs a friend right now."

"I think you're right. And I know I can count on your discretion," he added.

"Now if only we could say that same thing about Ted. It's men like him that make me appreciate what I've got," Lydia said. She reached down and kissed the top of her husband's head. "You're a good man, Charlie Brown."

He reached up and took her hand. "And you are the little red-headed girl of my dreams."

A MIXED BLESSING

Karen joined Toni and Alex in front of the elevator after leaving the title office. The elevator doors opened, and the three of them boarded.

Karen patted Toni's arm. Her eyes were red and puffy from crying. "Ain't it great ya sold your house in time to rent from the Thompsons?"

When Toni broke into fresh tears, Karen turned to Alex. "You know what she needs? This woman needs a dose of Mrs. Fields cookie dough!"

Toni managed a weak smile. "Is that a kind of over-the-counter antidepressant?"

"No prescription needed!"

Parting ways with them in the parking lot, Karen waved. "I'll bring over that cookie dough after we both get settled. Got some in the freezer."

As soon as Toni was into the passenger seat of their car, the floodgates opened. "Oh, Alex! How can I stand it? Watching Karen Donaldson, of all people, live in my dream house? What more can God ask of me?"

"Much more, I'm sure," her husband replied gently. "It's a house, Toni. It's a blessing that we found a buyer so quickly and that another home in the same ward is available. We won't be uprooted for another three years. By then, I'm hopeful both our daughter and our finances will be in recovery. The Thompsons' home is very nice."

"Not compared to the one we're leaving." She wiped at the tears on her cheeks. "I'm not sure staying in the same ward is a blessing. Too many people will enjoy watching our comedown."

"Yes, honey, and I know exactly who they are. If the misfortunes of others are what they take joy in, we can only hope that someday they have the opportunity to bring such joy to others." He started the car and pulled out of the parking space. "I'm trying to convince myself that this is an opportunity for us to show grace under pressure."

Toni frowned, still caught up in her negative thoughts. "Karen wants to bring me cookie dough? I think she's serving up a big ol' slice of humble pie! You know what I mean, Colleen?"

"Say what?"

"Just a new saying that's going around Relief Society. I don't have the energy or inclination to explain it. Suffice it to say, Karen was involved."

Alex signaled to turn onto the street. "If humble pie is what's on the menu, maybe we better dig in."

"What in the world do you mean by that?"

Alex kept the brake on and turned to his wife. "I can't help feeling like all these trials are putting me through a kind of emotional chemotherapy to kill my pride. Selling the restaurant and still working there as manager; selling the house and yet living nearby. It's all part of the refining process. Corina's cancer has forced us to realize what is truly important."

"Oh, Alex, I know." Toni sighed. "But our gorgeous home! Our Christmas card every year with the whole family posing by the fountain."

"There's definitely been some nausea involved," he allowed, pulling out of the parking lot at last. "It wasn't easy for me to sign over our home to Sister Donaldson. You know how hard I worked with the architect, designing that house and yard. But then I looked at her, sitting there beaming like she was lit from the inside out, and I had a strong impression she honestly did this to help us out."

"A part of me believes that, Alex, but . . ."

"Do you realize how long that house might have been on the market in this economy? What a blessing it is to have found a cash buyer. We didn't have to wait around forever or have a deal that fell through because somebody couldn't qualify for their loan. No one else would have paid our asking price."

Toni sighed again. "Yes, that's all true. And this proves it's true that Karen won the lottery," Toni added. "Nobody believed the rumors. I mean, there she was, still wearing that red vest with all the little pins like it was designed by Ralph Lauren, same old ponytail, same old Fruit Loops T-shirt and worn-out shoes. Seriously, Alex, seventy-five percent of that woman's wardrobe consists of freebie advertising T-shirts from grocery store suppliers. Most women would have been in a high-end department store ten minutes after the numbers matched."

Alex laughed. "I know *you* would have, sweetheart." He patted her knee. "It will be interesting to see what she does next."

"Oh, Alex, I don't want to watch that train wreck! She'll let her dogs and cats run rampant through my prize-winning flower gardens. My daffodils are coming up so beautifully this year. She'll probably hang a velvet Elvis painting in the master bedroom. Where I had the grand piano, she'll . . ."

Alex interrupted. "Toni, it isn't our house anymore. If she puts a foosball table where you had the baby grand, so be it."

"I will never set foot in that house while she owns it! You can't expect that of me, Alex. No one can!"

When he spoke again, his voice was firm. "You need to dwell on the positive, Toni, or this will eat you up. The Thompsons have been good to us, renting us their home for a more-than-fair price and putting their things in storage so we can move in and feel at home while they're gone. We still *have* a home, Toni."

"Not that 'the glass is half full' thing again! The next person who says that to me is going to get the contents of that glass poured over his head!"

Alex continued in a firm tone. "Facing the possibility of losing Corina has made me realize that today is all we really have. We have to enjoy our daughter—all our kids—today. We have to love each other today. Lots of people are taking a step down right now. The kids will take their cues from us, honey. We are going to face this with dignity, hope, and gratitude."

Alex glanced in the rearview mirror and pulled off the road. He turned to face his wife. "I have an overwhelming desire to kiss you right now and tell you how much I love you and what a faithful, caring companion you have been all these years, what a wonderful mother you are to our children, and how dedicated you are to the well-being of our family."

Tears of a different sort welled in Toni's eyes. "Oh, Alex! If only I were half the things you've always thought I was. I'm so weak sometimes. You have no idea."

"I beg to differ. I know your weaknesses better than anyone else on earth, and I love you in spite of them." He leaned across the seat and took his wife's face in his hands, looking deep into her eyes. "I love you, Toni." He kissed her gently, pulling her close and stroking the long, dark hair that most women her age could not still wear and look good. "Let's sit here for a few minutes and make the rest of the world go away."

KAREN MOVES IN

Karen thanked the elders quorum moving crew for their help. "As long as we've got the beds in and the big pieces of furniture, we're okay. Austin can help me get the rest of the boxes with his truck." She grinned. "Sorry about the reporters. My attorney said this would probably happen. Hey, maybe it'll make you all famous, huh?"

Austin stood transfixed, looking at the house.

"Thanks for coming down to help me move in," Karen said.

"Are you kidding?" Austin came alive. "Do you think I'd miss the chance to see the looks on people's faces when you moved in here? How many bedrooms does it have? Have many square feet is it? And the Cirronis will still be living in the ward while you live in their big fancy house. That's the best part!"

"Austin, didja think it was right how people treated us like they were better than us because they had money?"

"You know I didn't, Mom. That's why I'm so excited that—"

"Then why do you think it would be right for us to act like we're the bees knees because I've got a kazillion dollars? Ain't it the exact same thing?"

He sighed. "Okay, you're right. I know you're right, but dang, you're raining on my parade, Mom. And not just any parade. You're raining on my Macy's Thanksgiving Day Parade."

"How about you go back to the apartment and get the last few boxes before you get any wetter?"

"Okay, sure. I'm going. I'm going."

Karen went into the kitchen through the door adjoining the garage as Austin drove away. Wide-eyed, she looked around once more. She had only seen kitchens like this in the pages of magazines. *I can't believe this is all really mine.*

She opened a box marked "kitchen" and took out a neon-green plastic cup. She felt as if she did not dare touch anything. She pressed the cup against the ice dispenser on the outside of the refrigerator door and watched as crystal clear cubes popped into her cup. Then she switched the button to "crushed" and got a second layer of ice.

Wow! Now I gotta decide which I like best—cubed or crushed. I don't know how many more of life's big decisions I can take. She pressed the cup against another lever to fill it with cold, sparkling water. "Zippity-doo-dah! This is the life!"

Karen opened the freezer and took out a box of Mrs. Fields cookie dough, leaving several more boxes of cookie dough, two pot pies, half a bag of fish sticks, and a bag of frozen corn. She set it on the granite countertop, opened the plastic wrapper, and reached in for a couple of chunks of ready-to-bake dough. The magnet already stuck to the front of the fridge said it all: "Life is short. Eat dessert first."

She opened a cupboard and noticed the three thin dividers. *Wow! Look at this! One cupboard just for cookie sheets!* Water and treat in hand, Karen headed for the sofa. It looked shabby and forlorn in the spacious living room. The ornate built-in shelves on either side of the marble fireplace yawned empty, crying out to be filled with expensive collectibles. Karen spoke to the sofa. "You look as outta place here as I do. But you're still as comfortable as any sofa I've ever met."

She looked around for a pillow but spotted only a pile of dish towels. She grabbed them, stuffed them under her head, and stretched out, setting her drink on the nearby end table. Closing her eyes, Karen nibbled on the cookie dough.

A feeling of gratitude overcame her. *Never again will I have to spend the day standin' on my feet checkin' out groceries. I can go around helpin' people instead. This is gonna be so fun!*

Karen opened her eyes to look at the collection of gift cards that covered the ancient coffee table. She had spent an entire day purchasing the gift cards, going around to different stores in an effort not to draw too much attention to her expenditures.

The result was a large assortment of cards for everything from airfare to home improvement stores. She had cards for video rentals, office supplies, groceries, books, baby stuff, gas, and a wide assortment of all-purpose cards loaded with different amounts of money.

Now when I see someone who needs help, I can give them one of these. That way I won't give money to someone who won't spend it on what they need, and I don't hafta carry around a lot of cash.

A sudden thought struck. *I could buy one of those safari vests with all the pockets.* Karen took another bite of cookie dough and chewed slowly. She sighed contentedly. *Now I can buy as much Mrs. Fields cookie dough as I want—the best stress-reliever on the planet.*

At that thought, she jumped up from the sofa. "I can't believe I almost forgot! What will Toni think if I don't come through?"

Besides the cookie dough, she located the hat she had crocheted and looked around for the stuffed cat she'd doctored up for Corina.

• • •

The Cironnis were clearing the dinner table when the doorbell rang. Alex opened the door to a smiling Sister Donaldson, a red and white box in hand.

"Who is it, honey?" Toni asked.

Karen piped up. "I didn't forget ya!"

"Of course you didn't," Toni said under her breath. "Come in, Karen."

"I see you guys are a little more moved in than I am," Karen observed. "Of course, you got a head start on me." She held out the box to Toni, who took it and headed toward the kitchen. Karen padded along behind and watched as she opened the freezer door.

"I'll bake these for the children. I'm sure they'll be very grateful, Karen."

"Oh, no!" Karen objected. "That ain't how it works. No sirree bob! Brother Cironni, get your wife over there to the sofa and put one of them big fluffy pillows under her head. Then get her a nice cold glass of milk." As he complied, Karen retrieved the cookie dough from the freezer and pulled an ottoman alongside the sofa where Toni reclined, duly propped up by pillows.

Alex looked on, unable to keep the grin from his face.

Karen opened the box and tore open the plastic wrap surrounding the dough. "Now you just reach right in there and grab yourself a hunk. You don't even need a spoon 'cause they come in little balls, ready to plop down on the cookie sheet. Sister Arletti would turn over in her grave if she saw this—except that she's still alive."

Toni couldn't repress a smile in spite of herself. Karen held out the box. "Well? Go ahead! By the way, I sure do love that automatic ice and water thingy on the front of the fridge. It sure beats havin' to wrestle ice cubes outta plastic trays." Back to the matter at hand, she added, "So go ahead, Toni. Dig in!"

"Oh, what the hay!" Toni reached into the box for two clumps of chilled cookie dough. "Don't make me do this alone, Karen. I know how much you love the stuff."

"Don't mind if I do." Karen reached in and took a small clump for herself.

Toni took a tentative bite. "My mother used to whack us with a wooden spoon if we came close to her cookie dough."

Karen chomped away. "Think of it as feedin' your inner child."

How long before my inner child has a weight problem like yours? Toni wondered. She took another bite, this time a larger one. "You know, I think you're onto something, Karen. My inner child is quite enjoying this. In fact, I am secretly glad the children aren't around so I don't have to share."

"Speakin' of your inner child," Karen said, "I was with Mandee the other day at one of them play places with the tubes and the balls, wishin' I wasn't a grown-up so I could kick my shoes off and play."

"You're rich enough to build your own, Karen," Toni observed.

"Ya think? Bishop Parley said the key to a successful business is to find a need and fill it, do something nobody else is doing."

Toni sat up. "That's definitely something no one would think of." She turned to her husband. "Why didn't *you* buy a lotto ticket, Alex? It's much more fun spending someone else's money." She turned back to Karen. "You could have themed rooms and cater grown-up birthday parties."

Karen took another bite of cookie dough and talked as she chewed. "What a great idea!"

Toni was only getting started. "You could have an over-the-hill theme in one room and paint vultures all over the walls." She reached into the bag for another piece of cookie dough.

Karen continued. "We could have a gift shop with all kinds of over-the-hill gag gifts." She beamed. "Thanks for the idea. I'll be sure to give you a free birthday party after I build it. Gotta finish my dog park first." She rose. "I don't want to overstay my welcome. I ain't in no hurry to get everything put away back at the house, but I gotta at least find my toothbrush."

"Dog park?" Toni asked.

"Up in Heber. I'll tell you all about it one of these days. By the way, our dogs sure are happy to have a nice fenced-in yard. Speakin' of dogs, how's George? He still got the mange?"

"The vet is doing what he can," Alex told her. "Funny thing is his fur started falling out just as Corina started losing her hair from chemotherapy. She's convinced he shed out of sympathy."

"She made a list of service projects, you know," Toni said quietly. "Things she wanted to do before she . . ." Toni stopped herself short of the word. "One of them was to rescue an animal from the pound. I wasn't thrilled," Toni admitted, "but even though George is as ugly as sin, he's been a blessing, so therapeutic for Corina."

"If you ask me," Karen said, "a four-legged shrink's the best kind."

"You can't beat them for maintaining confidentiality," Toni observed.

"I bet George really did lose his hair so Corina wouldn't feel so alone," Karen said. "That reminds me. I've been workin' on this for Corina."

She held up a stuffed cat in a knitted cap. "I ain't knitted much since I was in Primary. The first time, I mean." She reached into her pocket. "I made a matchin' hat for Corina. I bought this fuzzy cat and gave him a haircut. See? Take off his cap and he's bald too. Then I knitted 'em both matchin' caps. I was thinkin' I was pretty clever, but it looks like the dog came up with the idea first." She laughed. "Scooped by a dog. When it comes to dogs, usually it's me doin' the scoopin'."

Toni forced a smile as an image of dog doo on her polished floors came to mind.

Karen noted the pained look on Toni's face. "My knittin' is probably a little lopsided, but it ain't too bad."

"Corina will love it," Toni assured her. "Thank you, Karen."

"I call him Kimo Kat. K-I-M-O. He's Hawaiian, you see. I might name a kitty of my own Kimo one day. I think Miss Scarlett is expecting. She's a bit of a floozie. With all this excitement goin' on in my life, I sort of forgot to get her in to the vet so she could have a career instead of motherhood."

"You mean it isn't Rhett's?" Toni asked.

"Nope. It's probably Colonel Mustard. It couldn't be Mister Magoo. We'll see who the kittens look like before we bring a paternity suit."

Toni's face clouded over again at the reminder of how many animals and litter boxes now occupied the showplace that had been her pride and joy.

Karen stooped over and gave Toni an awkward hug. "See you Sunday."

Toni remembered her manners. "Thanks for the cookie dough, Karen, and for the stuffed animal."

Toni rose and walked Karen to the door, thanked her again, and then returned to the sofa. She gestured for Alex to join her.

He sat on the end of the sofa, cradling his wife's feet in his lap. Picking up the red and white box from the end table, Toni sighed. "Karen Donaldson, multi-millionaire, and her menagerie live in our home." She held out the box. "Have some raw cookie dough, Alex. It'll make you feel better."

OUT OF THE BAG

Ignoring the pained look on the salesman's face, the overweight lady in the navy blue sweatpants and tacky Orange Crush T-shirt stretched out on yet another sofa, without even bothering to remove her scruffy brown shoes.

"I still ain't found one as comfortable as my sofa at home."

"Ma'am, you've been prone on every sofa on the showroom floor."

"Sorry, but I ain't *prone* to buyin' any of 'em. I'll just get another roll of duct tape for back-up repairs. Good looks is overrated."

You would know, he thought.

"I'll take comfortable any day." Karen struggled to sit up. "Wanna give me a hand here?"

Reluctantly, the salesman reached down to pull her to a sitting position.

"Thanks. I was kinda like a potato bug stuck on his back, huh?"

His smile was patronizing, his remarks pointed. "Is there anything *else* I can show you?"

Karen ignored his attitude. "Nah, I'll just look around a little more," she responded cheerily.

As she was ready to lie back for a serious mattress test, she overheard a husband and wife on the other side of a thin room divider.

"I know the youth bed is cheaper," the woman said, "but if we get a full-size bed, it can double as a guest bed when my folks come for the baby's blessing. When the baby is older, the two girls can share the bed."

"A larger bed isn't in the budget right now."

Karen rummaged in her purse and pulled out one of the prepaid credit cards. She stood up and walked nonchalantly around the divider. "Didn't mean to be listenin', but I can't help but think you oughta get the bigger bed. Here." She handed them the credit card. "Maybe this'll help. It's got a thousand bucks on it. Enough to get some extras even."

"I don't understand," the man said. "Why are you doing this?"

"Because I can." Karen smiled. "Ya never know. Maybe I'm one of the Three Nephites in drag."

• • •

A few minutes later, a salesman wrote up the young couple's order. "You have $127.42 left on your card."

The husband gaped at his wife. "It's for real!"

She turned to the salesman. "A woman in an orange T-shirt just walked up and gave that card to us."

"Orange Crush?" the salesman asked. "Was she short, sort of plumpish, with light brown hair?"

"Yes, that's the one."

"Go figure." He shook his head and finished the transaction. Returning to his desk, he opened that morning's *Salt Lake Tribune*. There was yet another story about the mysterious lottery winner, this time showing a picture of the magnificent home she'd purchased. He read the first few paragraphs and turned the page to where the story continued.

"It can't be!" he exclaimed. There she was, the sofa tester, unloading a box from the back of a pickup truck. "And I work on commission!"

OUT OF THE WOODWORK

Karen took a seat in Barry's office. "I got a visit from a couple of my cousins today."

"After the latest article in the paper, I expected you'd receive a little extra attention."

"It ain't what you think," she said. "Sure, I've had a few calls from old school friends and long-lost relatives. I done what you said, told them my attorneys have to approve everything." She smiled. "You're right. That puts the kibosh on things."

"Good. So, tell me about your cousins."

"Victor and Jerry—they're kinda the Harley-ridin' Hell's Angels type. They offered to come by my house every morning, them or some of their friends, to make sure nobody's botherin' me."

"'*Kinda*' Hell's Angels?" Barry repeated. "Isn't that like being a 'little bit' pregnant?"

"Okay," Karen conceded. "They're all-the-way Hell's Angels."

"What did they want?"

She shrugged. "Nothin'. They said I could donate to their toy collection drive at Christmas if I wanted to."

Barry laughed. "Perhaps you should take them up on it."

"I did. They came by this morning and scared off a few Charlotte Anns." At the quizzical look on Barry's face, she added, "You know, people trying to take advantage of me."

"The word is *charlatans*, Karen."

"Too late. That's what we call 'em now. I tried to look up aer-i-o-dite. I couldn't find it nowhere in my dictionary."

"Er-*YOO*-dite," Barry corrected her pronunciation.

"I don't have a gigantonormous dictionary that has to have its own piece of furniture like you do."

Barry walked over to the dictionary open on the stand and thumbed through it until he found the right page. He ran his finger down the list of words. "E-R-U-D-I-T-E." He read the definition. "'Characterized by great knowledge; learned or scholarly.'"

"So if I was *er-YOO-dite,* I would have known the definition."

"You underestimate yourself. You're a bright lady. A little work on your grammar, a few classes in something that interests you, and you might surprise yourself."

"I'd surprise everybody." She pulled a few papers from her briefcase. "I got two brothers, Lyle and Roger," she informed her attorney. "They ain't asked me for nothin', but I told them I wanted to pay off their mortgages. Here are the papers showin' how much they owe."

"That's very generous of you."

"Then if they ever need sumpthin, they can borrow against their homes. They helped me as much as they could when Ray left. My mom's home is paid off. She's a stubborn old goat that ain't gonna take nothin' from nobody, but I'll make sure she's taken care of."

"Your father is deceased?"

"Died seven years ago."

"Karen, helping your immediate family is fine. My hope, though, is that you can do your good works without further publicity. I've been getting calls lately from a very persistent tabloid reporter. His publisher has offered quite a sum for an exclusive about you."

"Won't this all die down soon?"

"You're an everywoman, Karen. Everything you do is newsworthy."

"I'm a *celebrity*? Will there be pictures showing me trying to act just like everybody else?" She held up an imaginary magazine. "'Julia Roberts Walks Her Dog.' 'Brad Pitt Takes Out the Trash.' 'Karen Donaldson Buys a Twinkie.' Wow!"

"Fame will get old fast, Karen. Trust me."

• • •

Jerry and Victor parked their intimidating Harleys in the circular drive and followed Karen into the house. A few minutes later, Jerry wiped muffin crumbs from his mustache and said, "What's up with all the beat-up cars cruising your house, Cousin Karen?"

"Last week I bought a new van for a family I met at Costco. They had kids crammed every which way into an old car that had overheated in the parking lot." She shrugged. "I don't know how anybody found out about that. I especially don't need Dee knowin' I bought somebody else a new car."

"Some stranger buys you a new car, you tell people about it. We're on the job as long as you think you need us. Thanks for the muffins. We'll go out there, rev our engines some more, clear the place out."

"Good. I gotta get to my meeting with Barry. He wants me to bring in all the mail I been gettin'. I got a *plethora* of proposals," she proclaimed. "*Plethora* is my vocabulary word of the day. I gotta prove to Barry that I can be *erudite*. That means scholarly and learned. *Plethora* means a whole bunch."

"You trying to impress him?" Jerry asked. "You two really got a thing going, like that one article said?"

Victor nodded. "Is that why he wants to see the proposals? He jealous, or what?"

"That's prob'ly it." She laughed out loud. "Wants me all to hisself."

I better not tell them about our upcoming trip to Vegas, she thought. *Don't want to take a chance that sumpthin' could mess that up.*

OUT OF THE GATE

"K aren, we've installed a direct phone line for the Undercover Angel Foundation," Barry told Karen at their next appointment. "From now on, Melinda will answer it with the official name of your foundation."

Karen turned to Barry's secretary. "Thanks for everything you do, Melinda."

"You're welcome. It's all part of the job."

"What a pretty dress. I love purple."

"It's my favorite color," Melinda said, kicking out her nearest foot and showing Karen a purple high heel.

"Don't those kill your feet by the end of the day?"

Barry cleared his throat and brought the conversation back around to business. "Every worthy cause from here to China wants your goodwill, not to mention a few unworthy ones."

"They've all got my mailing address too."

"It was almost inevitable."

"Let's don't forget about the proposals. I brought in a *plethora* of proposals."

Barry smiled in acknowledgment of her new vocabulary word. "We'll get to those later," he said. "For now, let's review your most recent expenditures."

"Suit yourself." Karen pulled a large checkbook from her briefcase. "For starters, I went to church in my mom's ward up in Coalville and made a big donation to their fast offering fund. Lotsa people are out of work. I figure that's the best way to help." She paused. "I realize I just assumed you're a Mormon and you'd understand about my church donations."

"Yes, Karen, I am."

"I thought so. Good, because I want to donate to the Perpetual Education Fund and the Humanitarian Fund regular-like. I'd like to consider some of the other organizations I get mail from. There's hungry kids all over the world. Every time you turn around, there's a hurricane or an earthquake somewhere."

"Just tell me which ones you want to consider, and I'll check them out first. That's all I ask. I'm sure you want your money actually helping victims, not lining someone's pockets." Barry looked at her over his reading glasses. "And Karen, about your business cards, we've already tracked down and will prosecute a person who duplicated your cards and then used one to try and get the Foundation to cover some major expenditures. It had the Undercover Angel logo, the angel with the nose glasses and . . ."

"You're kidding!"

"I am quite serious. I'll make sure there's news coverage about the outcome to discourage anyone else from trying that stunt, but please give the cards out more sparingly from now on. You might consider changing to an unlisted phone number as well."

"I'll be more careful," she promised. "I been helping people here and there."

"It's fine to help people as you see fit, but you must remember to try and be discreet."

"Sure thing, Mr. Luskin. And thanks for everything you did helpin' Austin set up his business. I got another business idea."

Barry smiled patiently. "I suppose we could get started on something new while I help him fine-tune his operation."

"I saw a video at the Church humanitarian office about moms in poor countries bringing their babies home wrapped in newspapers."

"I've seen that movie. Very touching."

"I was thinking that maybe we could get a bunch of ladies who need work and a bunch of sewing machines. They could make baby blankets and hats for the Foundation to donate all over the world. Homeless people could learn how to sew. There are women at battered shelters and women who sometimes need to make a little extra money to help support their families."

"A non-profit organization could be a good tax shelter. These days anything that creates jobs is welcome." He began to take notes. "I know you'd like to take people off the streets, Karen, but we'd have to screen applicants to make sure they were healthy, clean, and sober."

"Or we could help them get that way." She continued. "I want people to be able to work full time and have insurance and stuff, but I also want somebody to be able to come in who just needed a job for a short time, like if they just needed some money to get out of town, or if they had an unexpected bill come up, they could come work there for a while."

"When you're the boss, you can make the rules," Barry told her. "I'll look into it for you, Karen. There are enough vacant buildings these days. It would be a challenge, but I love a good challenge."

"Good deal! I got a safari vest with all the pockets to organize my gift cards. I got a system now. Airline cards are under my armpit, gas and grocery cards are over my gut . . ."

"I get the idea."

"Some people only need temporary help," Karen said, "but there's no better help than a good job. Like what I done for Carl."

"Who is Carl?"

"An artist guy I cleaned up and apprenticed to the guy who was painting the advertisements in the windows of the place where I bought my SUV. I got his card because I figured I'd need an artist for the party rooms at Second Childhood." She scooted forward on her chair. "So is that building you found gonna work?"

"Our architect is preparing a few preliminaries for the renovation," Barry confirmed. "We'll want to meet with him soon."

"Wow! Toni is gonna be so surprised to hear I used her idea."

"I've been busy with your dog park myself," the attorney continued. "That's quite a piece of land we bought up in Heber. There is a nearby vet's office in a strip mall with quite a few vacancies. What do you think of trying to attract some pet-related businesses? Quite a bit of your land is zoned commercial, as well. We could interest a big pet supply store in building nearby."

"Dang, you're good, Barry! You take my ideas and make them better."

"It could become an animal lover's paradise, with businesses making use of their proximity to the dog park and each other. I don't think there is anything else like it around."

• • •

Ben leaned in the doorway of Rex's office. "Remember our little unofficial wager? I hear your Mrs. Donaldson just bought the biggest home in Holladay, has hired bodyguards, and is headed to Vegas."

Rex looked up from the stack of papers on his desk. "Things are not always as they seem, Ben."

"I wonder what someone with money to burn will do in Vegas."

"Ben, *I'm* not going to gamble on whether or not *Karen* is going to gamble."

"Nothing to lose. How could she resist?"

"Speaking of gambling, I've got some elderly clients coming in momentarily to sign their estate planning documents before they head to Disneyland with their grandchildren."

"Sounds like a safe bet to me. You never know when those spinning teacups will be too much excitement. Okay, I'm going, but I still say you're going to be buying me dinner before too long."

FEELING LONELY

Camille sank onto the small sofa in the break room, grateful she was alone, hoping to lose her problems in a book.

It would be nice to have someone to talk to, she thought. *It was nice to go to lunch with Mr. Parley's wife, but I can't burden her with my problems.*

The door opened. Another secretary entered, got a soda from the machine, and sat on the other end of the sofa to drink it. She glanced at the book in Camille's hand. "I love that author. I read a lot of historical fiction too."

"You do? I picked this one up because it's set in Atlanta, close to where I grew up."

"How do you like Salt Lake?"

Camille hesitated only a moment. "The job is good. I'm still adjusting to everything else. My husband was transferred. He works in customer service for one of the credit card companies. I'd hoped moving here would be a fresh start."

Camille was gratified by Caroline's apparent interest. It had been too long since she'd had someone her own age to talk to. She found herself opening up more than she'd intended.

"A fresh start?" Caroline asked.

"We've been struggling. Jarrod is the jealous type. He gets suspicious if I have to work late or if I say something nice about a male coworker. He actually requested this transfer because he thought there was something going on between me and a coworker. The funny thing is, I couldn't stand the guy."

She looked down at her hands, wishing they had a friendship close enough that would allow her to share what was really going on with Jarrod. She also needed someone she could confide in about Ted Simon and his offensive remarks.

"I'm sorry," Caroline said. "I hope things will be better for you here."

"Me too." Camille wiped a single tear from her eye and quickly apologized for her show of emotion. "I'm sorry for having a pity party. A few minutes ago, Mr. Parley told me his wife wasn't feeling well. He told me to be sure to find him if she calls." She gazed down at the polished platinum band on her hand. "I wonder what it would be like to have a husband like that."

• • •

Now an old pro at navigating the maze of offices, Karen made it to Barry's office in record time.

"Afternoon, Mr. Luskin," she said cheerfully. "Here are the *important* documents you wanted to see." She held up a plastic grocery bag. "A whole new batch. They ain't all proposals, though. Some of 'em just want a date."

Karen upended the bag onto Barry's desk blotter. Guiltily, she fingered the lone letter she had stuffed into her pocket. She almost had it memorized she had read it so many times.

Dear Karen,

(I hope that isn't too friendly.) I used to come through your checkout line at the grocery store. I'm one of the folks that always nominated you for Most Friendly Cashier. My name is Harold, but all my friends call me Hal. I'm not writing this letter because I heard you won a lot of money, because money isn't what I'm all about.

I don't know if you ever noticed the guy in the blue baseball cap, but I noticed you. When I heard you'd quit, I was sad. Coming through your checkout line was the only time I got to see you. I knew you wasn't married, and before I could get up my courage to ask you to go to the Subway with me on your lunch hour, I heard you weren't going to be there anymore.

If you don't think this is too forward, would you consider meeting me sometime for a sandwich? I'd love to get together.

Sincerely,
Hal Braithwaite

He'd included a phone number that Karen now knew by heart.

Barry surveyed the pile of letters. "I've already drafted a letter from the law firm to send to those with return addresses or email addresses. Often a letter from an attorney is all it takes to get people to cease and desist." He looked up at Karen. "I think you would do well to heed Rex's advice for your family to confine your social contacts to people you already know."

Karen fingered the letter in her pocket. Hal was sort of somebody she already knew. "That makes sense," she said, "except that we ain't had no luck with people we already know."

Barry sighed. "Karen, you are free to exercise your own best judgment, certainly, but I'd hate to see your trust misplaced."

"Ain't that why we're on our way to the Chapel O' Love?"

"Yes, indeed. I have the tickets. I'll pick you up at six Thursday morning."

THANK YOU, THANK YOU VERY MUCH

The lady at the airport security gate recognized Karen at once. "Hey, aren't you—?"

Barry interrupted. "On the flight to Vegas and pressed for time."

"Nice save," Karen remarked as he shepherded her through the rest of the security process.

"We don't want to draw attention to ourselves."

"I thought that was what we were tryin' to do."

"Not on the flight over. In Vegas, leave the attention-getting to me."

Seated in the second row of the plane, Karen buckled her seat belt and turned to her traveling companion. "Okay, Barry. Tell me the plan again."

"We'll have our picture taken at the wedding chapel," he said, his voice low to avoid being overheard by the other passengers. "I had my secretary call the *National Enquirer* to say I couldn't meet with their reporter after all. She let it 'slip' that I was going to Vegas. Melinda's good. She knew exactly how to make him think he was getting a scoop." He took a sip of his bottled water. "We'll get a marriage license to make it look authentic and . . ."

Karen held up her hand to stop Barry as the flight attendant began the safety speech. "We gotta listen to this!"

Barry rolled his eyes. "I've heard it a thousand times."

"Well, I've only heard it that once when we flew to Texas." Karen hung on the flight attendant's every word, noting the location of the exits and studying the card in the pocket in front of her. When he was done, she turned back to Barry. "Can we find a wedding chapel with an Elvis?"

"If that's what you want." He glanced across the aisle. "We need to speak softly. For all we know, the person sitting in front of us is a reporter."

She lowered her voice. "You know, Barry, this ain't very honest. I always told my kids that deceptive and dishonest was the same thing."

As the plane lifted off the runway, Karen forgot again to keep her voice down. "Hey, Barry! We're flyin'! We're really flyin'!"

"Yes," he said calmly, hoping she would follow his lead and quit drawing attention to herself. "I'm aware that we are airborne."

"Well excuuuuse me, Mr. Frequent Flier."

"I thought you might be able to contain yourself on your second flight," he said dryly, "but obviously I was mistaken." Barry returned to the previous subject. "If it puts your mind at ease, Bishop Parley knows this was all my idea."

"It ain't the bishop I'm worried about," Karen said. "It's the Big Guy upstairs."

"There are numerous instances in scripture where deception was necessary. When Jochabed volunteered to nurse Moses, did she mention she was his mother?" He was on a roll, an attorney making a compelling argument backed up by the Almighty's case law. "What about the Lord telling Abraham to say his wife was his sister—for her protection?"

Karen shot him a look. "Barry, I don't know if you've noticed this, but you ain't God."

He laughed heartily. "You aren't the first person who thought I had a God complex." He leaned back slightly and looked straight ahead. "Be honest, though. In profile, don't you see a little family resemblance?" He chuckled at his own joke and then grew serious. "Look, Karen, whatever we do that doesn't mesh with your ethics, I'll take full responsibility for before the judgment bar of God."

"I hope you ain't been disbarred before you get there."

"My dear, Mrs. Donaldson, you've been spending way too much time in the law office. You fear I'll fail you in the heavenly jurisdiction?"

"I don't know how far that retainer extends," she said. "I'm kinda worried about the bill at the end."

Barry placed his hand over hers, all business now. "Karen, we're doing this for your protection."

She frowned. "But I *liked* getting the proposals."

"That's exactly what I'm afraid of."

• • •

Once they were underway, a flight attendant removed a heated towel from a wicker basket with a pair of tongs and held it out for

Karen. She took it, a little too eagerly. "This is my favorite part of first class, these hot towels!" She rubbed the towel over her hands and face. "Give me three or four of these and I'll just give m'self a sponge bath right here in muh chair."

The male flight attendant grimaced, and Barry choked on his soda, using his hot towel to staunch the flow of ginger ale from his nose.

"Dontcha just love the hot towels, Barry?"

• • •

Karen was surprised to see slot machines in the airport as they deplaned. "Boy, they don't waste any time gettin' ya to gamble, do they?" A teenage boy stood near one of the machines. Karen approached, dug a quarter from her pocket, and pulled the lever. Nothing happened.

"There ya go," she told him. "A quick lesson in gamblin'. You put your money in, and most of the time you don't even get a gum ball back."

"It looks like your luck didn't hold," Barry observed as they walked down the corridor toward the front of the airport.

"Ya think? I hope losin' that quarter won't set me back too much." She stopped to stare at a series of large ads on the wall. "Think our foundation could buy clothes for some of these poor half-naked girls?"

"Too bad we didn't think ahead," Barry said dryly. "You could have brought a couple of cases of knee-length shorts from Orem."

Karen turned to survey the other side of the hallway. "Those Thunder from Down Under guys don't look like they're keepin' very warm at night, either."

"I'm sure there are those who would beg to differ."

At the curb, Barry hailed a cab while Karen picked up a free local newspaper from a stand. "Tell him we want a place with an Elvis," she instructed Barry as the cab pulled up. "Can I buy a weddin' gown?"

"We'll head to the Strip," Barry said. "You can buy whatever you want there. You're rich, filthy rich."

"Why d'ya think they call it filthy rich?"

He opened the door of the cab and paused to consider the question. As he did, he glanced over his shoulder and saw someone he'd observed behind them for some time getting into a second cab. "Because of all the germs on a dollar bill," he told her. "Get in the cab." He added under his breath, "I think we're being followed."

"I thought we *wanted* photographers to follow us."

"We want them to show up at the wedding chapel," he clarified. "We don't want a tail to discover that this is all a fraud." He climbed into the cab after her. "Act natural. Never mind, you will anyway. What I mean is act like we didn't notice anything."

• • •

Karen's eyes darted from one flamboyant advertisement to the next as they headed away from the airport while Barry watched the cab behind them.

She turned the page in the free newspaper she'd picked up. "Here's an ad for Gamblers Anonymous," she said with a note of dismay. "You know my business cards—Ann O. Nymous? It's only got one 'n' in it! Dang."

"Technically, it has two."

"Not in the 'An' part! I spelled it wrong." She continued reading the ad and then set the newspaper down. "I'd like to go to this meeting, if we have time after the pictures."

"We do have a late flight," he said. "Karen, you bought one lottery ticket and lost twenty-five cents in a slot machine. I don't think you have a gambling problem."

"No, I want to give some of this gamblin' money back to people who are really tryin' to break the habit."

• • •

Karen smiled for the cameras. "We're gettin' our money's worth here, huh, Barry? Look at all those wedding photographers."

"They're mostly all reporters, Karen."

She leaned close and whispered, "I know! I ain't stupid! I was actin' natural, like you said." She smoothed her taffeta dress. "Me and Ray didn't have a big wedding. I borrowed a dress from my cousin because we was so young and poor."

"You look lovely," he said. "Smile for one last picture."

"Thank you! Thank you very much." The Elvis impersonator's words signaled an end to the ceremony.

Soon Karen was changed, her wedding gown stuffed unceremoniously into a large shopping bag since the garment bag it came in had gone missing. Barry scrutinized the dispersing crowd.

"Are all these reporters from around here?" Karen asked.

"I don't know," he responded. "We only leaked it to the *Enquirer* and the local press. I figured it would be more credible to have Salt Lake pick it up off the wire service." He looked down at the shopping bag. "I'm sorry your nice bag was stolen. I'm sure it was some reporter looking for more information."

"Like what?"

"Like where you bought the dress. Even now somebody's probably pumping the employees to find out everything you said and did while you were trying it on." He switched gears. "You still want to make that Gamblers Anonymous meeting?"

"Yeah, it starts at three."

"Early enough so they'll still have all evening to gamble," Barry commented wryly.

● ● ●

Once again, a second cab pulled up shortly after theirs. Barry led the way into the basement of a local church. A sign tacked to the door announced that the meeting was a regular occurrence. He steered Karen toward a metal folding chair in the last row and took a seat beside her.

The wooden pulpit had seen better days. A nearby table, covered with a faded pink tablecloth, held a coffee pot, a water pitcher, and an assortment of day-old donuts. He leaned over to Karen. "Good timing. Looks like they're just starting."

One after another, people took turns at the pulpit. "My name is Robert," an unkempt middle-aged man began. "I'm addicted to gambling."

This guy would sell his own grandmother, Barry thought.

"My name is Michael, and I have a gambling problem." Barry sized him up as well. *Overwhelmed by life and looking for an easy out.*

"My name is Rosemary. Gambling broke up my marriage. My husband got custody of our three children, but I still can't quit."

She's in pretty deep. Probably won't ever beat it.

He looked over at Karen and could practically see wheels turning in her head. He produced a small notepad and scribbled a hasty message. *"Whatever you do here tonight, discretion is of the utmost importance."* He passed the note to Karen.

"Gotcha."

"You know what 'discretion' means, don't you?" he whispered.

"Sure, like in the hymn," she whispered back. "'Let no spirit of discretion overcome you in the evil hour.'"

Barry sighed and put the notepad back in his shirt pocket.

• • •

As people filed out after the meeting, Karen approached one of the men. She extended her hand, spoke quietly, and led him over to a private corner.

"José, I was touched by the things you shared," Karen said. "I believe you really are tryin' to quit gamblin'. I run a charitable foundation and would like to pay off your gambling debts and give you a fresh start. You said it was about $60,000, right? What's your last name?" Karen quietly pulled a check from her purse and motioned for Barry to come cosign it. She knew he would approve. Of all the stories they'd heard, this man's had been the most believable and compelling.

"Maybe you really do know what discretion means," Barry whispered to her as he added his signature. He inclined his head slightly. "Don't look now, but the man at the refreshment table has been following us all day. Let's keep this quiet."

However, José had no investment in keeping a low profile. He threw his arms around Karen's neck. "Thank you! Thank you! You are one of God's angels! You have saved my life! You have saved my marriage! I will not have to look into the hungry eyes of my little children again!"

Although most of the group had departed, every remaining eye turned toward the trio in the corner. Soon Robert was at Karen's side, his eyes riveted on the check in José's hand. He looked from it to Karen and then back again.

Putting on the most downtrodden expression he could muster, Robert hung his head. "I could use some help feeding my poor, starving children too."

Karen reached into her purse. After fumbling around for a moment, she pulled out a gift card. "There you go. You got Smith's here in Nevada, don't you? That's got three hundred dollars on it to buy food for your children."

"That's it?" Then, realizing from the look on Barry's face that he might lose even that, he snatched the card from Karen's hand. "Gee, thanks!" he said sarcastically.

Karen ignored his tone. "You're welcome! Don't spend it all on beer and smokes." She reached down and picked up the shopping bag, shaking her head. "Almost forgot muh weddin' dress."

When they were finally out of the church and alone again, she turned to Barry. "Another good day's work. Let's head over to that *Star Trek* restaurant at the Hilton like you promised me."

RULES OF ACQUISITION

Soon Barry and Karen were in the back of another cab, headed to the Hilton for dinner.

"I think we finally shook the guy who was following us, but I've been aware all day that several dogs have picked up our scent," Barry whispered. Resuming a conversational tone, he commented, "Karen, I had no idea you were a Trekkie."

"It was like secondhand smoke. I was exposed to it from Austin watching. Sometimes you watch to spend time with people you love."

Barry's voice grew wistful. "Kathleen did that. I realize now that she probably hated my favorite legal drama. I fear I failed to return the favor."

"She dragged you off to the ballet or something, didn't she?"

"I did take her to *The Nutcracker*." He cheered up somewhat at that realization. "I didn't mean to get melancholy on you, Karen." He cleared his throat and refocused his attention. "So you want to eat at Quark's?"

Remembering they should stay in character in case a reporter interviewed their cabbie, he added, "I suppose that would be as good a way as any for us to celebrate our nuptials?"

"Our *what*?"

"Our wedding, dearest."

"Right!" She held up one hand in the Vulcan "V" and then said to the cabbie, "That's part of our weddin' vows—to live long and prosper. Now take us to the Hilton so we can get started." She scooted closer to Barry and whispered, "How'm I doin'?"

• • •

"This way, please, and get your wallet out." A big-eared Ferengi showed them to their table. "I am Cyron, your server. I desire to earn a big tip. I will do this not by giving you stellar, attentive service, but by using my powers of persuasion to entice you to order the most expensive items we offer." He handed them each a menu. "I will give you a moment to look over the selections and assess your finances."

Soon their otherworldly waiter reappeared. "Have you decided?"

Barry nodded. "I'll have the hamBorger."

Cyron turned to Karen. "Perhaps you will be available later after you have dumped this cheapskate."

"I couldn't do that on our weddin' day."

Cyron fixed Barry with a cold stare. "Your wedding day? Sir? And you can't pull out all the stops?"

Barry cleared his throat. "You're right. I'll also take some Rings of Betazeel."

"That's it? I certainly hope your date—oh, excuse me, your wife—makes up for it with her order. Ferengi Rule of Acquisition #188: A fool and his money is the best customer."

"I'd like the Klingon Kabob and Glop on a Stick," Karen said.

"No doubt you will want one of our overpriced desserts after you have cleansed your palates with those appetizers."

"Can I get a Vulcan Volcano without the booze?" Karen asked.

"Ferengi Rule of Acquisition #208: The only thing more dangerous than a question is an answer. You are requesting a virgin Vulcan Volcano?"

"Yup."

"Certainly, I can get you a VVV. But be aware of Rule #266: When in doubt, lie." He turned to Barry. "No libation for you to celebrate this momentous occasion?"

"Water will do."

"Water? *Water?* You bring your new bride to a theme restaurant on your wedding day—a place where underpaid waiters don excruciatingly uncomfortable latex masks in a desert climate and attempt to extort money from skinflint customers by impersonating minor characters from a show in syndication for decades—and you order *water?*"

Suddenly, the fellow at the nearby table rose and pointed a camera. By the time the flashes stopped and Karen and Barry could see again, the table was deserted.

After a pause Cyron asked, "Are you persons of interest to the paparazzi?"

"We're very famous, infamous really," Barry answered. "I'm surprised *you* didn't recognize us. Maybe they need to cut your eyeholes larger." He smiled. "Of course, I've been told, when in doubt, lie." He glanced around the room. "Where might I find a restroom?"

• • •

By the time Barry returned to the table, the food had been served.

"What took so long?" Karen asked. "Your hamBorger's getting cold. And can I try one of those thingies?"

"Onion rings?"

"Don't you get in trouble if you don't call the food by its *Star Trek* name?"

He handed the breaded ring across the table. "Your Ring of Betazeel, my dear."

After they finished their meal, Cyron launched a valiant attempt to get them to order dessert, with no success. "If this charming woman leaves you because of your penury, sir, it will be your *just deserts*." He nodded his head and placed the bill on the table. "I have three other tables of patrons to harass, if you'll . . ."

"I'll get the tip," Karen said, depositing a one-hundred-dollar bill on top of the check.

Barry raised an eyebrow, but said nothing.

Cyron was momentarily speechless. "In Ferengi society, women do not own property, but in light of this generosity, perhaps it is not altogether a bad thing to allow women some limited access to funds."

He disappeared with Barry's credit card and Karen's tip before "the female earthling" could think better of it. He returned shortly and handed Barry his receipt and credit card. "Thank you, Cyron, for a memorable evening," Barry said.

"Please give us a chance to further exploit you in the future." He bowed slightly and walked away.

As Barry pulled out her chair, Karen asked, "Are we headed to the airport now?"

He leaned close to whisper in her ear. "Actually, Karen, I disappeared on you to make other arrangements." He reached into his pocket and withdrew a card key. "I changed our flight to tomorrow morning. We're spending the night here at the Hilton."

• • •

Barry opened the door to Room 1422 and motioned for Karen to enter.

"Are you next door?" she asked.

"Karen, several reporters are still following us. All signs indicate they're digging for the complete story." He closed the door behind them. "There's some legitimate investigative journalism going on out there. We can't do anything to lead them to believe it was all a ruse. Who spends their wedding night on an airplane?"

"So we're fakin' a weddin' night too?"

"Not exactly. Marriage records are public domain; they're not something you can fake. We'd obtained the marriage license to make it look real, so it wasn't hard to take it a step further." He cleared his throat. "We're really married, Karen. It was a judgment call on my part. We'll get it annulled, of course, after the publicity dies down. We can probably sell our matching wedding bands on eBay, unless you'd like to keep yours as a souvenir." He waited for her response, which was not forthcoming. "So if you don't mind me sleeping in one of the two beds, it would certainly simplify things."

Karen stood for several moments with her mouth open. "We're *married?* I can't believe you did that, Barry! You didn't even ask me!"

"We've been watched since we got off the plane this morning. There was no time or place for a conference, and I felt it was best if you didn't know." He set his room key on the small end table. "Karen, if I take another room, somebody is bound to pick up on it. We'll both sleep here. In the morning, we'll make up one of the beds and order room service. That way, even if some guy bribes a desk clerk or maid, it will look legit."

"I don't like this, Barry. No way, no how!"

"Do you think I'll ask for a big divorce settlement?" Barry asked sarcastically. "I'm quite well-to-do all on my own, despite what Cyron thinks of my penury." He hesitated. "That's P-E-N-U-R-Y. It means—"

"I got a dictionary!" Karen snapped. "Picking up a new vocab word is not exactly at the top of my list right now!" She glared at Barry. "What would your wife have to say about you makin' a mockery of marriage?"

"Good alliteration," Barry said. "But I'm not making a mockery of the sacred institution of marriage as we know it. I'm making a mockery of a Chapel O' Love wedding."

"Don't give me that lawyer crap!" Still glaring, Karen pointed toward the door. "Go buy a newspaper or something while I take a shower. When you get back, I'll be in bed with the covers up around my ears. I don't exactly keep my favorite jammies in my purse."

Barry turned and went obediently to the door. "And for a weddin' present, how about gettin' me a toothbrush and toothpaste?" she said.

With his hand on the knob, he added, "Karen, please know I've done all this only for your protection. There are people out there who would take every advantage of you and your family to get your money. You can't be too careful."

"I still don't like it."

"Nor do I." His tone was sincere. "I regretted it the moment it was done. It was impulsive and thoughtless. I don't know what came over me. I've put my career at risk, Karen. If I am asked in the future if I have ever sworn falsely, well, a wedding vow would certainly qualify. Even if I pled extenuating circumstances, the consequences could be serious. I'm sure the executive committee at the firm will convene and dress me down, as well. And as you so aptly pointed out, so will Kathleen when I see her again."

Karen softened. "Ya risked your professional reputation to protect me?"

"Believe me, nobody could be more surprised than I am."

DELIA MOVES IN

When the latest tabloids hit the supermarkets, Barry was proven right on all counts. The public bought the wedding story, and Karen's proposals all but ceased. A few weeks later, the temporary marriage was quietly annulled. Karen was relieved but somehow it saddened her to slip off the inexpensive gold band. Even though it hadn't been a real marriage, her ethics had kept her from contacting Hal, the man from the grocery store who had written her the letter.

It was Saturday. Mandee was downstairs, practicing a simple song on their new piano. Other than her granddaughter, Karen was alone. She fished the crumpled letter from her purse and picked up the phone.

When there was no answer, she froze at the sound of the beep, wondering if she should leave her name and number. With the annulment, she supposed the charade was over. Or was she still supposed to be pretending she was married? Why did she feel she was cheating on her husband? Would someone show up and take pictures of her having a sandwich at Subway? Barry had been right that the fun of being famous would wear thin.

Because of the recent dinners at her home with Barry, she had gotten used to having him around. There had even been a few nights he had slept on the Murphy bed in the room over the garage so that his car could be seen leaving her home early in the morning. She'd pored over her dictionary late at night, looking for new vocabulary words with which to impress him. She forced her thoughts back to the man from the grocery store.

I like Barry, and I kinda miss havin' him around, but he could never be seriously interested in someone like me, and I wouldn't fit in his life. Besides, if fake marryin' me was a violation of his ethics, getting involved for real with a client would be even worse. Hal was friendly before I won the lottery. Ain't that what they told me to look for?

At the sound of a car pulling up, Karen quickly hung up the phone. From the window she watched the small U-Haul truck pull around in front of the garage. She looked regretfully at the phone, promising herself she'd call the next time she was alone. The last thing she needed was to have Dee find out she was calling a man to set up a date.

Downstairs, Karen pushed a button to open the garage, marveling at yet another piece of new-to-her technology. The truck backed into place. Delia got out of the orange hatchback and went to talk to the driver.

Dee's friend got out of the truck and opened the back doors. "I thought you said your mother worked at Smith's Food King," he said, looking admiringly at the fountain, the landscaping, and the house. "She own them all, or what?"

"You can bring the stuff in through here," Karen directed.

Curious, he continued. "You said your dad never helped out, right?"

Dee did not respond to either comment. Karen surveyed the young man carefully before extending her hand. "I'm Dee's mom, Karen," she said at last. He was not the only one making an assessment. She could not take her eyes off his face. He had at least twenty piercings—four in each eyebrow, several in his nose, lips, and cheeks, and one in his tongue. "Don't those set off metal detectors?" Karen inquired.

Dee turned to Karen. "Mother, meet Zhon."

"Are you French?" Karen asked.

"No. It's Z-H-O-N." He was still clearly marveling at the house. "Nice place you've got here. It looks like maybe I ought to get myself a job at Smith's."

"Smith's was good to me, but not this good."

"Been playing the ponies?"

"Nope. Ducks."

"Didn't know there was big bucks in ducks."

"You learn sumpthin' new every day, dontcha?" Karen motioned toward the wide curved stairway in the entryway that led up to the bedrooms. "You can take this stairway. It's wider. Delia's room is the big one at the end of the hall." *And this is the first and last time I want to see you in it.*

He picked up a box and headed into the house.

"Where'd ya meet *him*?" Karen asked, once he was out of earshot.

"Out dancing last night. I mentioned I was moving today, and he volunteered to drive the truck. A couple of other friends helped us get things loaded, but they would have been more help if they hadn't been so loaded themselves."

• • •

Karen watched from the window as Dee said good-bye to Zhon, trying to remember if she had ever experienced a kiss that lasted as long.

"That was mighty friendly for someone you just met," she said when Delia came inside. She couldn't keep herself from asking, "Is it weird kissin' somebody with a pierced tongue?"

"You get used to it."

"*Used* to it? I thought you just met him last night." Karen shook her head. "Never mind. I don't wanna know."

Dee turned away. "No, you don't. Jessie dumped me, so I'm getting some action wherever I can."

Karen furrowed her brow. "Dee, you're a grown woman and free to make your own choices, but there ain't gonna be any *action* in this house, especially not with your daughter in the next room." She turned away. "Besides, we ain't supposed to be datin' people we don't know."

"He's new in town," Delia argued. "He doesn't know nothing about me. He's just a guy I met in a bar."

"Like that makes me feel better," Karen muttered. "Just remember what I said. No foolin' around in my house."

"Yeah, Mom, I get it."

"You didn't tell him about me winnin' the lottery, did you?"

"No! He doesn't know anything, Mom. I guess he ain't very well read."

"I don't know how anybody missed them tabloid stories," Karen mused, "but maybe he ain't the sharpest knife in the drawer."

"He is curious about how you can afford this house."

"Whatcha gonna do? Tell him we live off the coins people throw in the fountain? Tell him I'm the cleanin' lady and the real owners are on vacation? He'll put two and two together soon enough, I imagine. Bishop Parley said we should date people we already know and trust."

"Yeah? Who exactly would that be?"

"Not some stranger you picked up in a bar."

"Mom, I agreed to your rules for living here. I won't bring my social life home, and I'll be more involved with Mandee. No drinking. No partying. Now here's my rule for you. You can't be nagging me all the time about going to church. They're a bunch of self-righteous hypocrites. They preach brotherly love, but they pick and choose who is good enough to love."

"It ain't the Church of Alison Arletti, Dee," Karen told her tiredly. "It's the Church of Jesus Christ. I'll quit naggin', but you know the door's always open." She changed the subject. "Do you hear Mandee in there practicin' the piano? Toni givin' her free piano lessons, that was someone bein' kind to us."

Dee softened. "Mandee does love her piano lessons. And thanks for fixing up such a pretty room for her. She thinks she died and went to heaven. I would have killed for a room like that when I was her age."

"I was gonna fix your room up too," Karen said, "but I thought you'd wanna pick out your own furniture."

"I made forty-seven bucks off my yard sale," Dee said. "Knowing you would buy me new furniture sure made moving easier. I just packed up my clothes and stuff. The closet in there is about the size of my room in the apartment."

"I know Mandee ain't the only little girl who dreamed of havin' a pretty bedroom. I couldn't give it to you then, so I'll give it to you now."

Delia gave her mother a hug. "Thanks, Mom. I'm sorry about earlier. And thanks for giving us such an awesome place to live and for getting a piano for Mandee."

"She practices every day. She wants you to be proud of her."

"I guess that's what all kids want, for their parents to be proud of them." Delia paused. "Are you proud of me, Mom? Are you proud of my many attempts at relationships? For having a kid when I was still a kid myself? Are you proud of my job at the Corn Dog Connection?"

Karen faltered. "Dee, I'm . . ."

"I didn't think so. Don't try to make something up. That's worse. I know I haven't exactly done anything you could be proud of."

"You've given me a beautiful granddaughter."

"Not exactly the way you'd hoped."

"That don't change how much I love her."

"I've neglected my duty to her, as you've let me know at every turn."

Karen took Dee's hand, and she felt her daughter's resistance soften. "Let's think of this as a fresh start, Dee. Listen to her play. It reminds me of when you was little, before your dreams got beat out of you. There are lots of paths besides the one you're on. You could get training in something, go to college." She took Delia's other hand as well. "I can't fix those dreams that didn't come true, but I can help ya see if some new ones might."

Delia's eyes filled with tears. "You'd help me go to school or something—like you're helping Austin?"

"Of course I would. We just need to put our heads together and figure out what's a good match for you." Karen listened to her granddaughter plunking away at the same simple tune on the piano. "It'd be a good example to Mandee. I'll do anything for you but pay the bills while you sit around doing nothing."

"There goes *that* plan," Dee joked. "What do you think I'd be good at, Mom?"

Karen's face broke into a smile. "Let's talk about it when we drive up to Jackson Hole for Austin's grand opening."

∙ ∙ ∙

Later that night, Karen thought about the man who had written her the letter and the man her daughter had introduced her to. *Men, they're trouble.* She took the letter from her purse and tossed it into the garbage can. *How can I be tellin' my daughter to be careful about who she hangs out with and then hook up with some guy who writes me a letter?*

16

• •

ROLLIN' IN THE DOUGH

Olive Arletti added a quick reminder before she turned the time over to Louise at the beginning of another quarterly Relief Society evening activity. "Please remember to keep the Cironni family in your prayers as Corina starts another round of her treatment." She continued, "Next, Sister Potter will share some much-needed information for our 'Homemakers' Hints.'"

Sister Potter rose, brandishing a woman's magazine. "I found an article on careful food preparation that I thought should be brought to our attention. Raw eggs can cause food poisoning. Any kind of uncooked batter with raw eggs in it is not healthy. This includes cake batter and cookie dough. Heaven knows children love to lick the bowl—"

Karen Donaldson spoke up. "And when all the kids have left home, you can have the bowl and beaters all to yourself!"

A couple of sisters snickered. Sister Potter continued. "I'm sure you've enjoyed that pleasure, Karen, now that your children are older, but now that you understand how dangerous the practice is . . ."

Karen countered. "So is skydivin', but it's a risk some people are willin' to take. At Smith's they stock Mrs. Fields cookie dough you can bake yourself, only when I buy it, it don't get cooked."

Sister Potter pursed her lips. "I'm sure it's not intended to be eaten raw. You shouldn't promote what could be a dangerous, even life-threatening, practice, Karen."

"But there ain't nothin' so comfortin' on a bad day as a good old chunk of cookie dough. What about that ice cream that has cookie dough in it? They don't expect you to fish out those little pieces and bake 'em, do they? I don't see how ya could. The government lets them sell it that way, so it must be okay."

Flustered, Sister Potter thumbed through the magazine in search of a quotation to counter Karen's position. "It's very clear this is not something to trifle with."

Karen responded, "Oh, yeah. There's lots of good stuff in them ladies' magazines. Of course, I don't leave *Good Housekeeping* lyin' around my house, on account of it looks a little hypocritical since housework's not exactly my cup of cocoa. But I did read in one of them about throwin' denture tablets into the toilet bowl to keep from havin' to scrub. I'm tellin' ya, it worked pretty good—got the porcelain shinin' just like Grandma's dentures. So, you might be right about the cookie dough, Sister Potter, but food poisonin' is a chance I'm willin' to take. In fact, I think that's the way I want to go. I could die with a smile on my face, and all I ask is that they bury me with a chocolate chip stuck in the corner of my mouth!"

Sister Potter said a few final words, none of which were heard over the laughter, and sat down, humiliated. She leaned over to whisper to Olive, "That woman is too much!"

"And she never misses a meeting," Olive whispered back.

• • •

Arthur dog-eared the page in his book, closed it, and set it on the night table, awaiting the barrage as Olive prepared to turn in for the night. "Karen Donaldson was even worse than usual tonight! I try to imbue our meetings with dignity and good taste, and there she is every single time to thwart my every effort." She put her brush down on the vanity and turned toward her husband in the bed. "In March the bishop forced her on me as an emergency teacher. You did talk to Rex about that, didn't you, Arthur?"

He mumbled something incoherent into his pillow.

Olive moved to the side of the bed, dotting cream on the delicate skin around her eyes. She imitated Karen. "'Why clean the oven anyway? Won't the heat kill the germs? Ain't it dangerous to breathe in all those fumes? The Scrubbin' Bubbles are the only ones doin' any scrubbin' at my house!'"

She tucked the loose tendrils of her hair under the stretchy band of ivory terrycloth around her head and began to apply her night moisturizer in upward strokes.

"Louise once told the sisters to microwave their kitchen sponge for ten seconds to kill the bacteria. At the next meeting Karen said she tried that and forgot to take her sponge out of the microwave and mistook it later for a chicken-fried steak. Can you imagine?"

Art smothered his laughter into his pillow and tried to disguise it with a cough.

Wrapped up in her commentary, Olive didn't notice. "Tonight, poor Louise was trying to educate the sisters about the dangers of eating anything containing raw eggs. Karen turned it into an advertisement for eating uncooked cookie dough. After all the things we've done for her family over the years, you'd think she could give me one meeting where she doesn't heckle my teacher."

"Hope springs eternal, dear," Art managed to respond in a serious tone.

"It's worse now that she's got all that money. Heaven knows Karen hasn't changed an iota, but there are some sisters who give credence to the things she says now just because she's wealthy beyond belief." She sat down on the bed. "It goes to show that you can't buy good breeding and class. No matter how many millions Karen has, she'd go broke trying," Olive stated definitively.

Art reached over to pat his wife's moisturized hand. "I'm sure the ladies enjoyed your meeting, Olive. You always take such care to make it special."

"Yes, I do, and to what avail?" She rose again. "I've got to take something for this headache."

In the bathroom, Olive got out the bottle of aspirin. She closed the cabinet, pondered a moment, and then opened it again. Rummaging around, she reached to the back of the top shelf and found a package left behind on her mother's last visit. Discreetly she tore open the wrapper and plopped two denture tablets into the toilet bowl.

Olive watched them fizz as they dissolved. When the process was complete, she swished the toilet brush around the bowl and flushed. "My, it really does shine!" she exclaimed.

"Olive, are you admiring your reflection in the toilet bowl again?" Arthur asked wearily. "Come to bed."

After a final, fleeting look, Olive joined her long-suffering husband. She crawled into bed beside him, but she was not done. "And then there was the time I talked about the importance of having the exterior of your home pressure cleaned. There was Karen. 'Ain't pressure cleanin' what you do when the home teachers are on the way over?'"

Arthur hid another smile. "Now Olive, getting all worked up about Karen won't help your headache go away."

"But the sisters laugh, and it only encourages her. Ruining my well-planned meetings is her only hobby."

"Maybe she'll find a new hobby now that she has more funds at her disposal."

"She *enjoys* it, Arthur!"

"Karen enjoys everything, haven't you noticed? She doesn't let things get to her. Maybe you could take a page out of her book and calm down a little about things that aren't so earth-shatteringly important. It might help stave off those awful headaches."

"Really, Arthur? You want *me* to be more like *Karen Donaldson?*"

"I just mean you never think about anything besides housework. Maybe Karen isn't the only one who needs a new hobby."

Olive pulled the ties at the top of her nightgown into a nice tight bow, her fingers jerking in angry emphasis. Leaving them untied had always been her signal to Arthur that he might have a chance for a little romance. "Well, I never! I work my fingers to the bone around here, and this is the thanks I get? I suppose you and Karen *both* think the Scrubbing Bubbles do it all!" She turned onto her side with her back to her husband and pulled the bedcovers up around her neck.

Arthur sighed and turned away and muttered under his breath. "Just me and the dust mites . . . again." After another couple of seconds, he exploded. "Dadgummit, Olive! I don't want a toilet I can drink out of or floors we can eat on. How about a little affection now and then without you worrying it'll muss your hair? Is that too much to ask?"

• • •

Karen made a quick stop at the grocery store after Relief Society to pick up a couple of things. Back home, she remembered to turn her cell phone back on and saw she had a message. She pushed the button for voice mail.

"This is Hal from the grocery store." There was a moment's hesitation. "I hope you'll call back."

Karen hit the button to return the call, but then she looked at the clock. She reconsidered and flipped the phone shut. It was almost ten. *Kinda late to call. Maybe tomorrow. Maybe never.*

She contemplated the fact that it was flirting with an unknown clerk at a convenience store that had landed her in such a complicated situation in the first place. Maybe Barry was wrong. Surely every person she'd ever meet again wouldn't want something from her.

What if Hal really is just that nice guy I remember from the store? I'll never know if I don't call him back.

GOT A MINUTE?

R ex Parley looked up to see Ted Simon in the doorway of his office. "What can I do for you, Ted?"

Ted entered, closed the door, and took a seat. "I could get used to the view from a corner office."

"Do you want the problems that come with the view?"

"If I could have Cami just outside my office, I'd handle whatever they threw at me." Ted laughed jovially.

Rex did not respond in kind.

There was a tap at the door. "Yes?" Rex asked.

"It's just me," Camille said, opening the door. She entered and blushed when she saw Ted. "Here are the documents for your two o'clock meeting. I won't go on break in case you need me to make copies after they sign." She walked to his desk and handed him a stack of papers. Rex noted how Ted followed her every movement.

"Thanks, Camille," Rex said. "I'll give you a buzz if I need you to witness the will. It's good to know you'll be nearby." He set the papers down as she left.

"It must be nice to have her nearby," Ted remarked.

Rex frowned. "Ted, was there a reason you came by—other than to discuss the finer points of my secretary?"

"Tell me you've never noticed she's attractive."

"Of course I've noticed," Rex said. "But even if I weren't married, there are boundaries, personal and professional." He leaned forward. "Didn't that verbal warning we gave you sink in, Ted?"

"I thought that thing with Melinda had blown over," Ted said. "Secretaries compare notes in the break room, and the next thing you know, there's some overblown accusation. You compliment them and suddenly you're in the doghouse. All I said was 'Nice dress, Mindy.' "

"Perhaps it was the *way* you said it."

"It wasn't even Mindy who complained. It was that prissy Barbara who sits by her. I apologized as suggested, but it was no big deal to Mindy. We always kid around." He grew serious. "I'm a top litigator in this firm. If some secretary thinks she can nail me because I said 'nice dress,' she hasn't seen me in action."

"I'm sure we've all seen only the tip of the iceberg."

Ted smiled at what he thought was a compliment. "Which brings me to why I stopped by. Am I going to be made partner this year?"

"Do you know how many years I worked here before I was made partner?" Rex paused. "We promised you early *consideration* as a partner, so we're considering you."

"Like I didn't know that."

Rex looked at his watch. "I'm expecting a client momentarily."

Ted stood. "I hope my contributions to the firm won't be overlooked—especially the new clients I've brought in through my political connections."

Rex reminded himself that the firm had spared no effort or expense in recruiting Ted. It was no wonder he had an ego to match his accomplishments. "Yes, Ted," he responded. "We're aware of what you do here." *In fact, I'm aware of more than you think.*

• • •

On the way back to his office, Ted passed the copy center and saw Camille alone in the room.

Camille jumped when someone came up behind her.

"I didn't mean to startle you," Ted said. "I just need a ream of copy paper." He moved closer and reached around her for the paper, "accidentally" brushing his arm against her in the process. "I was just telling Rex how much I enjoy the view from his office," he whispered. "He thought I was talking about the view outside the window."

Ted disappeared as quickly as he had come. Camille was hard pressed to hide her tears from the two secretaries who entered the copy room a few moments later. She heard a hushed comment about her marriage problems as she left, feeling as alone as she had ever felt in her life.

RIDING THE RAPIDS

Grant showed up immediately to help Austin book the four friendly, twenty-something girls.

"I'll take this group out," Austin told him.

"How about we flip a coin?"

"No, I'm pulling rank," Austin said. "They're hot!"

"Fine! I quit! You're the boss, maybe, but you haven't got anybody to boss now, except the people counting up how much money we're losing. Chad told me he'd take me back any time."

"But if I let you run this trip, you won't quit? What makes you think I want an employee who thinks he can bully me? Go ahead. Chad's waiting."

• • •

Chelsea Krumperman from Shelley, Idaho, gave Austin her phone number at the end of their trip, and it was the beginning of a beautiful friendship that lasted until she found out that he hadn't served a mission and didn't often go to church.

Grant went back to work for Chad, armed with insider information about Austin's business, which Chad made full use of. As summer's end neared, Austin wasn't sure whether to shut down for the winter or shut down for good. When Chad undercut him on his last big booking of the summer, Austin closed up shop and headed to Utah to talk things over with his mother.

• • •

"Mom, I let you down. I tried so hard, I really did!"

"I know ya worked hard, Austin. You've always been a hard worker."

"Barry said you can work for someone else for forty hours a week or yourself for sixty, but turns out it was more like eighty." Austin frowned. "Part of me would like to keep trying, but I can't keep mooching off you." He slumped down on the sofa, his discouragement showing in his body language. "I figured in all the start-up costs, the equipment, and getting the location set up. But I also figured once we opened for business, we'd start making money and I could start paying you back or at least stop borrowing from you."

"Maybe things ain't workin' out in Jackson Hole because that ain't where the Lord wants ya to be," Karen suggested to her son.

"Like God cares what I do."

"That's just it, Austin. How's God supposed to work in your life when you keep slammin' the door in His face?"

"What evidence did we ever have that God cared?"

"We had the Thompsons," Karen said. "We had a place to live where they never raised our rent. You didn't have to change schools, and you got to grow up with all the same kids."

"Who *all* thought they were better than us."

She changed the subject. "Hey, didja know Adrienne is doin' a semester abroad?" Just then Karen's cell phone rang. She picked it up and looked at the number. *Dang! He always calls at the wrong time.*

"What do I care what Adri's doing?" Austin replied.

"Just thought you'd wanna know she ain't married."

"She sure didn't stick around here very long after her mission."

"Did you give her any reason to?"

Adrienne Thompson represented everything Austin had wanted in life and couldn't have. He could still picture her in the burgundy dress she had worn when he'd taken her to junior prom. Even now he could bring to mind her long, silky, chocolate-brown hair, sparkling dark eyes, and the way she had looked at him when they slow-danced. That night he had known God loved him. Not so much since.

Karen feared the change of subject had not been helpful so she tried again. "If things don't work out in Jackson Hole, you wanna help me with my dog park?"

"How's that coming?"

"We got most of the landscapin' done, been sellin' bricks that people can personalize with their pet's name. There's gonna be a path that goes all the way around. We've made a dog restroom in the back with five old fire hydrants."

"It sounds great, Mom," Austin said flatly.

"We've got a bunch of businesses openin' in a strip mall nearby—a dog groomer called Groomingdales and a kennel called Bark Place. There's already a vet's office. There's gonna be a bakery that makes dog biscuits and stuff called Café Canine. It won't all be done until next year. There's gonna be a pet superstore on the other side."

"I'm sure Boomer and Butterball can't wait."

"Café Canine has a room where you can have a birthday party for your dog," Karen told him. "They'll let the dogs loose on the birthday cake, and then they'll hose down the room. It's all tile with a drain in the middle. I think my next kitchen'll be like that."

Austin almost smiled. "I wonder why Sister Cironni didn't think of that for this house, with all those kids."

"We just gotta come up with a name for the park."

"'Gone to the Dogs?'" Austin suggested.

"I think your recent business experience is affecting your suggestions."

"Or my love life. Take your pick." He frowned. "I let you down, Mom. I worked hard, but . . ."

"It's okay, Austin. Now that you've tried your hand at business, why don't you go to school and study business management?"

"I've already cost you too much money."

"It didn't break me," she responded. "Barry told me the interest my investments made last month was more than I could have made checkin' groceries my whole life. Not too shabby!"

"Thanks for the offer, Mom." He switched back to the previous topic, preferring to talk about a dog park rather than his own lack of direction. "How far is it from the dog park to Park City?"

"That's it!" Karen said. "Bark City. That's what I'll call it. Thanks, Austin."

"Yeah, sure. Well I can't help you with the dog park until I go back to Wyoming and figure out what I'm gonna do about my business there."

⑲

FOUL BALL

H iya, Camille!" Karen said, pausing at the young woman's desk on her way to Mr. Luskin's office. "Hey, keep your eyes open for an article in the paper about my latest big win at Swiss Days in Midway. Cow Pie Bingo they call it. I won two free movie tickets!"

Camille was still smiling to herself about Karen's news when Ted came around the corner shortly after Mrs. Donaldson headed down the hall to Barry's office. "Playing ball with the firm tonight, Cami?"

She looked up from her proofreading. "Yes, I am. We have enough people for a team, don't we?"

He lowered his voice. "More than enough, but don't use that as an excuse to stay away. I wouldn't have volunteered to coach the team if it wasn't for the pleasure of watching you run the bases."

Camille blushed and looked down at the papers. "I have to finish proofing these documents. Rex is waiting for them."

"Rex? Not *Mr. Parley?* That's mighty friendly. When are you going to get friendly with *me?*" Ted put his palms on her desk and leaned down. "I hear there's trouble in paradise, Cami." His voice was as smooth as silk. "I'm here if you need someone to talk to."

Camille blanched. Was there anybody in the office who hadn't yet heard about her marriage problems?

She blinked back the tears. "Please leave me alone, Ted. I've got a lot of work to do."

When at last he left, Camille found the words of the document swimming before her eyes. She was sorry now to have confided in

Caroline, who was apparently more curious than caring. Her lack of discretion led Camille to withdraw even further from contact with her coworkers.

Nor could she talk to Jarrod about Ted. He'd quiz her about what she'd worn that day or how she had been sitting, implying that somehow she'd encouraged his advances.

She was embarrassed to tell Rex. The worst of Ted's comments weren't things she'd repeat to a conservative Mormon bishop.

Unable to concentrate, Camille grabbed her novel and retreated into the break room. She sank into the nearest of two small sofas, desperate to lose herself in someone else's life and trials.

Before she finished a page, Barbara entered to put something in the fridge. Camille looked up and caught her coworker staring at the cover of her book. Barbara looked away, but not before Camille saw the disapproving look on her face.

Camille had heard several of the Mormon women comment on Barbara being too prim and proper even for them, so she ignored the look.

She never knew what to expect from her Mormon coworkers. She'd overheard the strangest bits of conversations. Once Caroline had remarked that another of the secretaries was in her ward. Knowing that Caroline had a new baby, Camille asked which hospital they'd been in together. The secretaries had all laughed until Erica kindly explained what a Mormon ward was.

Since then, Mr. Parley had clarified a few things for her because as bishop, his ward members sometimes called the office, and he had wanted her to understand how to deal with them. It amused her that Mormons referred to their assignments as "callings." Moses had a "calling." Mother Theresa had a "calling." Apparently, God not only handpicked who would lead the congregations, but He also personally selected who would lead the singing and work with the Cub Scouts.

After re-reading the same paragraph three times, Camille closed the book. *I could tell Rex some of the milder things Ted has said. It could still get the message across without being too embarrassing.* She stood up. *I need to stop being such a doormat—with Jarrod, with Ted, with everyone. I'm going in there right now before I lose my nerve.*

Camille picked up her book and headed back toward her desk, hurrying to pick up the ringing phone.

She announced the call and quickly put it through to Mr. Parley. "Rex, it's Greg Andrews from your church. He says it's an emergency."

A few seconds later, Rex appeared in the hall, suit jacket in hand. "Camille, I need you to reschedule my eleven o'clock meeting with the Langtons. I'm headed to the hospital." Forgetting that Camille was not familiar with such things, he informed her of the reason for his departure. "Someone in my ward needs a blessing."

Camille nodded, and he was out the door. *Someone needs a blessing? If Rex can give out blessings, maybe I can ask him to make Ted go away.*

• • •

Camille gathered up the stack of documents as the last page fed out of the printer. She headed to Rex's office, where she set the draft on the one clean corner of his desk and put his granite paperweight on it, the signal that it was something he needed to look at.

With the proofing done and the appointment cancelled, Camille headed back to the break room, novel in hand. She wasn't the only one with the idea for an early lunch. Two secretaries were already seated at one of the tables. Camille retrieved her sandwich from the fridge, sat down on the sofa on the other side of the room, and opened her book. She hadn't begun to read before her concentration was interrupted by a lively conversation between Barbara and Lynette.

"I'm sick of being made to feel guilty about being a working mother," Lynette said.

"My children won't be in day care," Barbara stated.

"You mean your *imaginary* children, Barbara? The little Eagle Scouts and Mia Maids all in a row?"

Camille pretended to read.

"It is counsel from a prophet," Barbara said.

"So, you're saying that if I had enough faith, I'd stay home with my children," Lynette asked.

"You said it, not me. Amber's making it work."

Lynette became angry. "Amber's husband makes quite a bit more than mine! We're supposed to store food and pay tithing and not put our education ahead of having a family, provide for our children and yet stay home and raise them but not be in debt. I work because I have to!"

"Often, the things we need to hear are the things we don't want to hear."

Annoyed by Barbara's self-righteous tone, Lynette's voice rose. "Since you're single, you can imagine you'll marry a rich man so you can stay home and be the proverbial baby-factory. Come see me when you're really trying to *do* it, Barbara, somewhere besides in your imagination."

Barbara wasn't finished. "You could budget more carefully."

Now Lynette sounded as though she was about to cry. "It's not just you. All the other leaders in Young Women are stay-at-home mothers. Sister Granger can't understand why I won't use my week of vacation to go to girls' camp with the Beehives."

Camille puzzled over that one. *Beehives? I know the Mormons store wheat. Do they produce their own honey too? Is that why Utah is called "the Beehive State"?*

"I spend Sundays and Tuesdays with the Beehives. I'm not spending my vacation with them too," Lynette said.

Barbara lowered her voice. "You shouldn't talk so negatively, Lynette, in front of a nonmember." She motioned toward Camille.

"Oh, yeah," Lynette said, "I forgot. I'm also supposed to be doing missionary work. Not to mention writing my personal history, searching out my kindred dead, sewing all my own clothes, and baking bread."

Camille's reading was barely a pretext at this point. *Wow! Their church expects all that? Maybe I should rethink considering the Mormons in my search for a religion.*

Lynette rose. "Camille, don't mind me. I'm just venting."

"Go ahead, vent," Camille said. "It's hard for me to leave my little girl too."

"You have a daughter?" Lynette asked, realizing she still knew very little about the shy new secretary.

"She's two. Her name is Jordan." Camille dog-eared the unread page in her book and stood up.

"Don't let us run you off," Lynette apologized.

"You're not. I've got an errand to run. Anyway, um, good luck with your, uh, beekeeping."

Camille blushed at the ensuing laughter. *What did I say now?*

HIT A HOMER

Rex drove directly to the ballpark from the office. His unexpected trip to the hospital had necessitated him staying late at work. The game was well underway by the time he reached the field. He sat down next to his wife on the blanket she had spread out, gave her a quick kiss, and grabbed a sandwich from the cooler.

"Sorry I'm late."

"We're used to it," she said with a smile. "This was a good idea for family home evening. You ought to sign up to be on the team."

"They don't need an old codger like me in there flubbing up."

"At least loosen your tie, Rex. Relax a little." She leaned against him as his youngest daughter climbed onto his lap. "What's the update on Sister Bodily?" Lydia asked.

"She's been downgraded from critical to stable. It looks like she'll be okay."

"That's good to hear." Lydia gazed out at the field. "Who is this we're playing tonight anyway? Some of the faces on the opposing team look familiar."

"It's Chivers & Taylor, the firm Jeff Chivers and Trudy Taylor left FB&M to start. It should be real competitive. Plus it's our last game of the season."

• • •

Nicholas Parley, Rex's thirteen-year-old son, turned off the faucet in the restroom and reached for a paper towel. The voices he heard from outside carried through an open window high in the cinder block wall. One of the voices sounded familiar, but he couldn't place it.

"What are you talking about?" the woman asked.

An angry man answered, "I saw how he looked at you. It happens everywhere we go. You and Blaine in Atlanta and now . . ."

"If you knew me at all, Jarrod, you would have known that I couldn't stand Blaine Goodrich. I haven't done anything to lead Ted on! If you weren't so paranoid and suspicious, I could confide in you and get some help when I have to deal with men like him."

"You're awfully friendly with Rex too. Got a little hero-worship going on there, Cami?"

It's Dad's new secretary! Nicholas realized. He tossed the damp paper towel into the wastebasket but stayed in the restroom, eavesdropping on the heated conversation.

"Honestly, Jarrod. Listen to yourself! First you think I've got something going on with the office jerk, and then when I say something nice about a man who's *not* the office jerk, you turn that around too. Yes, my boss is a nice man. Yes, we've worked a little late once or twice, but I've always called and . . ."

"What am I supposed to think?"

"That being your wife means something to me! If you don't trust *me,* consider the fact that the man is a Mormon bishop, for heaven's sake!"

"A man is a man."

"I've had enough of this, Jarrod. I don't have to listen to any more . . ."

"I'm not done."

Nicholas imagined what his favorite on-screen hero would do, emerging powerfully from behind the cinder block wall, muscles rippling. *"Oh, yes you are,"* he would utter, in a deep voice years past puberty. But a return to reality reminded Nick that he didn't have a build that could intimidate his little sisters, much less a woman's angry husband.

"Let go of my arm. You're hurting me."

"Are you going to tell all your new friends what a horrible, abusive husband you have? I wouldn't be this way if . . ."

Forget the movies. What would Dad do? Nicholas wondered. He didn't know for sure, but he was pretty certain Rex wouldn't cower behind the Scott towel dispenser and do nothing. Nicholas opened the door to the restroom and stepped out. He spoke to Camille, but his gaze was fixed on Jarrod. He did his best to deepen his voice. "Every-thing okay here?"

Jarrod immediately let go of Camille's arm. "Just having a little discussion. A *private* discussion," he added.

"Okay, um, well, if everything's okay, I guess I'll just get back over to the ball game." Nicholas headed toward the bleachers, not sure he should sit by his family and have Jarrod make the connection.

• • •

A couple of minutes later, Rex's cell phone rang.

"Don't get it, Rex," Lydia said. "It's Monday night. Church people know they shouldn't be calling you."

"Which means it's probably an emergency. It could be about Sister Bodily." Rex opened the phone and moved away from the blanket. He was surprised to hear Nick's voice.

"Dad, I just saw a guy being abusive to his wife. It's somebody you know. I don't know if I did the right thing, but I kind of interfered, well, enough for him to let go of her, anyway. I'm sitting on the bleach-ers. I don't think it would be a good idea for me to sit with the family right now. I'll tell you about it when we get home."

"If you want to talk about it now, I'll come over . . ."

"I think it can wait. They're back over at the game now."

"We'll talk about it when we get home."

• • •

When Camille went up to bat, Ted yelled from the sidelines, "Hit a homer, Cami!"

Camille turned and gave him a dirty look. She swung at the first pitch, a ball so low it practically rolled along the ground.

"Strike one!"

She swung at the next ball which was high and outside.

"Strike two!"

The third ball was the wildest of all. Cami swung fruitlessly a third time.

"Strike three."

She threw down the bat and stomped off the field.

Lydia turned to Rex. "I wonder what's eating Camille."

Rex let out a long breath. "Why do I have a feeling I'm about to find out?"

WHAT'S EATING CAMILLE?

First thing at work the next morning, Rex rang his secretary's extension. "Camille, could you come into my office?"

When she arrived, Rex smiled and motioned for her to sit. Camille noticed right away it wasn't his usual smile. She hesitated before taking a seat.

"I don't know quite how to approach this, Camille," Rex began, "so I'll come right to the point. Last night, my son Nick was the young man who came out of the restroom in the middle of the, uh, discussion with your husband. He told me your husband had you by the arm. I'm concerned that you might be subject to more serious abuse privately."

Camille did not look at him. "Did your son overhear everything?" *Where is a trap door when you need one? I'll die of embarrassment if he told Rex all the accusations Jarrod made.*

Rex cleared his throat. "Yes, he told me the gist of the conversation." He tried to lighten things up a little. "You'll be relieved to know that I didn't believe the gossip about us."

"Oh, Mr. Parley, this is so embarrassing."

"Forget embarrassment, Camille. I'm concerned that you are being emotionally, and possibly physically, abused. I won't turn a blind eye to that."

She looked up at last and met his eyes, seeing nothing but compassion. Tentatively, she began. "When we were dating, I was flattered that Jarrod was a little jealous and possessive. But now that we're married, he turns my every interaction with a man into something." She looked out the window at the mountains and continued. "If I sign for a package, he'll think I slipped the UPS man my phone number. I've done all I can to earn his trust—sought out female doctors, barely talked to my friends' husbands, let him order for me when there's a male waiter."

"My wife now and again will draw a glance, and I always tell her it's a tribute to my good taste."

"Not all men are like you, Mr. Parley." Camille used the more formal address in light of everything. "Not very many at all." She started to cry. "The worst thing is that Jarrod tries to convince me it's my fault he gets angry or . . ."

"Or what?"

"Or physical." She hung her head. "Sometimes he'll grab my arm or shove me. He's never hurt me seriously, but there were times when I thought he might."

"Do you think he would consider counseling?"

She raised her reddened eyes. "I think we're past that." Rex handed her a couple of tissues from the box on the side of his credenza. "Last night Jarrod told me he's going back to Atlanta. He's been threatening to leave for a long time. He confessed that he had an affair with a girl in Atlanta to get back at me because of his suspicions about me and a coworker. Only there was nothing going on. In fact, I couldn't stand the guy."

Rex nodded. "Go on."

She blew her nose. "He somehow justifies what he *actually* did because of what he *imagined* I did. He says I ruined our marriage. He got back in contact with the woman in Atlanta because he thought I had . . . you know . . . here. He is suspicious of my friendship with you, and he thinks I have something going on with Ted too, which is preposterous. I constantly worry about how all of this is affecting Jordan."

"Is he filing for divorce?" Rex asked.

"He said he's going to start the process."

"People like Jarrod often bail out, thinking they are leaving the source of their problems, only to find that they surface anew in their subsequent relationships."

"I guess we'll see," Camille said.

"I am a proponent of marriage, Camille, but not toxic ones. In this case, you and your daughter might be better off outside the bonds of matrimony. There are holy bonds, and then there are just *bonds*. If it comes to that, we'll see to it that you have good legal representation."

"I appreciate that," Camille said. "He said he won't fight me for custody. He wants to be totally free. His new woman doesn't like kids, apparently."

"That in itself is an enormous blessing. Often, controlling men like Jarrod engage in heated custody battles as power plays. You don't want your daughter to become a pawn in that chess game." He paused. "You don't have roots in Salt Lake. Does this mean you may be leaving us?"

"I think I'd rather try to rebuild my life here than to go back to a place with unhappy memories." She frowned. "My mother will tell me I should have shut up and put up with it, that if he works and helps pay the bills, I'm luckier than a lot of women."

"You haven't had much of a support system anywhere, then?"

"No, not really."

"Let's see what we can get set up for you here, Camille."

She rose, tempted to show him the bruises underneath the long sleeves of her sweater. "You've already helped me more than you know," she said. "Thank you. I feel so much less alone."

"If you need a female friend, Camille, please feel free to call Lydia. She enjoyed getting to know you over lunch." He stood and opened his arms for a fatherly hug. As he took Camille into his arms to comfort her, he looked up as someone passed the open door. Catching only a fleeting glimpse of purple fabric, he wished he had thought better of the hug. His counsel to others had always been to avoid any familiar contact with a coworker that could possibly be misconstrued. He released her quickly, and she moved toward the door, unaware that someone had passed by and seen their embrace.

"There is one more thing I want to say before you go, Camille." She turned. "If you ever have problems with anyone in this firm, you can come to me about it." He cleared his throat. "It would be best if it came voluntarily from you, rather than me asking pointed questions, because that would appear I was leading you."

That was all the prompting she needed. Instead of walking through the open door, Camille closed it and went back to the chair. She sat down, leaned forward, and looked her boss in the eye. "Yes, there *are* some things I'd like to tell you. I'm through being Jarrod's doormat, and I'm not going to let anybody else treat me disrespectfully anymore."

"Go on," Rex prompted.

And she did.

AUSTIN MOVES IN

Austin opened the *Jackson Hole News and Guide* and was greeted by a picture of his mother's smiling face. The caption read: *Lottery winner's luck is holding.* Karen stood in front of the cow that had made her a two-time winner. A close-up of the winning cow pie, smack dab in the middle of square seventeen, accompanied the brief story.

Austin cringed as he read his mother's quote: "I just plopped down my money, and the cow did the rest of the plopping."

Austin wondered how widely this latest story had spread if it had reached the little hometown paper in Jackson Hole. *Gosh Mom, don't you want more grandchildren?*

Austin's day got worse from there. The only people with a booking cancelled when their son ended up in the emergency room as a result of a skateboard stunt gone wrong. Jen announced her engagement and let him know she would not be back the following season. He heard through the grapevine—Grant was always willing to let Austin know how successfully the competition was cleaning his clock—that Chad had beat him out yet again by sealing a deal with the developers of a new hotel.

Too proud to ask his mother for more funding for his failing business, in mid-September Austin sent his boats "Down the River" one last time. His competitors took advantage of his going-out-of-business sale and swooped down on his top-of-the-line rafts and other equipment like a bunch of vultures picking a carcass clean.

He'd found someone willing to take over his lease. His location was being turned into an ice cream parlor by the time he finally pulled up the last stake and headed out of town with all his worldly belongings in the back of his pickup truck.

In no particular hurry, Austin headed to Salt Lake City by way of Yellowstone Park, stopping to watch Old Faithful erupt. He had taken that route because he'd thought of possibly calling Chelsea Krumperman in Rexburg, where she was attending BYU–Idaho.

The internal debate continued as he stopped in Ashton, Idaho, to fill up with gas. As the numbers on the pump ticked away, Austin argued with himself. *I don't even know if she'll still be interested, but if she is, do I want a long-distance relationship? A girl like her is worth the drive, even with gas prices this high, but I'd have to admit defeat, tell her I closed down the business. . . .*

The pump clicked off. He retrieved his receipt. *I could act like I've seen the light and didn't want to run a business that interfered with church.* He climbed back into the truck. *Then she'll probably bring up the mission thing though. She's probably involved with someone else by now anyway. On the other hand, what have I got to lose? She might be desperate to ditch that last name.*

Before he headed back onto the highway from the gas station, he dialed her cell phone. There was no answer, but in her message she gave the number to her apartment. He left a quick message and then called the other number, only to be informed by her roommate that she was out.

"May I tell her who's calling?"

"Austin from Jackson Hole."

"The river rafting guy?"

"She's talked about me?"

Sensing she had said too much, Melanie did her best to cover. "We always catch up with each other's summer activities. Are you still running the river trips?"

"Uh no, it's a little late in the year. I'm headed back to Salt Lake, actually."

"Does she have your number there?"

"She's got my cell number."

"Okay, I'll tell her you called."

He flipped his phone closed and got back into the truck. *So much for that detour.*

• • •

It took Austin a couple of days to get settled in the basement at his mother's new house. It was several times larger than the apartment he had just left. There was a huge family room with a kitchenette on one end and an imposing stone fireplace at the other, still with hooks in the mantle where the Cironni children had hung their Christmas stockings.

His black futon looked kind of lonely there all by itself. He moved his things into two of the bedrooms, both adjoining the same bath, using one for his bed and mismatched dresser and nightstand, and the other for his computer, desk, and bookcases.

He plopped down on his bed. *Now what do I do with myself? I'm a bum, but at least I'm a first-class bum. I'd better find a job or go to school or something.*

He was jarred out of his thoughts by the sound of his cell phone. He grabbed his jacket and pulled the phone out of the front pocket just in time. "Hello?"

"Austin?"

"Speaking."

"This is Chelsea. I got your messages."

"Hi, Chelsea. I'm glad you called back. I was going through Rexburg and thought I'd buy you dinner or something. Unless one of those BYU guys had a vision that you're 'the one.' "

"I'm sorry I missed you, Austin."

"So no vision yet?"

She laughed. "The semester just started."

"Right. All things in wisdom and order. Register. Buy books. Find wife."

Chelsea laughed again. He loved the sound of her laugh.

"Are you going to be up this way again soon?"

Definite interest. "I hadn't planned on it, but . . ."

"Actually, in a couple of weeks I'm going to Salt Lake with some friends. Maybe we can get together then."

"It would be great to see you."

"Give me directions, and I'll have my friends drop me off at your house."

After he hung up, Austin had a feeling he'd never experienced before. *She's going to come here and see this house. I don't have to be embarrassed about where I live.*

He began to make plans. *I've got to keep Dee and Metalface out of sight. I need to find a job or at least have something on the horizon. I need to get more furniture, and maybe a couple of churchy pictures on the wall. Mom told me to use the money from my going-out-of-business sale to furnish the basement. I bet I could get this place looking pretty good.*

• • •

By the time Chelsea arrived a couple of weeks later, Austin had put together a very livable bachelor apartment. After he served a nice lunch, they settled in on his new couch. "So, Austin," she said, nestling into the plush forest-green sofa. "This is really nice! I'd move back home if my parents had an awesome basement like this. What does your mother do anyway?" Chelsea asked.

"What does she *do?*"

"Professionally. You said your parents are divorced, right."

"Mom's got her finger in a few pies, and she got a good, um, settlement. She does some work for a charitable foundation too." It wasn't exactly untrue, just a little white lie. He didn't want Chelsea to be interested in him because of the money—although he preferred that dilemma to his previous life situation.

"What does your dad do?"

Good question. I have absolutely no idea who he is or what he does. "You know, Chelsea, I don't know the man. He disappeared before I was old enough to remember him. We've got what we need, and he's not around, never has been." He said it in such a way as to discourage further questions.

"At least he left you well-provided for."

Yeah, right.

Chelsea reached out to touch his arm. "I was so happy to hear you've gone back to church."

"Well, my business interfered with church attendance." He hesitated. "So I closed it down."

"I'm sorry I let that bother me so much, Austin," she said. "I judged you unfairly. You obviously have your priorities straight. Not many guys would close down a successful business and . . ."

"I'm thinking about going back to school," he interrupted. "I never really had enough . . . *direction* the first time. Now that I've run a business, I'm thinking about pursuing a business major, probably at the University of Utah."

"That sounds like a good idea, I guess."

"You *guess?*"

"I thought you might still go on a mission."

"Okay, Chelsea. I thought we were having a good time. Now you're trying to convince me to leave for two years?" He turned to face her. "Do you like me or not?"

"Yes, I like you, Austin, a lot. I see great potential in you."

Austin nearly spat out the word. *"Potential?* Telling a guy he has potential is like calling a girl a sweet spirit."

"A mission is an important part of holding to the iron rod."

"I'm more of a Liahona guy, myself," Austin said, leaning back until the footrest on the reclining portion of the sofa popped out.

"Okay, a Liahona guy, sure."

"Liahona people realize there can be more than one way to do things, right?" He clasped his hands together and put them behind his head. "Admittedly I got off track from my plans to serve a mission, but presently I'm more interested in that whole eternal marriage thing."

"Okaaaaay . . ." She drew the word out long enough that he knew it was anything *but* okay.

"I'm a little old for a mission now, Chelsea. I wouldn't fit in with all those nineteen-year-olds."

"I wouldn't rule it out."

"We'll see," he said.

" 'We'll see' always meant 'no' when my mother said it," Chelsea observed.

He pushed the footrest closed and turned to face her. Moving closer, he said seductively, "In case you hadn't noticed, I'm *not* your mother."

"So what does your Liahona say *today?*" she asked, playfully responding to his flirtation.

"Just this morning it told me that I would have a visit from a beautiful girl and that I should make her lunch." He twined his fingers in her honey brown hair. "It told me that no matter how much I felt like I wanted to kiss her, I shouldn't because iron rod girls don't kiss on the first date. See, that's the difference. A Liahona person doesn't count the dates. He goes by his feelings. He may date someone five or six times without kissing her."

He leaned even closer and whispered in her ear. "He may never kiss her—or he may feel so close to someone after a brief time that he really,

really wants to kiss her. He follows his feelings, unless he realizes it's going to mess up what could be a beautiful relationship."

Chelsea drew in her breath and with it inhaled the scent of his expensive cologne. Tanned and toned from running the river, Austin looked even better than she remembered. Truth be told, this tall, blond fellow with green eyes was the reason she and her friends had decided to run the river in the first place.

She sighed and snuggled into him. "I'm thinking that if I, uh, held onto the iron rod with *one* hand, I might be able to see a *little* of what is written on your Liahona."

Austin caught his breath. *She wants me to kiss her. All right! Maybe I shouldn't, just to make a point. On the other hand, if I can resist a beautiful woman who obviously wants to be kissed, I might as well go into cold storage for two years.*

He brushed the hair back from her cheek and made the world go away for a few glorious seconds. Then he looked into her eyes. *Our kids are going to be so good-looking.*

The magic of the moment was shattered when his mother yelled down the stairs that Chelsea's friends were there to pick her up. Austin cursed the timing but walked her out, his arm comfortably around her shoulder. On the way up, he stopped for one more pulse-quickening kiss on the stairway.

At the car, Chelsea introduced him to her three curious girlfriends. He leaned down to greet them through the open window. They watched wide-eyed as Chelsea rose to give Austin a quick kiss before she got into the backseat. Already awed by the big house, Chelsea knew her friends would not lack for things to ask about on the drive back to Rexburg.

Austin was still smiling when he went inside.

"So that's Chelsea?" his mother asked.

"Yup."

"She's very pretty."

"You noticed too?"

Austin headed downstairs, his step a little lighter than in recent times.

• • •

Feeling a bit wistful and wishing she had someone to connect with, Karen went upstairs and took the next baby step.

After a tutorial from her son, she'd learned how to add contacts to her cell phone. She'd retrieved Hal's number and added it to her list of contacts after several tries. It was time to use it. She brought up his name and pushed the button. This time she got a live man and not a recording.

"Hi," she said. "Is this Hal? This is Karen Donaldson. You know? From Smith's Food King . . ."

GIVE, OH, GIVE

After Sunday's block of meetings, Toni picked up her two youngest children from Primary. Karen looked up from loading up her singing supplies. "Little Alex did such a good job today," Karen reported.

"I was the little stweam!" Alex Jr. beamed. "I made the gwass gwow gweenoo still."

"I'm so proud of you, honey," Toni said. "Karen, can I help you carry some of that?"

"Sure thing, Sister C." Karen handed her two posters. "If you can get these, I'll get the rest."

Toni followed Karen out to her vehicle. "Did I tell you Corina always takes Kimo Kat with her to chemotherapy? Recently several parents of the other patients asked me where they could get one."

"Really? I'll see if I can find more of the stuffed cats. It's makin' the hats that takes time. Do you crochet?"

Toni smiled. "Not very well, but if you find the stuffed animals, I'll help make the hats." She got a faraway look in her eyes. "You grow to care about the other children and their parents. We've all become one big, not-necessarily-happy family."

Toni handed over the posters and quickly changed the subject, not wanting to think about the little boy who had died the week before. "Alex and I were in South Jordan and saw a sign for a business called Second Childhood. We knew it had to be you. It is, isn't it?"

Karen loaded her vehicle while she talked. "They're finishin' up, gettin' the party rooms painted. It's amazin' how fast things can come together when you got a little extra money to motivate people. Of course, we renovated a building, so we didn't have to build it from scratch."

"How are you doing all this, Karen? I mean I know you've got the money, but . . ."

"I've got Bishop Parley's law firm workin' for me—got my own personal attorney on retainer. I tell Barry what I wanna do, and he makes sure I have what I need—realtors, architects, a construction company. Everybody kind of jumps at the chance to work for the Undercover Angel Foundation because they know we pay our bills and that we'll probably have other projects." She closed the back of her vehicle. "I'm workin' on an idea for a used toy store called Grandma's Attic. I got Dee buyin' vintage toys at yard sales and on the Internet to keep her out of trouble and give her something to do. I've almost filled your whole three-car garage."

"With toys?"

"Yup! Barry's still workin' out the bugs. He says that with all the recalls on toys and problems with lead paint, we have to be careful about the toys we resell. I found a guy who makes old fashioned wooden toys and boxes of blocks, so there will be some new stuff too, but old fashioned."

"Blocks will always be in style."

"Our architect is designin' it to look like a real attic. There are lots of grandmas and grandpas out there who still need something to do."

"You amaze me, Karen. I mean you could just sit around living the high life and . . ."

"So when's your next milestone birthday, Toni? I'm gonna give people I love a free birthday party at Second Childhood."

"You don't really expect me to tell you when I reach forty, do you?"

"People who lie about their age don't get no free birthday party."

Toni laughed. "I'll have to weigh my options."

"We're looking for somebody to manage the place. I think Alex should apply."

"Are you serious, Karen?"

"Barry tells me everybody says I'm the best employer they ever had. People are anxious to work at one of my companies."

"That little stream's got nothing on you, Karen." Toni took her young son by the hand. "I'll certainly tell Alex. I know it's been hard on him managing the restaurant when we no longer own it." She felt tears come to her eyes. "Karen, you've been far better to us than we—than I—deserve. I know I haven't always treated you . . ."

Karen cut her short. "Apology accepted. God's workin' on all of us, Toni." She tossed her purse into the open window and onto the passenger seat. "I'll call ya when I find the stuffed animals, and you can come over, and we'll crochet some hats."

"Will you be serving cookie dough for refreshments?" Toni asked.

"Well, I don't know about you, but I can't crochet on an empty stomach."

• • •

Toni hesitated at the ornate front door. It felt foreign to knock on what she still considered her own front door. She swallowed hard, remembering her resolve not to enter the place as long as Karen lived there. She forced herself to think of the ailing children for whom they were crocheting hats. *If this is what it feels like to swallow your pride, it doesn't exactly go down easily.*

Karen answered the door. Toni took a deep breath and stepped inside. The house did seem to be cleaner than Karen was known for. Toni tried not to think about where she was as Karen motioned toward her secondhand sofa. *I suppose this is Karen's idea of interior design—colored duct tape to patch the sofa.*

She winced at the large plaid doggy bed in the alcove with the bay window, her personal sanctuary where she had studied her scriptures each morning. The built-in bookcase near the window seat that once displayed her personal library of gospel favorites now held chew toys and boxes of dog biscuits.

"I found six more of the fuzzy cats, so I bought 'em all." She motioned toward her battered coffee table. "I got a bunch of different colors of yarn—didn't want the kids gettin' their hats mixed up." The multi-colored yarn balls sat next to a platter of cookie dough balls.

Toni caught sight through the window of a brightly colored plastic play fort near the gazebo, where she'd shared so many romantic anniversary dinners with her husband. She picked up a ball of yellow yarn, forcing herself to concentrate on the job at hand.

"Too bad you can't figure out how to mass-produce these, Karen. There are so many kids who could use one."

After some time of companionable chit chat, Karen paused in her work and looked up at Toni. "I ain't told nobody else this, Toni, but I got a date comin' up in a couple of weeks, and I been wonderin' what to wear."

"A date? *With whom?*"

"A guy I knew from the grocery store."

"Where are you going?"

"To the Subway sandwich shop."

Toni racked her brain to remember anything noteworthy from Karen's wardrobe. It hadn't changed much even though she'd come into money. "Your usual *shabby chic* should do fine."

Karen laughed out loud. "Is that what you call my style? I used to be sloppy, but now that I'm rich it's called *shabby chic?*"

"You want him to like you for you," Toni said, "so you ought to be yourself." As Toni said the words, she realized with a start that she truly meant them.

"I heard that old beat-up furniture is in style now too," Karen continued. "What do they call that? Depressed?"

"Distressed."

Karen laughed again. "Oh, my furniture is in great distress, that's for sure!"

"It's none of my business, but why haven't you bought new things?"

"We got some new stuff in the bedrooms and downstairs. This is a really comfortable sofa. I ordered a slipcover for it. That's all I need."

"Karen, you're an amazing woman. You can really just say 'that's all I need' when you could buy yourself anything in the whole wide world?"

"I bought a new house and a car and a piano. What else should I do to make myself happy—buy the Hope Diamond and set it here on the coffee table to stare at?" She paused. "There's one thing money can't buy, though. I get lonely sometimes. Austin's got a girlfriend now that he sees as often as he can. She's in Rexburg goin' to school. And Dee, I ain't crazy about her new boyfriend—he's kinda scary—but whatcha gonna do? Sometimes I wonder if I'm gonna spend the rest of my life sittin' here watchin' *Wheel of Fortune* by myself."

"Tell me about your date."

"I ain't dated much since my divorce. I only ever had one real boyfriend—Ray Donaldson. We met when I was twelve, fishin' for pollywogs in the park. We was best friends after that."

"I married my best friend too," Toni said.

"I've had a bunch of marriage proposals since I won the lottery, you know. My little Vegas weddin' put a stop to that. Did you read about it, or don't you read the tabloids?"

"Yes, I bought one, Karen," Toni admitted. "It isn't often someone I know is front page news." She rolled more yarn from the pink ball.

"That's a good thing, ain't it?"

"I suppose so. I don't believe everything I read in the tabloids, though. So, tell me, what parts of that story were true?"

Karen suddenly became very engrossed in counting stitches. "The less you know about that the better, Sister C. It was all Barry's idea—to get guys to stop sendin' me marriage proposals."

"Did it work?"

"Yeah, it did the trick. But now I don't know how to find somebody who's interested in plain old Karen Donaldson. I ain't even sure why anyone would be, without the money throwed in. Winnin' the lottery almost makes it a sure thing I'll either be taken advantage of or die a lonely old woman." Her fingers slowed to a stop. "I ain't crazy about either of them options."

"I hadn't thought about it, but I guess you're right."

Karen lowered her voice as if someone might overhear. "So, this guy from the grocery store, he wrote me a letter. We been playin' phone tag since then, but I finally talked to him. Barry ain't gonna be happy about it. He makes me bring him all the proposals I get. But I didn't give him this one because it wasn't a proposal."

"Do you know the man?" Toni asked.

"As well as you can know somebody you only talk to while you're ringin' up their groceries. But Bishop said we should limit our social contacts to people we knew before we were rich. I figure this guy fits."

"You sound a little unsure."

"Have you ever made a plan and then something always comes up to get in the way?" Karen asked.

"Lots of times," Toni said.

"So what do you think when that happens?"

"Sometimes I think it means I'm not supposed to do it, that for some reason it just isn't right."

"I been wonderin' that," Karen confessed.

"Other times, though, I wonder if it is something I'm supposed to do and that's why there is so much opposition."

"That don't help none, Toni, givin' it to me both ways."

"So go have a sandwich with the guy. What's the worst that can happen?"

"Yeah, I guess you're right."

"What about Barry? I saw his picture in the paper. He looks rather distinguished, and he can't be married. No wife would have gone along with that Vegas trip."

"His wife died," Karen confirmed. "Are you sayin' I oughta make a play for Barry? For real?" She snorted. "I don't think you could find two more different people on the face of the earth. He's a really nice man, though. I did kinda get used to havin' him around."

"Stranger things have happened."

"I had my chance in Vegas, and I think I let Barry slip through my fingers." Karen chuckled. "On the other hand, he is the one who came up with that plan to keep me from gettin' all the marriage proposals. Maybe he was jealous, huh? Maybe he's got the hots for me, and I just don't know it." She laughed even louder at the prospect of that.

Toni laughed along, reaching for another piece of cookie dough, and trying to recall the last time she'd had such a relaxing afternoon. Once she'd stopped thinking about the house, Toni realized that spending a few hours crocheting with Karen wasn't half as bad as she had imagined it would be. *Who'd a thunk it?*

"I should prob'ly just keep drownin' my loneliness with the Mrs. Fields cookie dough," Karen said. "For now, anyways."

RAY RETURNS

R ay Donaldson looked at the directions Karen's cousin, Victor, had given him and signaled to turn right. He was glad Vic remembered their friendship from years before and had been sympathetic to his reasons for showing up now.

"Everybody else knows where Cousin Karen lives," Vic had told him, "so I guess it won't hurt if you do too. Be prepared to be greeted by a couple of biker brothers. Just tell them Victor sent you. We got extra security on duty today, because she's throwing some kind of a shindig at the park."

Is the Good Lord smilin' on me, just a little, maybe? Ray wondered. He answered himself. *Nah! I don't deserve help from on high, much as I could use it.* He ran his fingers through his thinning hair—a habit he'd had since his youth, back when there'd been a little more hair to run his fingers through.

Ray had never been good at speeches. He rehearsed as he drove through the streets of Holladay.

Karen, it ain't what it looks like. Victor told me you came into some good fortune. Now it'll look like that's why I showed up. Truth is, I wanna try and get acquainted with my kids and try to make amends to all of you for not being there.

He turned onto her street, growing more nervous by the second. *Face it, buddy. You left her to provide for them two kids alone. She ain't gonna be glad to see you, and nobody's gonna believe the real reason you tried to find her now.*

He parked in the circular driveway and took a deep breath, his eyes widening at the sight of the huge stone house. Stepping out onto the brick-paved drive, he got back into his car and backed up, parking on the street. *It ain't gonna impress her if my car leaks oil all over her fancy driveway.*

He flipped a nickel into the fountain and wiped his hands on his pants. *Step eight, making restitution. How do I do that now? Even though it took me forever to save up, that few thousand dollars I wanted to give her is gonna be like the nickel I just threw into the fountain. And any way you slice it, I'm gonna look like a scum-sucking freeloader.*

Before he could jump in his car and drive back the way he'd come, he spoke sternly to himself. *Time to be a man, Ray, and face up to what you done and what you ain't done. The worst they can do is tell you to get lost.*

Suddenly sweating something fierce, Ray resumed his positive self-talk. *I have turned my life over to a power greater than myself. I will trust God. I have turned my life over to Him. He will help me.*

A banner was strung in front of the house. It proclaimed: *Bag Boy Appreciation Day.* A long winding driveway through a wooded area led to their nearest neighbor's home, so Karen's impressive home appeared to stand alone at the end of the street, bordering on a park to the east.

Ray headed toward the park. Broadcasting from what looked like an oversized boom box, a disk jockey announced the next tune. Ray headed in that direction when a dog across the grass diverted his attention. It was a chocolate cocker spaniel, attached by a leash to a good-looking tall blond fellow. He veered off to the left where the young man stood with his dog.

Ray had always been an animal lover. "Mind if I pet him? He looks like a dog I used to have." Ray patted the dog's head, and the friendly pup squatted at his touch. Ray enthused. "Just like Buster. Greets you with a little piddle."

"Your dog was named Buster?"

"Yeah, it was short for Buster Brown, 'cause he was brown, like this one. What's your dog's name?"

"Boomer. We had a dog named Buster that died when I was about four. We kept one of the puppies from a litter he fathered. We named her Butterscotch, 'cause she was caramel colored. She died when I was sixteen, but we kept two of her puppies." He looked the man over. "Are you one of the bag boys?"

"No. I'm, um, looking for Karen Donaldson. Do you know her?"

"She's my mom. Last I saw her . . ."

Ray's jaw dropped open, and he missed the rest of the sentence. Here was Boomer—son of Butterscotch, daughter of Buster—with a definite family resemblance, yet he was face-to-face with his own son who did not resemble him in the least. "You . . . you're . . . you're . . . Austin," he stammered.

"Boy, word travels fast when you come into money. Nobody used to know who I was. Yeah, I'm Austin. My mother's over there." He called out to Karen, who had her back turned. "Hey, Mom! Somebody's looking for you."

Karen turned around, looked, and then squinted.

Ray wasn't sure she'd recognize him after all these years, and he was reasonably sure that this wasn't the best way to introduce himself to the son who had grown up without him. But Karen was coming toward him and he had to do something, say something. She came closer.

"Karen, it's me, Ray."

"Ray?" Karen's eyes went wide.

Austin looked at him warily. "Ray *who?*"

Ray went white and stood in awkward silence, staring at his son. *He does have my green eyes.*

Karen answered for him. "Ray Donaldson. Austin, this is your father."

Ray stood frozen. *Austin looks about as thrilled as Luke Skywalker was to find out Darth Vader was his dad.* At last he managed, "The dog, he looks just like Buster."

"Yeah," Karen said, "Buster's his grandfather."

"So I understand." He ventured a weak smile at Austin, but it was not returned.

"Looks like this dog has a better sense of where he came from than I do," Austin said. "What're you doing here, anyway?"

"It ain't what it looks like, the money and all."

"Of course, it's not." Austin rolled his eyes. "None of the people always hanging around now are interested in us because of the money, right, Mom?"

"Austin, let's the three of us go back to the house. This party'll go on just fine without me for a few minutes."

"You go if you think you've got something to say to him."

"Austin, please. I wish you'd . . ."

In answer, Austin turned away from her—away from the man he had just learned was his father—and walked off.

•   •   •

It wasn't long before Dee came home and found Karen and a strange man seated at the small dining room table. They were looking through photo albums.

That's weird, she thought. *Why would some guy wanna look at baby pictures of me and Austin?* She turned to her mother. "I'm gonna be out late with some friends tonight. Can you keep an eye on Mandee?"

"Dee, there's somebody I wanna introduce you to." Ray stood, doing his best to be a gentleman. Karen began, "Dee, this is. . ."

Ray interrupted. "Let me do this, Karen."

All at once Dee put it together—the interest in the photo albums, his obvious nervousness around her. *This is one of the guys that sent mom a proposal in the mail.* "You ain't one of the bag boys, I suspect," she said.

"Nope." He extended his hand. "Name's Ray. Ray Donaldson."

Delia's outstretched hand fell to her side and her eyes opened wide. She looked past him to her mother, who nodded. It took a moment for the shock to wear off, but when it did, Delia was dismissive. "So, you're my dad. Hi, Ray." She said it as if he was a new neighbor. "I'm Delia, but everybody calls me Dee. By the way, you're a grandpa, and you're babysitting tonight." She turned to Karen. "I'll be out late, Mom, maybe all night. Don't wait up." And then she was gone.

Dee's cavalier attitude wasn't what Ray had hoped for. He didn't know *what* he had hoped for, but he was reasonably sure this wasn't it. Still, Delia's indifference was better than Austin's hostility. He looked over at Karen. "Well, what'd I expect? Somehow I thought you'd be the one that was spittin' mad at me."

She shrugged. "What'd be the use of that?" She turned another page. "Wanna see more baby pictures?"

RAY MOVES IN

Karen turned the last page in the photo album and sat back. "So, that's our kids."

Ray was stunned. "Yeah . . . wow . . . our kids. I mean, they ain't kids no more. And I'm a grandfather?"

"Dee had a baby when she was in high school. We'll try to arrange a better way to introduce you to Mandee. She's over at the park with my friends from the store."

Karen got a bag of potato chips and poured them into a bowl. She set the bowl on the table between them and sat back down. Ray took a handful.

"When I got the job at the Smith's on 45th South, the chance to move into this neighborhood seemed like a blessing straight from heaven."

"So you lived around here before you bought this mansion?"

"A couple of streets over, in a basement apartment."

Still thinking about Austin and Delia, Ray switched gears. "Do you think they'll give me a chance?"

"Only one way to find out. You plannin' on stickin' around?"

He took a deep breath. "I'm a recoverin' alcoholic, Karen, and I'm tryin' to get my life right—with you and the kids and with God. I figger you and God might take it easy on me, anyways. I ain't got a place to stay yet, but if I can find something around here, I'd like to try and be part of their lives from now on."

"You been gone a long time, Ray."

"I never meant for it to be this long. I always planned . . ."

"I ain't tryin' to make you feel guilty," Karen interrupted. "I'm just saying you can't come back after twenty years and expect to help out with burpin' and changin' diapers."

"Austin hates me."

"Austin don't know you. What he hates is that he never had a dad."

"Delia doesn't seem to care. I don't know which is worse."

"At least you got an honest reaction."

Ray pushed the bowl aside. "What about you? How do you feel about me showing up?"

"You got my honest reaction too—surprise. I never thought I'd see ya again, Ray."

"Yeah, I know you was surprised, but now that the shock's wore off a little, how do you feel?"

"I ain't sure the shock's wore off, Ray."

"You got a problem with me stickin' around to try to get to know the kids?" He took a deep breath and let it out. "I know this ain't gonna make a difference now, but I saved up some money to give you to help make up for all the time I wasn't there to help."

Karen responded slowly. "About havin' you around, I think it'd be better for you to stay than poppin' in, introducin' yourself, and then disappearin' again. I know the kids ain't exactly rolled out the welcome mat, but if you stick around, maybe they'll believe you really wanna be part of their lives."

"I ain't expectin' it to be easy."

She closed the photo album. "About the money. Austin was ready to go on a mission once. I'm still hopin' he'll go. You could offer it to him for that, but he'd probably just use you as another excuse not to go."

"You need to trust that God'll help out."

Karen raised an eyebrow. "That don't sound like the Ray I know."

"I ain't the Ray you knew anymore. I been workin' hard on a lot of stuff." He looked hopeful. "Then you don't mind if I stick around?"

"Suit yourself."

"That's what I've been doin' my whole life. I'm tryin' to break that cycle, Karen—and a couple of others. After I split, the guys I hung out with went out drinkin'. It was just social for me at first, but always in the back of my mind was the fact that I left you alone with two little kids."

"We wasn't ready to get married, Ray," Karen said. "Neither of us."

"Yeah, but you stepped up to the plate once we had the babies. Me? I started drinkin' to try to forget what a poor excuse for a man I was." He folded his hands on the table. "I've been goin' to AA meetings regular for a couple of years now. I've got a sponsor. It wasn't hard for me to get through the first few steps, acknowledgin' a higher power and all. I always believed in God, and when I started talkin' to Him again, I started seein' ways that He cared, even about a guy like me."

He continued, "I ain't had a drink in nearly two years now. When I got to step eight, I knew I was never gonna go no further until I found you and the kids and made amends . . . whatever I could, anyways."

"So you were plannin' to come back before I got rich?"

"Yup, but I dragged my feet, because I was thinkin' maybe you'd hit me up for back child support—not that you didn't have a right to—but I figured I'd go to jail or the poorhouse if you did. So I waited until I had some money saved up, at least as a start and as a show of faith."

"How did you find out I was rich?"

"Vic told me about you winnin' the lottery. I called him because I thought he'd know where to find you. I know this sounds stupid, but I felt like you bein' rich was another answer to my prayers. Felt like the way back was bein' made easier for me."

Karen laughed. "I dunno, Ray. Bishop Parley's got me convinced God don't run the lotto, but I got my own theory. You know how the devil takes good things and twists them for evil purposes? Well, I figure maybe God can take something that ain't good—like the lotto—and turn it to a good purpose."

"Maybe so."

"We tried to keep the news from spreadin'," she said, "but there's only so much you can do."

"I looked up some of the articles after I talked to Vic." He frowned. "He told me he thought you wasn't really married to the attorney guy."

"We was trying to keep the marriage proposals down."

"Did ya get a lot of them?"

Karen smiled. "More than before I was rich."

"Anyways," he continued, "I knew how bad it would look if I showed up right after you struck gold. I hope you believe that money ain't the reason I'm here now."

Karen looked across the table at Ray, and he met her gaze unflinchingly. She finally spoke. "I do believe ya, Ray. Can't speak for what everybody else is gonna think, though."

"I'll deal with everybody else—even the kids. I just need to know you believe me." He reached across the table and took her hand. "I'm sorry, Karen, for all the hard times ya went through on account of me."

"What's done is done," she said. "I forgave you a long time ago. I had to. I couldn't go through life angry. You made choices, and now you got your consequences—two kids who might never let you in their lives. I can see God's workin' on ya, and I try not to interfere in His work."

"Will ya help me with the kids?"

"I ain't got much influence myself these days."

"What've you told them about me?"

"That we got married way too young and that you wasn't ready for the responsibility."

"I guess that's more than fair." He took a sip of the soda Karen had provided.

"Ya know, Ray, maybe you're an answer to my prayers too. Dee don't wanna admit it, but I'm pretty sure she's got a drinkin' problem."

"That don't surprise me." Ray cracked his knuckles. "You know, Karen, maybe we could get together—once a week or something—and talk about the kids. You could help me catch up and try to understand them. Would you do that?"

Karen nodded. "Sure, Ray. You wanna come here?"

"Let's pick a restaurant and talk over dinner."

"Sounds kinda like a date," Karen said.

"It's for the kids," he assured her.

"Okay. For the kids." She felt herself begin to blush and quickly changed the subject. "Hey, I just remembered, I got a party goin' on over at the park."

"Oh yeah. The bag boys."

"I better get back on over there." She paused. "Ya wanna come over tomorrow and meet Mandee, after I've had a chance to talk to her?"

"Sure. What time?"

"Just call first."

"Okay, sure. How old is she?"

"She's six." Karen hesitated, knowing she should probably consult Barry or Bishop Parley before she made the offer. "Above the garage, there's a big room."

"It's a big garage," Ray observed.

"It used to be Brother Cironni's home office. They got one of them cool built-in Murphy beds in there. Ya move the two bookcases to the side and there's a bed, made it so it could double as a guest room, I guess, or maybe so he'd have a place to sleep if they had a fight. There's a bathroom with a shower. There ain't a kitchen, but there's a little mini fridge in there and you could get a microwave."

"What're ya sayin', Karen?"

"Even with Dee and Mandee and Austin livin' here with me, we got way more room than we could ever use. I don't need the space. It has its own entrance, and I own it, so . . ."

"Really? I don't much need a kitchen anyways, and I don't have much in the way of worldly goods."

"You'd hafta pay me some rent," Karen added.

"Well, yeah. Of course. And I need to find a job."

"Ya want it, then?" Karen asked.

"Sure, why not?"

As if in answer to that question, it suddenly dawned on Karen that she had a date the following Saturday and that her ex-husband living over her garage might be a detail that was hard to explain to anyone with whom she might become involved. *I guess I wouldn't hafta bring it up on the first date. He ain't comin' to my house. We're just a couple of old friends havin' a sandwich together. Yeah, that's all.*

CUT TO THE CHASE

Rex was already backed up on his workload due to an unscheduled meeting of the executive committee in which he had brought up Camille's complaints against Ted Simon. The members of the committee had been split, as he had feared they would be. Besides the obvious problem of lack of evidence, Ted had fierce allies. Rex had taken a firm stand against two members of the executive committee who were staunch in his defense.

He had pushed the replay button on his final remarks several times already, wondering if, as had been suggested, he was equally biased in the other direction. "We cannot let Ted's prowess as a litigator cause us to overlook these serious infractions. I will get to the bottom of this."

Ted's cocky attitude in the face of the latest allegations had alienated Rex further. He'd met lots of egos over the years, but Ted won the grand prize. He stood firm, not so much in defense of his innocence as in his ability to face down any opponent. The bottom line was that they needed some indisputable evidence of Ted's wrongdoing before they could do anything but issue a warning.

• • •

"Bishop," Karen said, as she popped her head into his open door. "Ya got a new member in the ward."

Rex looked up from the papers on his desk. He'd long ago given up reminding Karen to call him "Mr. Parley" at the office. "Who is that?" he asked curtly, not his usual patient self. The time he had allotted to

Karen while Barry was at a doctor's appointment had long since been eaten up by the meeting. Still, she was on the schedule, and she was definitely a paying client, even if none of his other clients paid to discuss the minutia of their lives.

Karen came into the office and took a chair. "You know that party I had at the park? Bag Boy Appreciation Day? They work hard, and most places tell them not to take tips. They have Secretary's Day, but some employees, like bag boys, nobody ever notices."

"'Executive Assistant Day' is what they call it now." Rex had learned he had to cut to the chase with Karen. "But I doubt you came in today to discuss the bag boys." He immediately regretted his sharp tone. "Or bag persons, as they will someday be called."

"Bag lady don't work either, does it?"

Rex softened. "I apologize for being short with you, Karen. I'm kind of backed up today."

She paused. "That happens to me sometimes too. Hope ya get feelin' better."

It took a moment for Rex to realize that she thought he was talking about intestinal woes rather than workload. He didn't even bother trying to correct the misconception. It was Karen, after all. Rather, he did his best to steer her back to the topic at hand. "Who is this new member of the ward?"

Karen remained evasive. "Barry always looks at what checks I been writin'." She fished in her attaché for her checkbook. "He looks at my personal ones too so he knows what I've been up to." She opened the checkbook. "See? I been keepin' good records, just like you said."

Glancing quickly through the ledger, Rex noted several checks had been made out to the same person. "Who is Gwen Michaels?"

"She's a college student who's been helpin' me with house cleanin'. I thought when I hired her maybe she'd hit it off with Austin, but he's got a girlfriend up at BYU–Idaho. She keeps findin' excuses to come down here, and he's goin' up there this weekend to take her to some big dance. Who knows? Maybe it'll get serious with him and Chelsea. This weekend I got a . . ."

Karen caught herself. *I can't believe I almost told him about my date with Hal.* She switched back to a safe topic. "So anyway, the house looks so good now, I'm thinking about havin' Sister Arletti over to eat off my floor."

"My goodness, Karen. How many hours of cleaning does this represent?"

"That's for six hours."

"This is more than we pay highly educated law clerks!"

"Law clerks do the stuff real lawyers don't wanna do, right? I don't wanna do housework. That's what it's worth to me not to have to do it. Besides, Toni Cironni was comin' over, and I couldn't have her thinkin' I wasn't takin' good care of the place."

"Toni came over?" He didn't even try to mask his surprise.

"We're workin' on a project together."

Despite his curiosity, Rex continued to try to steer Karen back to the original subject. "This looks fine, Karen. Now, what's this about a new ward member?"

"Oh, yeah! Like I was sayin', I was havin' that party over at the park and I heard my name and looked up and there . . ."

Rex glanced impatiently at his watch. "Karen, I'm afraid I'm going to have to ask you to get to the point."

She blurted it out. "Ray Donaldson, my ex-husband, is gonna be livin' in our neighborhood."

"Your *ex-husband?*" Rex put his head in his hands. "In our ward?"

"Yup."

"Where?"

Karen looked down and mumbled the answer. "Over my garage." She continued before Rex had time to react. "I was as surprised as you are. He wants to get to know the kids."

"And your newfound wealth has nothing to do with it?"

"He ain't asked me for nothin', Bishop."

"You're giving him a place to live."

"But he didn't ask. I volunteered." She hurried on again. "He's gonna pay rent."

"Does he have a job?" Rex asked.

"Well, not yet, but Ray's a real good handyman and good at yard work, and with him around, the guys on the Harleys wouldn't have to come by as often."

Rex continued to hold his head in his hands, mostly to keep it from exploding.

"He can help me at Bark City when it warms up again."

"I imagine the grass will always be well fertilized at your park," Rex observed.

Karen was more than willing to abandon Ray's return as a topic of discussion. "Oh, there'll be pooper scoopers available and a fine if you don't clean up after your dog."

When she smiled, Rex saw the braces on her teeth.

"Getting some orthodontic work done?"

"Oh, yeah. Me and Dee both. Teeth are like kids, best to straighten them out early, but it ain't never too late." Her smile broadened. "Don't worry, Bishop. I ain't getting a boob job or a face lift."

"Far be it from me to suggest that you would. There is nothing wrong with having your teeth straightened, Karen."

"I admit I thought about liposuction," she said wistfully. "Some days I look in the mirror and say, 'Karen, you're rich. Why don't ya go get some of them bacon double cheeseburgers sucked outta yer hips?' I'll probably just stick with the braces, though. I don't want you all to think I've turned vain."

Rex consulted his watch again. He had another client arriving soon. He'd have to move Karen along somehow. Whereas most of his clients were downright succinct when paying by increments of an hour, this was not a worry for Sister Donaldson.

He dispensed a bit of parting advice. "I'm not sure it's a good idea to involve your ex-husband too closely in your business dealings."

"Ray's a hard worker."

"Karen, this man left you with two very young children and never helped support you afterward—financially or otherwise."

"I forgave him that a long time ago. That's what we're supposed to do, right?"

"Yes, but . . ."

"If I get angry all over again now, it won't change nothin'. I don't hafta punish him. Austin's so angry he won't even talk to him. Ray sees how Dee's been tryin' to fill the void in her life with relationships that don't work—and who knows what else. He's here to get to know the kids, and he ain't backin' off from the fight again."

"That all sounds very admirable, Karen, but . . ."

"Did I tell you Dee was trainin' to become a veterinary assistant? She was gonna work with the vet by my dog park, but she missed a couple of classes because she'd been drinkin' and didn't finish the trainin'."

"I'm sorry to hear that." Rex grabbed a slip of notepaper and quickly jotted down the number of the ward executive secretary. "Karen, this discussion would be best carried on in another venue. Call Brother Jensen and come see me at the bishop's office."

She took the paper but didn't shut off the sound. "Ray says he understands what's goin' on with Dee," Karen continued in a rush. "With the drinkin', I mean. I know that don't sound like a good thing, but he's been there and maybe he can reach her. Besides, she's got this boyfriend that gives me the creeps."

Rex stood up to signal that their meeting was over, but Karen continued. "Since Ray says he wants to help with the kids, however late in the game, I thought if he was livin' nearby it'd at least give him a chance to try, so that's why I offered him the garage."

"Karen, I'm sorry to cut you short, but I'm expecting another client momentarily. Let's talk later—in my office at church."

She stood. "That's all I needed to tell you. I don't know if Ray ever goes to church, but he's a member."

"I'll visit with him soon, Karen. Thanks for letting me know he's here."

AUSTIN'S HOT DATE

Chelsea came to the door in jeans and a T-shirt. Austin was puzzled. "Chels, what's up?"

She motioned him in. "We're not going to the dance."

"Is there a problem with those guys you said could put me up for the night because . . ."

"No, that's not it."

"You sick?" he asked.

"No, I'm not sick."

Austin noticed a couple of Chelsea's roommates peek out before closing their bedroom doors.

"Sit down." It was more of a command than an invitation. Austin lowered himself onto their small flowered sofa.

Chelsea disappeared for a moment and then returned with a file folder bulging with newspaper articles. "Melanie found all these." She sat down next to him. "Why did you lie about your mother?"

He let out a long sigh. "Chels, you can't imagine the complications that come from something like this. People make friends with you for the wrong reasons and . . ." He grew defensive. "I didn't lie. I told you she got a settlement."

"You let me think it was a divorce settlement. I can't have a relationship with someone who isn't honest with me."

"So my mom wins the lotto and I'm toast? It figures! You could have done this over the phone and saved me the gas and time, not to mention the expense of renting the tux." He ripped the bow tie from around his neck and tossed it on the nearby end table. "You want the truth? Okay, here's the truth. My dad left when I was a baby because he couldn't handle the responsibility. Mom worked most of her adult life as a grocery clerk and, until recently, we lived in a basement apartment and were the ward's favorite charity case."

Austin was on a roll. "All my clothes were hand-me-downs, and the kids at church who accepted me wouldn't accept my sister. She quit going to church and got pregnant when she was seventeen. Her boyfriend checked out on her in the proud family tradition." He stood up. "Actually, you're smart not to get serious with me for fear the trend might continue. Basically, we were poor white trash. Only now we're *rich* white trash."

Her voice softened. "Oh, Austin, I didn't know." Chelsea took his arm and pulled him back down onto the couch. Then she pulled out one of the clippings and her tone again became confrontational rather than sympathetic. "What about this Vegas wedding?"

"Let me guess. You're upset because it wasn't in the Las Vegas Temple. Publicity trick. Mom was getting marriage proposals in the mail. Her attorney thought this was the best way to get them to stop."

Chelsea shoved the article in with the rest and dropped the whole folder onto his lap. "So you didn't think I could handle the truth," she said.

"*Are* you handling it?"

"Melanie found other articles about people who won the lottery and bad things that happened to them."

Austin scowled. "Isn't she thorough?" He tossed the file onto the table next to his bow tie. "I hope she gets school credit for all this research or at least scrapbooks it for you. Shall I thank her myself? No doubt she's got her ear to the wall somewhere around here."

Chelsea ignored the tirade. "Most people who win the lottery spend all the money within a few years and end up worse off than they were before. You should read a couple of the articles," she urged. "All kinds of bad things happened to one guy after he won. And people get addicted to gambling and can't stop."

"Then I hope she didn't miss the article about the Cow Pie Bingo, because that clearly shows Mom has a gambling addiction." He shook his head, wondering if he should just cut his losses and leave. "The first thing Mom did when she won was to go talk to our bishop. I'm pretty sure she'll squeeze by on her couple of hundred million and won't ever buy another lottery ticket."

Chelsea's eyes opened wide. "That much?"

"And then some," he added. "I haven't done an in-depth study like you obviously have," he replied sarcastically, "so what can you tell me about someone who is merely the *son* of someone who bought one lousy lottery ticket? You know, before you make any judgments, my mom has helped more people than anybody realizes. She started a business making baby blankets that's full of people who were down on their luck and now have some dignity."

He picked up his bow tie. "So, now that I've come clean, why don't you change and we'll go to the dance? I didn't get dressed up and drive all the way to Idaho to sit in your apartment reading newspaper clippings about . . ."

She stood up abruptly. "I can't."

"*What*? Why not?"

Her words tumbled out. "Don't you see, Austin? The curse of the lottery may not happen to your family the way it did to the guy in the article, but your family is still incredibly rich. If we keep dating, we might get married, and then we'd have kids, and then all the while we'd be trying to teach them good values, but we'd still be giving them everything they wanted—or at least letting your mother do it. Didn't you say she bought your niece a piano and bought her new bedroom furniture?"

"That'll ruin her life, for sure."

"Don't you see? I can't take the chance that I might set my heart on the things of the world," Chelsea said, "instead of laying up treasures in heaven."

"You're breaking up with me because my mother is rich? *I* don't even *have* any money, Chelsea. I'm unemployed and living in my mother's basement."

"You're not going on a mission and you're not running a business anymore. What are your plans for the future, anyway?"

Austin threw up his arms in disgust. "Make up your mind, Chelsea. Do you want to break up with me because I'm rich and materialistic or because I'm poor and directionless? Or are you just off your meds?"

Chelsea began to cry. "A lot of women suffer from depression. My doctor told me there's no shame in taking an antidepressant."

Good grief! Austin thought. *What did I start now?* "Chelsea, I didn't know. I'm sorry. I was joking. I had no idea . . ." A light went on. "Hey, isn't that something kind of major that *you* didn't tell *me?*"

She ignored that observation. "People don't tell jokes about physically handicapped people, but they joke about people who struggle emotionally."

Austin sighed. "We're not going to the dance, are we?"

"I'm sorry, Austin, but I don't think things can work out between a Liahona guy and an iron rod girl."

He tried to lighten things up. "Liahona Guy and Iron Rod Girl. Sounds like a couple of religious superheroes. I bet if they teamed up, they'd be awesome together."

"I'm serious, Austin. I don't think we should go out anymore."

Austin picked up the file folder. "Do I get to keep this, as a souvenir?" He walked to the door, file folder in hand.

He wasn't looking forward to the drive back to Salt Lake City, especially since he'd be alone with his thoughts of yet another relationship down the tubes. He paused at the door. "For the record, Chelsea, my mother didn't pay for the tux rental. Have a good life."

He was out the door and halfway to his car before she uttered a quiet, "You too."

DELIA'S HOT DATE

While Austin was headed back to Salt Lake City, Dee was dining at the Outback Steakhouse in Sandy.

Zhon dipped a piece of the Blooming Onion in the sauce. "Wouldn't it be nice if we could treat ourselves to restaurants like this all the time, DeeDee?"

"Fine by me."

"Imagine if money was no object, the things we could do."

Before the evening was out they had done just that, planning exotic adventures all over the globe.

Dee sipped her drink. "Zhon, did you pick Australia as your first choice because we're eating at the Outback?"

"That's why I brought you here," he said. "I've always wanted to visit Australia."

"I've always wanted to visit Greece."

"We can stop on our way back from Australia."

They continued their date with a few after-dinner drinks at a local bar. Later, when they were back in Zhon's car, he said quietly, "We *could* make it happen, Dee. We could move to San Diego, travel the world—do all the things we were talking about."

"Sure. I sell corn dogs and I flunked out of vet assistant training, and you work in the stockroom of a mail-order company."

He pulled out of the parking lot. "Don't you get a third of your mom's money when she dies?"

"Yeah, in about thirty or forty years." She sighed. "I'll be too old to enjoy being rich."

Zhon leaned across the seat. She could smell the whiskey on his breath. "I saw an episode of a cop show where a woman killed her husband by putting antifreeze in some Jell-O." He paused for that comment to sink in. "They couldn't trace it."

Dee's eyes widened.

"It's the perfect crime. Just to be safe, we could plant evidence making it look like your brother did it."

Dee was incredulous. "You're not *serious?*"

"You and me, diving off the Great Barrier Reef, staying at posh hotels in Greece . . ."

"I was dreaming, sure, but I would never *off* my mom! Let me out of the car! Here! Now!"

"I was kidding, babe," he mumbled. "I've had a little too much to drink."

"All the more reason for me to take a cab home."

"Like you're not drunk yourself."

"That won't keep me from taking a cab."

When Zhon refused to pull over, Dee got out at the next red light. By the time she got home, all she could think to do was to call Bishop Parley. Dating a guy who wanted her to kill her mother was almost enough to send a girl back to Sunday School to find a nice church-going fellow. Almost.

· ·

KAREN'S HOT DATE

Delia answered Karen's ringing cell phone. Hearing a female voice, Hal verified their plans. "See you tonight, then." Dee might not have panicked if not for her recent date with Zhon. She alerted Bishop Parley, Barry, the Hell's Angels, and Ray. She knew now that you couldn't be too careful about who to trust. They could all be in cahoots—Zhon, Chelsea, this Hal guy.

· · ·

Karen headed to the Subway sandwich shop. She felt some misgivings. It wasn't her style to go behind anyone's back, but she was hopeful nobody would be any the wiser. It had been decades since Karen had been on a date, if she didn't count her dinners with Barry. The night before had been her first "summit meeting" with Ray at Chuck-A-Rama, but all they had talked about was the kids. That hardly counted. After her divorce, the couple of dates she'd been on had convinced her that dating wasn't worth the cost of a babysitter.

As she opened the door to the shop, she immediately noticed that it had somehow become the dining establishment of choice for some familiar people. In fact, the only person in the place she didn't know well was her date, Hal—although she recognized him from the grocery store.

He stood and greeted her shyly as she came in. Trying hard to ignore everybody else, Karen walked to the counter with Hal and ordered a sandwich. She itemized her toppings—green peppers, lettuce, and olives—lots of olives.

Ray fumed at his table. *I know she loves olives. I bet that guy don't know she loves olives.*

Karen was relieved that thus far her friends and family had kept their distance, but she knew they were all eavesdropping. Ray jumped up just as they headed toward a table in the corner.

"Karen!" he demanded. "Who is this man? What's goin' on?"

Hal's face turned red and he looked at Karen questioningly as he sat the tray down on the table.

"He's a friend from the grocery store," she explained. "Always came through my line and always voted for me as 'Most Friendly Cashier.' "

"I think you're bein' a little *too* friendly!"

"And I think you're bein' too bossy! Go sit down, Ray."

Karen looked around the room. "Sorry, Hal, but there are a few people here I've gotta talk to." She picked up her soda, took a sip, and turned to address the small crowd. "I don't think you're all here in case ya gotta Heimlich me if I choke on a pickle. What's goin' on?"

Barry cleared his throat. "I'm sorry, Karen, but recent events have made us especially aware of your ongoing need for protection."

Karen scowled. "What recent events? I'm gonna pretend you all ain't here, and Hal and me are gonna sit down and eat and get better acquainted. You told me I could date people I know."

She sat down, picked up her sandwich, and took a bite. Ray was still standing by their table. "Ray, I told ya to go sit down," Karen ordered.

"You really think I came back just because of the kids? Don't you know I suggested them meetings to spend time with you? Can't you tell that I've never stopped loving you?"

Karen put down her sandwich mid-bite. Her mouth gaped open with unchewed bits of turkey and ham visible to all the world. At last she closed her mouth and swallowed. "Hal, I think our date ain't goin' too well." She pulled out a twenty-dollar bill and put it on the table. "That's to pay you back for my sandwich and for your time and gas. Thanks for voting for me, Hal, but maybe Ray's right. I ain't sure our friendship should go any further."

His confusion showed. "I wasn't trying to cause any trouble."

"It ain't your fault. Sometimes things just don't work out. I've got some friends and family I'd like to introduce you to." She pointed to a table near the window. "That's my bishop and my lawyer, Barry, and for that matter, my bishop is my lawyer too." She pointed to the man still standing near their table. "This here's my ex-husband, Ray. And my lawyer is my ex-husband too. Not the bishop, the one with the glasses. Ray is my *real* ex-husband and Barry's my fake ex-husband. Well, actually . . . Oh, never mind." She pointed to another table. "Those are my two kids. Those three tough guys at the table behind them, they're some of my Hell's Angels bodyguards."

"Is . . . is that all?" Hal stammered.

"The sandwich makers are with the FBI, and with any luck, the photographer from *The National Enquirer* will show up any time now."

Wide-eyed, Hal suddenly decided to take his meal to-go and beat a hasty retreat.

Karen faced her friends and family. "I know you're here because you care about me, but he really was just a guy from the grocery store. I'm sorry I went behind everybody's back, but I was lonely. Barry, I shoulda given you the letter he sent me, but he didn't *propose* nothin' more than a sandwich at Subway. It was deceptive, but in the Bible, Moses's mother didn't say who she was and . . ."

She faced her ex-husband. "And, Ray, you're being mighty territorial for a man who's been gone over twenty years and back for a few days."

"I overheard the attorneys sayin' the one with the glasses was gonna play your jealous ex-husband, and I decided I was a better fit for the part," he said sheepishly.

Barry turned to Rex. "Why didn't you warn me I had an understudy?"

Karen pretended to rip open an imaginary envelope. "And the Oscar for overactin' goes to . . ."

"What if I wasn't actin'?" Ray raised his eyebrows and cocked his head. He stepped up to the plate. "Can I buy you dessert?"

She hesitated only briefly. "Them oatmeal raisin cookies look kinda good."

Ray purchased several cookies, brought them over to Karen's table, and sat down. Unconvinced that running off seemingly benign Hal had been such a good idea, Bishop Parley's disapproving look said it all. Barry didn't look pleased either, as he had grown increasingly protective of Karen the longer they worked together.

Ignoring everyone else, Ray looked across the table at Karen. "I ain't no good at romance, Karen. You know that. I never was and probably never will be. I don't deserve a second chance, but we made two kids together and if there is any way you could consider . . ."

A paper straw wrapper lay crumpled on the table between them. Karen removed her straw from her drink, holding the end with her finger, trapping a little soda in the end of the straw. She released the few drops onto the crumbled paper, causing it to unfold and writhe snakelike on the table. "You was the one taught me how to make straw wrapper snakes," she said. "We go back a long time, Ray, but still, this is all happenin' kinda fast."

"Pollywogs in the park," Ray added. "It ain't like we just met."

Karen pondered that comment. "Bishop did say to date someone I know. I can't take no more dates where the cavalry comes riding up. Besides, you all just scared off the only other man I might've dated." She put her straw back into her drink. "The one thing that could bring us back together is watchin' you tryin' to love our kids."

"I'm sorry I made a scene there. At first I was just pretendin', and then them feelings just came rushin' back like a flash flood in the desert. I mighta started hopin' maybe I'd have a chance with you when you let me move in over the garage. When Dee called me and told me to come to the Subway, she made it sound like this guy was up to no good, tryin' to take advantage of you."

"Dee ain't had real good luck with men. Maybe that clouded her vision. One thing I know. I ain't marryin' you or nobody else nowhere but in the temple."

Ray reached across the table, smashing her snake straw, and took her hand. "I'm gonna get things right this time, Karen. I promise you."

"I ain't makin' no promises yet. We'll see how it goes." She took a bite of cookie and chewed slowly, swallowing hard. "On the other hand, it'd save me a lotta time wadin' through the proposals."

"I'm here to stay, Karen, but maybe the kids ain't the only ones need convincin' of that."

GONE TO THE DOGS

Austin pulled an article out of his pocket and handed it to Dee as they walked in the park, a rambunctious cocker spaniel leading the way. "Chelsea gave me this article about the curse of the lottery, about some guy who won the lotto and had a run of bad luck."

"We were messing up relationships long before Mom won the lotto."

"Zhon and his evil plans does give me perspective on Chelsea, at least."

"What happened with her, anyway?"

"She went ballistic on me because I wasn't honest with her about Mom's winnings." He kicked a rock. "But at least I didn't have to get a restraining order."

"So Zhon wanted me to off Mom because I don't have money of my own, and Chelsea broke up with you because you might *have* money sometime. That's kinda crazy."

"Chelsea broke up with me because I wasn't honest with her and because she didn't want to set her heart on worldly things. This is the first time I've been dumped for having too much money." He pulled up the zipper on his jacket. "I used to try to make kids from school think we had money when we didn't. Now we have money, and we're trying to hide it. I'm not sure which is more messed up." He stopped to let Buster mark his territory. He circled endlessly before deciding on the right spot. "Maybe next time we should be like the dog, sniff around a little more." He elbowed his sister. "Especially you."

"How was I supposed to know Zhon was like that?"

"Didja ever take a good look at the guy?" he asked. "For starters, any guy you meet in a bar is probably not a winner."

"Name one guy from church who has ever been interested in me."

"Bishop Parley."

"Very funny."

They sat down on a bench. "You still haven't told Mom why you got the restraining order, have you?"

"She'd freak. Can't I just let her be glad I'm not seeing him anymore?"

"This is why you overreacted to Mom having a sandwich with a former customer at Subway, isn't it? Does she think he manhandled you or something?"

"I haven't asked her what she thinks. I guess she figures I'll tell her when I'm ready."

"You've gotta tell her, Dee. You think you can hide stuff, but it's not like we don't see what's happening in your life."

"I guess I should have figured out that Zhon was all about the money," Dee said. "I convinced myself that he really liked me for me. It felt good to belong to someone."

"Don't say it like that. You're not a possession."

"You know what I mean. It's nice to have somebody in your life."

"Yes, I had started to enjoy that." Austin reached down and patted the dog at his feet. "So what did you do when Zhon suggested you poison Mom's Jell-O?"

"I freaked. He wanted to make it look like you did it too, in case we got caught."

"Somebody better get a restraining order on me now," Austin said, "because if I ever see him again . . ."

"Let's hope he's smart enough not to come around," Dee interrupted. "I know I ain't the poster girl for Sunday School, but I'm not gonna off my mom for her money." Dee ripped off a broken fingernail and began to chew on the ragged edge.

"I'm glad you thought to call Bishop Parley. He knew exactly what to do."

"I thought he was gonna lecture me and make me feel guilty," Delia confessed, "but all he did was listen and help me get the restraining order. He did talk to me about naming a guardian for Mandee. He's gonna help me with that too." She switched gears. "Anyway, I know I have to tell Mom the whole truth. I'll tell her and Ray when they come back."

Austin's voice turned bitter. "Leave him out of this. It doesn't involve him."

"He *is* our father, Austin, like it or not. In case you haven't noticed, Mom and Ray are spending a lot of time together. You heard him at the Subway shop."

"I can't believe Mom's giving him another chance, just like that."

"You might try to get to know him a little. He ain't such a bad guy." When she bit into her quick, Dee removed the finger from her mouth and shook it in pain. "What am I gonna say to Mom, Austin?"

"Remember, Dee, this wasn't your idea. Tell her first thing you did was dump him and call Bishop Parley. But if I were you, I'd stop by Smith's and get some cookie dough first. She's running low."

"Good idea!" She touched his arm. "You're a good big brother, even if I am the oldest. After this thing with Zhon, I've been thinking about maybe going to church—or at least to a church dance—where I could meet someone who won't try to talk me into killing my mother."

"Hearing that'd cheer Mom up more than the cookie dough, Dee."

"Ray said he'd go with me."

"Is he going to bring a little Tupperware bowl full of Cheerios for you?"

"I'd rather have Mom dating our dad than some guy who comes outta the woodwork."

"I don't like it." He looked his sister in the eye. "You really plan to start coming to church?"

"Maybe. I mean, I've got stuff I'd have to give up, if I got serious about it."

"Dee, a couple of token visits to Sunday School won't help you get over any serious addictions."

"Don't get all self-righteous on me just because you've been going back to church for a few months."

Austin persisted. "If you need help, Mom and I will be there for you. Do you think we haven't seen all the signs?"

She turned away. "If you're so righteous, why don't you go on your stupid mission?"

"Don't change the subject just because you don't wanna talk about it. You and Ray can go sit on the back row at church in the lost sheep section for a couple of weeks if that'll make you feel better. But nothing will change until you admit you need help."

"I ain't addicted to nothing!" she insisted. "Okay, so maybe I've been drinking a little more than I should. Can you blame me, under the circumstances? I can give it up whenever I want to."

"Sure, Dee," Austin said with a sigh. "While you're at it, why not find yourself another guy like Zhon?"

• • •

Karen sat speechless on a stool in the kitchen as her daughter told her how and why Bishop Parley had helped her take out a restraining order on Zhon Thackeray.

Austin and Ray sat quietly nearby, watching as Dee pushed the plate of cookie dough across the granite countertop, closer to her mother.

Finally Karen spoke. "So if we see him around, we call the police?"

"That's what Bishop Parley told me."

"Thanks for bein' honest with me, Dee. Maybe some good can come of this."

"What's good about somebody wanting to kill you?"

"Give me a minute." Karen grabbed a piece of cookie dough. "It's good that you found out what kind of man he was." She took a bite. "It's good that you didn't go along with him." She swallowed. "It's good that now you'll be more careful about the kind of guys you pick." Karen paused. "But what ain't so good is that now I'm kinda afraid to eat Jell-O, and you all know how much I like Jell-O."

31

LIKE FATHER, LIKE SON

Austin surveyed his sister. "Dee, you can't wear that! Little Bo Peep in a miniskirt and fishnets?"

"It's my favorite Halloween costume. I look hot. Ain't that lost sheep theme still popular at church?"

"This is the young adult Halloween party. You've gotta tone it down. Trust me! No French maid. No Catwoman. No she-devil."

"What's left?"

"Mom has that Wicked Witch of the West get-up."

"That covers me from wrist to ankle," she protested.

"I'd go with that." He grinned. "Remember what they used to teach you in Young Women, 'Modest is hottest.' "

"Yeah, right." Dee rolled her eyes.

Austin shook his head, hoping his sister would take his advice, as he headed out the door on an errand for his mother.

• • •

Ray wiped his brow on his shirt sleeve and put down the rake as his son approached.

"Mom asked me to bring this over to you." Austin handed an envelope to Ray. "So you're doing yard work at the Thompsons' now?"

"You mean the Cironnis'? I don't know who used to live where. Alex saw what a great job I was doin' with your mom's yard. He said it would be great to have somebody reliable doin' the yard here."

"Somebody *reliable?* And they asked *you?*"

The derision in Austin's voice told Ray that his efforts to win over his son had thus far been fruitless. Austin turned to leave.

"I understand that you did the lawn when you lived here."

"I did."

"Karen tells me that when you were ten years old, you told Brother Thompson you could do a better job than the fellow they were paying."

"It was no big deal."

"You looked out for your mother. You have every right to be angry at me, Austin. I'm sorry I wasn't there takin' care of my family."

Austin's voice took on a bitter edge. " 'I'm sorry' ain't gonna cut it, Ray. You can't change the past so I didn't have Sister Arletti poking me to see if the pants she gave me fit. You can't make the kids be nice to Dee even though she doesn't dress like they do. You can't make up for any of that now!"

"I've got until my dying day to try," Ray said quietly. He pulled himself up to his full height of five foot ten. Austin had a good three inches on him, but Ray did his best to look his son in the eye. Austin returned his father's gaze, fire in his eyes.

"I know I can't change the past, but as long as there's breath in my body, I can work on the future. You can't take that away from me. Your mother is willin' to give me a second chance, and I hope that sometime maybe you will too."

"My mother trusts everybody—which is why she has to have a bunch of attorneys and Hell's Angels looking out for her."

Ray wiped his hands on his jeans. "I wanna talk to you about something. Will you give me a few minutes?" He hoisted himself up onto the cinder block wall that divided one yard from another.

Austin stood, hands shoved obstinately into his pockets, looking past Ray into space. "Five minutes."

"I wanna pay for you to serve a mission, Austin—pay it all myself, outta money I had saved up for you kids and what I'm making now. It'd come outta my wages—none of your mother's money, not a dime."

"As usual, you're a little late. I'm not going on a mission."

"You planned to once. Your mom told me you were excited about serving."

"That was a long time ago."

"Are you happy? Is your life goin' the way ya want it to?"

"Does anybody's? Ever since Mom bought that lottery ticket, there's been no chance for any kind of normal social life. I shouldn't go on a mission. I should go into a monastery."

"The Good Lord will help you find your way, Austin."

"Who are *you* to be talking to me about God?"

"God has a plan for you."

"And *this* was it?" He scowled. "Then it looks like I got hosed!"

"Your mother told me how when you went off to Wyoming you was gonna save up for a mission. What happened?"

Austin continued to stare off into the distance. "I got off track."

"You know, I was just a little younger than you when I got a job workin' outta town. I came home on the weekends to be with Karen and you two babies. We married right outta high school. I was nineteen when we had Dee, twenty when we had you. Delia, she had the colic, cried all the time. Karen had such patience with her."

Ray ran a grimy hand through his thinning hair. "I was a family man workin' with single guys. Only during the week, I sort of forgot I was a family man. I didn't go out with girls, but I was always hangin' out with the guys, and their freedom started to look pretty good to me. I just wasn't ready for those weekends home with the cryin' babies."

"Am I supposed to feel sorry for you now?"

"Just listen, Austin. When I told Karen I wanted a divorce, I promised I'd send her money and I did—for a while. But then I needed a new truck, and it had a pretty hefty payment on it. Before long I started sendin' less and less money to your mother. It was always my plan to catch up. Because I hadn't kept my promise, I was afraid to come around and see how you all were doin'. I knew it'd about kill me to see how hard you struggled on account of me."

The fury in Austin's eyes as he faced him made Ray wish his son had continued to stare off into space. "Ya think?" he exploded. "But now you come back, and you're romancing Mom, and it looks like your troubles are over!"

Ray took a deep breath. "There are troubles that don't have nothin' to do with money, Austin. As I was sayin', I told myself that with Karen being so patient and lovin', she'd be okay takin' care of the two of you. I know the Church helped for a while. That's one thing Karen ain't never wavered from, the Church."

"Can't say that for the rest of us."

"When we was first married, we used to go together, but when I'd come home on the weekends, it seemed to take too big a chunk outta my Sundays. Karen could've left the babies with me—a lot of women would have as punishment for my not goin'—but Karen wanted you there with her."

"I don't remember her ever letting me stay home."

"I know I've left a big hole in your life, Austin, and I can't just spackle over it, but I thought maybe you could understand I got off track from the important things I intended to do, seeing as how you . . ."

Austin narrowed his eyes. "Are you saying I'm like you?"

"I'm tryin' to keep you from being like me. I know from experience that no matter what else ya try, even if ya succeed, ya ain't gonna find happiness if ya don't do what you're supposed to. You'll be like Jonah in the belly of the whale, waitin' to be barfed out on a beach." He reached for Austin's arm, turning him toward him. "You ain't too old for a mission. Like I said, I wanna pay every last dime. Maybe then I could feel like I done something for my son."

"I'm not going on a mission." Austin yanked his arm free. "I gotta go. My *mission* tonight is to keep Dee from dressing up as Lady Godiva for the young adult Halloween party."

Ray lowered himself down from the wall and picked up his rake as Austin stormed off. *Guess that's my fault too. This ain't gonna be easy.* He repeated to himself the saying he had learned from his sponsor, Wendell. "Life is hard, but I can do hard things." An unmanly feeling came over Ray, and he fought back the tears. *It ain't good news that the biggest insult I could give my son is to tell him he's like me.*

THE ROADKILL MOBILE

Monday morning Rex turned on his computer to see how many emails awaited his attention. A little before ten, Barry Luskin entered his office, a recorded disk in hand. "You might want to see this. Overseeing Karen's business ventures has been an adventure in itself, to say the least."

He sat down in the nearest wingback chair. "When she started 'Senior Citizen Night' every Thursday at Second Childhood, I had to scramble to get everyone to sign a release. So far, we haven't had any major injuries, despite the employees privately referring to it as FHE— 'fractured hip evening.'"

Rex smiled as Barry continued. "Alex Cironni is doing a great job as manager. If the grand opening was any indication, this should be a profitable venture. Mr. McLelland told me he wants to have his nineti-eth birthday celebration there. I've reserved the whole place for the firm next August 14th."

"Sounds like a good time—stuffy attorneys going down the slides in suits and ties."

Barry smiled. "Wait until you see the latest. Karen set this whole commercial up herself. The expenditures weren't large enough for me to have to sign a check, so I didn't know what she was doing until it was done."

"She made a commercial?" Rex followed Barry into the nearest conference room, where he put the DVD in the player and turned on the television. After a few seconds, he saw Karen and Ray surrounded by several dogs and cats.

Karen spoke first. "Every year hundreds of animals are killed by motorists. Even when people try to keep their animals secured and other people try to drive safely, accidents happen."

It was Ray's turn. "If you hit an animal or come across an animal that has been hit in Salt Lake, Utah, or Davis county, call 1-800-ROADKIL, and we'll come pick it up."

The camera angle widened to reveal a truck in the background. Ray had painted over an old ice-cream truck, apparently only one coat, because the shadow of the ice cream bars still showed through. Bold red letters emblazoned on the side proclaimed: RAY'S ROADKILL MOBILE.

"This will give me a chance to keep my legal skills polished," Barry observed. "How many crank calls do you think this business will generate and how much fun do you think I will have tracking those people down?"

Rex nodded, knowing Barry would be in his element with such an opportunity to wield the long arm of the law. "Remember the talk we had with Karen about not funding the half-baked ideas of her relatives?" Rex said. "It seems we forgot to counsel her against funding her *own* hair-brained ideas."

• • •

"Karen," Rex began, "I understand you've, um, helped Ray start a new business." It didn't escape Bishop Parley's notice that now they were discussing business matters in the bishop's office. The lines were blurred beyond hope.

"You saw our commercial! Whaddya think? We set this whole thing up ourselves. Got us a refrigerated truck to put the animals in after we pick them up. The calls go to Ray's new cell phone. We was lucky that number was available. He does this in between doing yard work for people."

"I see."

Karen continued. "If the animal has tags, we contact the owner. At the end of the day, we take the unclaimed dead animals to a crematorium."

"Karen, there are statutes," Rex continued. "I'm not sure this is even legal. What if an animal is merely injured? What if it is sick or rabid? Surely there's a government agency already providing this service."

"Then they ain't doin' a very good job," she stated. "I once saw a dead raccoon lay by the side of the road for almost a whole month." She shrugged. "I know I don't understand all the laws, but if one of my kitties runs out into the street and gets hit, I've got the right to go get him and take him home and doctor him or bury him."

"Yes, you do," Rex acknowledged.

"So what's the difference between that and Ray doin' it for other people?"

Rex sighed. "It isn't quite that simple, Karen."

"Me and Ray, we brainstormed on how to make this work," she argued. "We been gettin' lots of calls already. There are always dead animals up in the canyons. We've removed a couple of pretty big dogs that could've caused accidents if people had to steer around them."

"I'm not disputing that there is a need, but . . ."

"You said the key to startin' a good business is to find something that nobody else was doing."

"Yes, but . . ." Rex used two fingers to massage his temple. "Sometimes there is a good *reason* nobody else is doing it. Is there a fee for this service? How does the business fund itself?"

"People ain't gonna call if it costs money. Besides, who would we charge?" She reached into her briefcase and pulled out a few sheets of paper. "Here's a list of the calls we got the very first week." She held up a couple of sheets of lined paper.

"So if the Foundation is supporting this business, in essence *you* are supporting Ray. I take it the two of you have been spending quite a bit of time together."

"We grew up together, Bishop, and we're thinkin' about maybe growin' old together too. We're workin' together," Karen said. "He works and the business pays him—a business I set up to help people, not to make money. He can do this in between all the yard work and handyman work he's been doing and support *himself.*"

Rex sighed. "Karen, get with Barry and have him work his magic on it."

• • •

Ray sat nervously on the small sofa outside the bishop's office. He knew Bishop Parley was skeptical about him. Who could blame him? He dreaded explaining himself to a man who had so obviously provided well and unwaveringly for his own family.

One thing Ray was particularly reluctant to share with his new bishop was his employment history—a few fast-food restaurant positions, including one as manager, and some time working construction. He had done handyman jobs and painting here and there, and he had worked at a logging mill in Idaho until he cut off the tip of his index finger.

Since then he'd washed and detailed boats in Poulsbo, Washington. He'd left his most recent job painting lines on the highways for the Oregon Department of Transportation to go in search of Karen and the kids. He was a hard worker, someone who could be trusted to show up and get the job done, but he didn't know how he could get the bishop to see that.

Ray fidgeted nervously. Karen had assured him that their bishop had said there was value in honest work, whether with the hands or the mind, but she didn't know what it did to a man's pride to sit across the desk from someone who had graduated from a fancy law school and have to admit that the closest thing you had to higher education was a stint at Hamburger University for management trainees in the fast-food business.

The door to the bishop's office opened. "Ray, why don't you come into my office?" He obeyed and took a seat across from the desk. His dress slacks were cutting into his midsection uncomfortably. Apparently the last time he'd gotten dressed up, he'd been a size smaller. The bishop closed the door and took his seat behind the desk.

"Ray, I wanted to talk with you and get acquainted. Also, when a new person moves in, we usually give them a chance to introduce themselves and give a talk in sacrament meeting."

Ray's face went white. "A *talk?*" he squeaked. "In sacrament meeting? In—in front of *everybody?*" How could he tell the bishop that he had a terrible fear of public speaking, that he would rather cut off another finger with a chain saw than face the congregation from the pulpit? He shook his head. "No!" he blurted out.

"I see."

"I mean, not now. I'm not ready, Bishop."

"Ray, I'm going to speak frankly with you. Twenty-some-odd years ago you left your ex-wife with two young children to care for and until recently you were never heard from again. There was little or no financial support or help of any kind. Now, miraculously, you reappear just as Karen has become financially well off. Karen Donaldson is one of the most loving and trusting people I have ever met. For some reason, she is willing to give you a second chance."

"I never expected that neither, Bishop."

"Now and then I suspect people are less than truthful with me as a bishop. I'd like you to tell me, Ray, and try not to insult my intelligence, what exactly transpired to bring you back."

Ray ran his hand across his balding head. It was cool in the office, but he was sweating something terrible. He wiped his palms on his slacks, leaving dark handprint skids. He took a deep breath and began.

"Karen and I got married right outta high school, and we had two kids right away. None of my friends was tied down to those kinds of responsibilities. I was tryin' to live in two worlds—bein' married and takin' care of a family and havin' fun with my buddies and bein' carefree."

He stared at the light fixture to avoid eye contact with Bishop Parley. "Changin' diapers and walkin' the floors at night with cryin' babies—'specially Delia, she had the colic—was awful hard on me while I saw my friends havin' fun."

"I have six children." It might have been a comment intended to show sympathy, but to Ray it sounded more like an indication that Rex had endured far more diaper duty than he could begin to imagine.

Ray continued, recounting to his new bishop the same story he had told Austin, feeling all the while that the sympathy level was about the same.

"And how did you come to reappear?"

"I kept tellin' myself that I was gonna save up and send a whole lotta money to Karen and the kids. I was too ashamed to go see 'em if I didn't have any money. Before I knew it, years and years had gone by."

"They have a way of doing that, yes."

"Recently I've been goin' through the AA program. I knew I needed to set some things right with Karen, you know, step eight. How could I have known all that would coincide with her gettin' rich? I know you think I'm here after the money, but that ain't true. I'm happy to just make a workin' man's wages."

"From where I sit, it appears that Karen is supporting you financially and giving you a place to live. How exactly is that considered *restitution?*"

SUSAN LAW CORPANY

"Bishop, you may not think I'm sincere, but what about all them guys that proposed? For sure they're after the money. At least with me you've got a chance that I'm a decent guy who means it when he says he loves her. I loved her before there was any money. There ain't gonna be anybody else that can say that."

"Perhaps not," he allowed.

"We've had two children together. Delia is out of control. It don't help that I wasn't around to lend a guidin' hand. Austin may never get over his anger at me. But I'm not runnin' this time. I'm here—I know I'm a little late—to take some responsibility for my family."

At that moment, Ray's cell phone vibrated. "This is my Roadkill Mobile line. Mind if I take this one?"

Ray was grateful for something, anything, that might possibly cut his interview with the bishop short. He spoke into the phone and took down an address, snapping his phone shut when the call was ended. "Looks like we got a dead deer up Parley's Canyon. Duty calls."

"We'll talk again, Ray," Bishop Parley said sternly.

Ray smiled a weak smile. "That's what I'm afraid of."

33

. . . .

EXECUTIVE COMMITTEE

C amille entered Rex's office, prepared for a briefing on that morning's tasks. "Close the door, please, Camille," he requested. She
complied and sat down in the usual spot, sensing that this was more
than a request for some revisions on estate planning documents.

"I want to give you an update on the situation with Ted. He was
asked to attend our recent executive committee meeting where I shared
the things you told me. It should come as no surprise to you that Ted
denied everything."

"Doesn't it make a difference that another secretary made a complaint about him?"

Rex shook his head. "I'm sorry, Camille, but the previous complaint has been recanted. Melinda now says it was completely blown
out of proportion, that all he did was compliment her outfit." *Melinda's
defense of Ted is so staunch that I am inclined to wonder if their friendship
extends outside the office.*

"What does this mean to me?"

"Now it's a case of your word against his. Ted, as you may be aware,
has some strong supporters in the firm. He has invaluable contacts
politically and has brought the firm some impressive new clients."

"Maybe you could say I brought Mrs. Donaldson in," Camille suggested, smiling weakly.

"Would that I could, Camille. The bottom line is that we need a
witness before we can take any kind of action against Ted. As it is, we
can only issue a warning."

"Which means that it is even more unlikely that I will ever find a witness."

"I'm sorry, Camille. I brought up my own observations about Ted and comments he has made about you, as well as how I've seen him look at you." Rex looked away, not wanting to embarrass her. "He suggested that if finding you attractive was a violation, we should string up every man in the office."

He made eye contact once again. "In addition, I brought up some things Ted said to my wife."

"Did that help?"

"First, she didn't tell me about it at the time, only recently, so it would appear that just when I need something against Ted, I have manufactured it. Or that is the way he made it seem. The man is a skilled manipulator in a courtroom and very good at what he does. Ted suggested I'm threatened by him, that I have a personal vendetta against him, and that I am using my wife and secretary as pawns to undermine his power."

"The other members of the committee, do they believe that? Don't they know you?"

"I'd like to think they do. I've learned not to second-guess what others think. In matters like this, you never know who gives outward sympathy but secretly belongs to the Old Boys' Club. A couple of the men on the executive committee are senior members of the firm who can almost remember the days when you called your secretary your 'girl' and expected her to press your pants if requested."

"Thank you for letting me know how things stand."

"I'm sorry, Camille, that I could not do more. We are, however, withholding partner status from Ted until we complete our investigation of his behavior, which will include his history prior to joining our firm."

A MAN WITH A MISSION

S oon Ray Donaldson had recruited nine other families in the ward for whom he was doing yard work—mowing in the summer, raking in the fall, snowblowing in the winter. Word had quickly spread that Ray Donaldson was saving up to support Austin on a mission.

In the affluent ward, many were willing to give up the dreaded tasks to Ray. Hard work was the one card he could play. He intended to show Bishop Parley a ward full of manicured yards and snow-free sidewalks. The snow blower had been a birthday gift from Karen, but he knew Bishop Parley would likely see that as another sign that she was supporting him. In the meantime, he answered calls for the Roadkill Mobile, picking up deceased animals in between his yard work tasks.

• • •

It seemed to Austin that anytime he drove through the neighborhood that winter, he passed his father, out running his snowblower down someone's driveway—a concrete reminder that Ray was putting his money where his mouth was.

• • •

"That's sumpthin' about your dad, huh?" Karen was obviously proud of her ex-husband.

"Gosh, Mom, have you forgotten about all those years we struggled?"

"I ain't forgotten. I just don't wanna live my life angry."

"All these people in the ward keep asking me whether or not I've got my call. He has no right to tell people I'm going on a mission!"

"He's just tellin' 'em that's what he's savin' for."

"He's getting other people to put that expectation on me."

"I never did think Ray was that clever, but you're right. He's got the whole ward goin' after ya. Have ya prayed about it, Austin, or don't ya wanna know the answer?" She quickly changed the subject. "I heard Adrienne is back from Europe."

"Adrienne's back?" She heard the hope in his voice.

"She'll be stayin' with the Morleys, so she'll be in our ward."

For the first time in a long time, Austin let himself consider the possibility of serving a mission. *Adri's coming back.* Adrienne Thompson had always said she was going to marry a returned missionary, no matter what. Adrienne—tall, slender Adrienne with the quick laugh and the dark sparkling eyes. *Suppose we started dating again? Would she still be around in two years? She could get a master's degree or something. Adri isn't the type to sit around pining or who would panic if she got to the ripe old age of twenty-five and was still single. Mom was right that I didn't give her any reason to stick around.*

• • •

The following Sunday, Austin followed Karen out of the house, her Primary bags in tow. "Sheesh, Mom, what have you got in here?"

"Stuff to get the kids to sing."

He loaded the rest of the Primary paraphernalia and jumped into the vehicle next to his mother. She rounded the corner and quickly covered the few blocks to church. Austin began to unload her visual aids. "Good grief, Mom, when you teach them to sing 'Popcorn Popping' are you gonna bring an apricot tree?"

"Austin?" He turned at the sound of his name.

"Adrienne!" He looked into the familiar dancing eyes. She was dressed in brighter colors than he remembered.

"It's the new me. What do you think? I've been studying in Spain. I decided to try out some bullfighter's red and some bright yellow and purple."

"The purple looks good on you. It reminds me of that dress you wore to the dance."

She grabbed his arm. "I was so glad to hear that you're going to go on a mission, Austin. I'm so proud of you! It must not have been an easy decision to make, but trust me, you'll never regret it. I kind of feel like I've been on another mission. It's great!"

Her enthusiasm was catching. Austin heard himself answering her back. "I wanna hear all about it. I'm gonna go in today and talk to the bishop about putting my papers in as soon as I finish unloading this Primary stuff." Karen's mouth dropped open.

"Hi, Sister Donaldson."

"Good to have you back, Adrienne. Why, ya look like a beautiful bright parrot next to all us old crows."

"Isn't it exciting? Austin going on a mission! I always knew he'd go someday. Some people you just have that feeling about."

Karen took a sidelong glance at her son. "I'm still gettin' used to the idea myself."

As Austin entered the church building to make an appointment to speak to the bishop, hopes renewed, Adrienne Thompson went back over to Liz Morley's car and slipped her arm through that of the young man standing there conversing with her friend.

• • •

Austin sat in the bishop's office, waiting for the bishop to start talking. A short time ago, he had enthusiastically made the appointment, but now he sat, head down, not meeting his bishop's gaze. The scene had replayed itself already in his mind a number of times. Young adult Sunday School class. Adrienne with that same great enthusiasm introducing some guy named Jason, her fiancé. They'd met in Europe on the study abroad thing. *She's in on it! She tricked me—tricked me into getting an appointment with the bishop. She's already found a returned missionary to marry, so what difference does it make? Now the bishop's gonna start tightening the screws too.*

Bishop Parley did not try to hide his surprise or his pleasure. "You wanted to talk to me about serving a mission, Austin?"

"Bishop, I'm not sure I really want to go." He waited, studying the different props in the office—the big ward map, the poster of the General Authorities, the picture of the Savior—anything to keep from meeting his bishop's gaze. He sat, arms defiantly folded, waiting for the inevitable lecture. *I should have told Mom not to wait.*

Bishop Parley flipped open his scriptures, turned a few pages, and began to read. "Then you're probably right not to go. Here it is, Doctrine and Covenants section 4, verse 3: 'Therefore, if ye have desires to serve God, ye are called to the work.' " He stood up to signal that the interview was over. Without a trace of malice, he said, "If you don't want to go, Austin, I don't think they want you. They're looking for missionaries excited about doing the Lord's work." He shook Austin's hand. "Come back and see me if you ever change your mind."

That's it? Austin felt as if he had been dumped by a girl he didn't want to date in the first place. He had been prepared for the bishop to try to convince him to go, not to tell him he was not wanted.

He found Karen waiting outside in the Lucky Duck running the heater. The yellow SUV was one of the few remaining vehicles in the parking lot. He got in and they headed home. He helped unload the Primary stuff on the other end, not saying a word.

"Well?" Karen questioned her son. "Ya just gonna clam up? What'd the bishop say?"

"He told me they didn't want me."

"What?"

Austin looked down. "I told him I didn't wanna go, and he said if I didn't wanna go, they didn't want me."

"I'm disappointed, Austin, but it's your decision. Did you decide to stick around and see if you've got a chance with Adrienne? You know she was always the one for sayin' how she wasn't going to marry anyone but a returned missionary, but maybe she'd . . ."

"Didn't you see him? She announced it in Sunday School. She's getting married in Denver so her parents can be there."

Karen busied herself putting her posters into the closet. "I guess that's what happens when young pretty girls go off to BYU. I'm sure Adrienne has found herself a nice fellow. Impressin' a girl ain't the right reason to go on a mission anyway."

"At least she's not marrying Brad Cooper. Spare me the lecture, Mom. And you can tell Ray to lay off too. I told the bishop, and I'll tell you. I'm not going!"

THE TOWN THAT DIED

When Karen decided to attend training in Boston to learn how to be a hospital clown, Ray had encouraged Austin to accompany her. He agreed with his father. Neither of them wanted Karen navigating an unfamiliar city by herself.

Their flight was uneventful, with Karen playing the role of the seasoned traveler to Austin's novice. They had taken a cab from the airport and were exploring the area outside their hotel.

Austin turned around but his mother was no longer behind him. "Mom?" He looked around and saw that she had gone across the street. He ran across the street, where she had purchased a newspaper from a roadside stand. "Mom, why'd ya take off like that?"

"I saw this stand that has newspapers from all over. I had a feeling I was supposed to buy a newspaper. I just ain't found the right one."

"The right one? What are you looking for?"

"I'll tell you when I find it."

A few minutes later, Karen held up a paper, the *Asheville Citizen-Times*, so he could see it. "The Town that Died" read the headline.

"I think this is it," she said.

"This is what?"

"I get feelings, Austin, when I know I'm supposed to do something, like the day I knew I needed to go to that laundromat the time I gave that young girl some money while her boyfriend, or whatever he was, was in the bathroom. Just now, when I read this newspaper, those feelings flooded over me."

"So what are you gonna do?"

"On the way back from Boston we gotta stop in Letherby, North Carolina. It says they closed down a big furniture factory that employed most of the people in the town."

"Let me see the article," he said.

She handed him the paper. "Some days I do stuff 'cause it seems like fun, like that day me and Ray went to the Deseret Industries and put twenty-dollar bills in the pants pockets, but sometimes I get feelings like I been brought to a certain place for a certain purpose. I've got those feelings today about this little town."

Austin felt a warmth come over him as he read, a confirmation of the feeling his mother had that they needed to visit the small town in the newspaper article. Reluctant at first to admit it, Austin finally said, "I feel it too. Okay, Mom, whatever you say."

• • •

Karen spent an enjoyable two days in the clown training, but the little town was always in the back of her mind. She was glad when she was finally on an airplane headed to North Carolina. "How long are we gonna stay in that town?" Austin asked.

"As long as it takes. I called Ray and Dee and told them what we're doin' so they know why we ain't back yet. I guess I oughta call Barry too." Karen pulled out the article again. "They got the headline wrong. The town ain't dead. It's on life support, maybe, but it ain't dead yet." She handed the article to Austin. "This is where we're gonna start. We're gonna visit this little bakery. That's the only business in town still open."

"So when we fly into Raleigh, we'll rent a car?"

"Yup. We oughta be in Letherby by two or three o'clock this afternoon near as I can tell."

• • •

It was closer to three-thirty by the time Karen and Austin entered the city limits. "How do we know where we're goin'?" Austin asked.

"We'll drive around until we see the bakery or until we see someone who can tell us where it is. This looks like the main road into town, and it ain't a big town. We're lookin' for a yellow building with white trim, from what I can tell from the picture."

They drove past an abandoned gas station and businesses with boarded-up windows. Then Austin spotted a yellow building, set back off the main road with parking in front. "I think that's it up there."

• • •

Our Daily Bread belonged to two spinster sisters who had lived in Letherby all their lives. When the furniture factory closed its doors, Eleanor and Lucille Mayfield, direct descendants of founding father Jonas Letherby, had stubbornly refused to close up shop, even though sustaining business had all but ceased.

One by one, the shops that had served the community had closed their doors for the last time. Some continued to offer services if there was a way they could do so without the overhead of a business location. The most recent casualty was Wanda's Cuts 'n' Curls. Wanda was now giving haircuts in her basement.

Between them, the sisters had squirreled away some money from the inheritance they had received when their parents had passed away. Deeply religious, they'd had no trouble deciding to remain open for business, providing the townspeople with their daily bread, whether or not they could pay.

Lucille, the one with a head for figures, handled the financial end of things. They had determined that for the time being specialty items would have to take a backseat to the basics. Eleanor had lettered a large sign that now graced the front window. "Fresh-baked bread, whatever you can pay or promise."

According to the article, the little bakery was the only thing keeping hope, and possibly even some of the inhabitants, alive.

• • •

Austin followed Karen into the bakery. "I'd like to get three loaves of wheat bread," Karen stated.

Eleanor thanked them as she bagged the bread. "We appreciate the business. You're not from around here."

"No, I'm from out west. Are you the owner?"

"I'm one of them. I'm Eleanor Mayfield. Folks around here call me Ellie. If they're old enough to remember *The Beverly Hillbillies*, they call me Elly May. Folks that aren't quite so old but remember when they shot J.R. Ewing call me Miss Ellie." She handed the bread to Karen.

"But you can call me plain old Ellie, on account of I'm both plain and old."

"How much do I owe ya, plain old Ellie?"

"Like the sign says, 'whatever you can pay or promise.' Times are tough right now for folks around here, and that's our new policy. They did an article in the Asheville paper recently, and folks've been right neighborly, coming by and putting a little extra in the jar here, but that's entirely up to you. Our regular price was $3.50 a loaf."

Karen looked at the oversized jar that held numerous bills and coins and IOUs written on little slips of paper. "Do you take checks?"

"Not unless they're local."

"What if they're out-of-town checks but for a lotta money?" Karen countered.

Ellie surveyed Karen's outfit. *She doesn't dress like someone well off.* "Lucy, come here a minute. We've got a customer with a financial question."

Karen handed Lucy a check made out for ten thousand dollars. "Will that keep you in business for a while? That's what I can pay, but I can promise more if ya need it," Karen added.

Lucille, the more skeptical of the two, narrowed her eyes and looked at Karen. "Are you having a go at us, because if you are, it certainly isn't very neighborly."

"I saw the article and decided to come over and see if I could help. See the name on that check? That's a charitable foundation I represent."

Karen overheard the last of Ellie's whisperings to her sister. "If she's a crackpot, then we're only out three loaves of bread. Take the check, Lucy. Maybe it's of the Lord." In tandem, the two sisters turned smiling faces toward Karen and Austin. "Thank you, Miss um . . ." Karen had taken to signing her name as illegibly as possible on checks from the Foundation.

"Ya can call me Ann. Ann O. Nymous." She handed Ellie one of her business cards.

Lucy squinted at the signature. *It looks like it says 'Kay' or 'Kari' or something. Yes, she's a crackpot.* "I can't quite make it out, but that doesn't appear to be the signature on this check."

"What matters is if it clears the bank."

"I suppose so." Lucille punched a button on the cash register and placed the check under the tray for safekeeping. "God bless."

"It ain't hard to see that you're religious."

Lucille spoke first. "We open our store every day with a little prayer. Lately other folks've been joining us, folks from the town who are out of work. If you're still in the area, you could join us tomorrow, at 7:45. We've been calling it 'town prayer.' We have all been exercising our faith together, calling on our dear Lord to bless our little town."

• • •

Soon gift cards started appearing in unexpected places in the town of Letherby—mailboxes, lunchboxes, toolboxes. But Karen wasn't done yet.

One afternoon, she and Austin drove to a nearby town. The first stop was the local bank. Karen called Barry and had him wire fifty thousand dollars. "I want twenties, fifties, and hundreds," she told the man at the bank. "We can come by later if it will take you a while to get that much cash together." Their next stop was a craft store where she bought wide green ribbon, a pair of scissors, large googly eyes, and a hot glue gun.

That night in their hotel room Karen wrapped an inch-high stack of assorted bills in green ribbon, piping a thin line of glue onto one end of the ribbon and pressing down to make sure it held. She turned the stack over and carefully set two large googly eyes into two waiting globs of hot glue, holding them until they were set.

She held it up for Austin's inspection. He began to laugh. "Mom, you're too much! It's the money that's watching you, the money from the Geico commercial."

"Yup! The money you could have saved by switching your automobile insurance. Now get to work. We've got a lot of these to make."

The following evening, under cover of darkness, wearing Undercover Angel nose glasses just in case they were spotted, Karen and Austin had gone around leaving the stacks of money on people's doorsteps, in unlocked cars, and any of a number of creative places where they would be found but not easily spotted from afar.

Karen and Austin had gone to town prayer the first morning they were there, but Karen had decided to keep a low profile so she would not be spotted as the do-gooder, especially once Ellie and Lucy discovered that the check really didn't bounce.

The next morning, Karen conferred with her son. "Austin, my pockets are all empty, but my winter coat fits better now. I was probably looking like a real Two-Ton Tillie with all them cards in the pockets and a coat over top. After last night, we'd better get outta town or we're gonna be found out."

"You're ready to leave? I was just starting to have fun."

"We got money to as many of the people as we could. They got a real sense of community here, so anybody we missed, hopefully somebody'll share with them. It ain't enough, though. They don't want handouts. They want jobs."

㊱

. . . .

CLOWNING AROUND

Karen had worked hard creating her clown's personality, and Dr. Ophelia Bologna was now set to make her first appearance talking with sick kids in the oncology wing at the Primary Children's Medical Center in Salt Lake City.

She surveyed herself in the mirrored closet doors. *Do I look funny? Heck, I could ask myself that and get a "yes" most days, even when I wasn't dressed like a clown. In disguise I can find out which families need help payin' their bills without anybody knowin' who I am.*

She picked up her Mirth Aid Kit and pinned a name badge onto her white coat. "Dr. O. Bologna" it read. She went down to breakfast and did a twirl for her granddaughter. "Whaddya think?"

"Can I come watch?"

"No, but maybe when you get older, you can go to clown trainin'. Would ya like that?"

"Can I really?"

"What's another clown in the family?"

. . .

Karen tentatively opened the door to the room housing the first patient the nurses had said needed some cheering up. Picking at the hospital food was a young man she judged to be around twelve years old. "Mornin', Jeremy. Dr. Ophelia Bologna at your services, but you can call me 'O. Baloney.' "

He looked up, annoyed. "Great! They send a clown in here. What, like I'm five?"

She reached into her black bag and took out a rubber hammer. "Let me check your reflexes." She hit his knee with the hammer, and it made a noise that sounded like breaking glass. No response.

"They said you been feelin' down."

"Yeah, cheer me up. I just found out that I don't get to go home for Thanksgiving. I'll probably miss Christmas too." He continued to pick at his food. "This food is crappy, but I'm gonna throw it up anyway."

Up to this point, Karen had been following the script she had mapped out for herself, but she realized that something was missing from Ophelia—her spontaneity.

"You're prob'ly right. Here, let me save ya some precious time." She picked up the vegetable beef soup and dumped it into the tray he kept nearby for upheavals. She followed that with some orange Jell-O and green beans. Turning the hammer around, she stirred up the mess with the handle and then bent to examine it. "I don't blame ya for not wantin' to eat this slop! It ain't fit for man nor beast."

She grabbed the corner of his hospital gown and wiped the reddish-orange residue from the handle of the plastic hammer, leaving part of one green bean clinging to the fabric.

"Hey, what are you doing? Are you *nuts?*"

"I'm cleanin' my instrument. We can't operate without followin' proper procedures." She reached over and pushed the nurse button. "Jeremy has tossed his cookies. We'd like to order a Big Mac, large fries, and a chocolate milk shake. Supersize the milk shake. Doctor's orders."

There was a pause and then Karen heard laughter from the nurse on the other end of the intercom, but more welcome was the laughter from the young man in the bed. Soon the nurse came in to check on Jeremy and to see what she was missing. "Have you got my order?" he asked. "A Big Mac sounded really good."

"Sorry, Jeremy, but we don't do take-out," the nurse apologized.

"But is he allowed to eat such food?"

"Jeremy is a very sick young man, and the hospital food is specially coordinated by our hospital nutritionist to be healthy and—"

Ophelia interrupted her. "And boring." She turned to her patient. "I'll be back in a few minutes with your order, Jeremy."

"Wait!" The nurse stopped her. "You can't bring in outside food."

"We don't hafta worry about him eating healthy, 'cause he's already sick, right? I've been visitin' with him for a few minutes, and he's a sick young man. Sick, sick, sick, he is. I'll be smuggling it in, under my coat." She picked up her hammer. "You just look the other way when I come back and nobody'll get hurt." Karen slammed the hammer against the dinner tray. She heard a chorus of laughter and breaking glass.

• • •

Ophelia sat nearby while Jeremy ate his Big Mac. "So, Jeremy, where are your folks? Are they close enough for visits?"

"They're in Nephi. They come up on the weekends, and my mom comes up during the week when she can."

"Are they able to cover your hospital bills?"

"I think we've got good insurance. At least, I've heard Mom and Dad saying how grateful they are for it."

"If you know of anybody in here whose family is strugglin' to pay the hospital bill, will you let me know?"

"My friend, Jenny, she's been in here a long time, and I think her family hasn't got very much money."

"What room is she in?"

"She's in room 405, two doors down from me."

"Maybe I'll give her a little visit."

"Dr. Baloney?" He paused. "Are you—will you come back and visit me again?"

She reached into her bag and pulled out a Popsicle stick glued onto a cardboard smile. "Sure thing." She handed him the smile. "In the meantime, if you're havin' a bad day, ya just hold this Smile on a Stick in front of your face and the doctor'll never know. It's called stuffin' yer feelings, something we teach all our young men."

"Yeah, the nurses come in here wondering why I'm not all happy and stuff, stuck in here while all my friends are out having fun and I'm . . ." He couldn't continue.

Ophelia stuck her neck out. "Certainly if you're dyin', ya oughta be cheerful about it. Hey, maybe ya could make a list of the bad things you'd miss out on."

"Like green beans?"

"Green beans is a good place to start, but I think there needs to be a few more things on the list to make it worthwhile dyin'."

He grabbed a piece of paper. "Broccoli too."

• • •

On her next visit, one of the nurses stopped Ophelia. "Um, Dr. Baloney, I wanted to tell you how cute that little stuffed cat is that you gave to Jenny last week, the one with the crocheted cap. It really seems to be cheering her up."

That was my last one. Wouldn't it be great if every kid had a creature that was going through something the same as they was?

"And how's Jeremy?"

"He whips out his cardboard smile every time someone comes into his room. He's been in much better spirits since your visit."

"Good to hear. So who else do you have this week that you think needs some special attention?" She surveyed the nurse's round belly. She pointed to her name badge. "I'm an OB too if ya need some doctorin'. See, OB—Ophelia Bologna."

"Thank you, Dr. B. I'll be in touch. I may need a Smile on a Stick if I get postpartum depression."

Ophelia turned serious. "How do ya do it, taking care of the sick kids? It must be pretty heart-wrenching when you lose one."

"Stick around long enough and you'll find out. I tell myself that if I make life a little easier for any of them while they're here, I've done a good thing. Some nurses manage not to get emotionally attached, but I don't do that very well." She patted her round belly. "Once I'm a mother myself, I'll probably have a whole new level of empathy for parents who lose a child." She smiled and took Karen's hand. "It's a wonderful service you're doing for the kids here, remember that."

Karen sighed. "I guess I'd better keep one of them smile thingies for myself in case one of these days I gotta stuff some feelings."

TWELVE STEPS

R ay watched in disbelief as his daughter stood up and headed toward the pulpit during fast and testimony meeting. *This can't be harder than speaking in front of all those people last week*, she thought.

Delia collected her thoughts as she sat in the choir seats and listened to the trials and tribulations of Sister Newport, who had beat her to the pulpit. "Brothers and sisters, this has been a hard month for our family."

Yeah, your dad died. He was old. Suddenly it hit Dee. *What am I doing up here? I wonder if anyone has ever come up here and then chickened out? I haven't done this since I was what, nine?*

Sister Newport tearfully wrapped it up, and Dee realized she was in the hot seat. She looked out from the pulpit at mostly familiar faces. "Brothers and sisters, my name is Delia Donaldson, and I am an alcoholic." It hadn't been what she had planned, but it was what came out. She realized, if nothing else, that she had everyone's attention.

"Last week I stood before a group of people and admitted that. Today I'm admitting it to you. The AA program includes steps that help you cope with life without the aid of a substance to dull your pain. One of the steps is making amends to those you've hurt."

Dee looked over the congregation and caught Karen's eye. "I have caused my mother pain. I have neglected my daughter. As for making amends to anyone else in this ward, I think it needs to work the other way around."

She swallowed and continued. "I've heard people come up here and say that if they've offended someone, they're sorry." Overlooking the fact that she herself had just made a public apology, she said, "I think apologies from the pulpit are insincere and basically a bunch of . . ." Dee searched for a word strong enough to convey her meaning but mild enough to be used in church. ". . . hogwash."

Emboldened, she continued. "I think most of the time people are aware of when they're hurting other people's feelings. One Christmas when I was a teenager, my mother saved up and bought me a beautiful dress. I was so happy to come to church for once dressed as nicely as the other girls."

She took a deep breath, determined to go on. "I walked into class and one of the girls said, 'Wow! The Deseret Industries has some nice stuff this year. I'm going to have to start shopping there!' Then they all laughed. Even when I looked nice, they made fun of me."

Out of the corner of her eye, Dee saw Austin get up and leave the meeting. She didn't look at her mother, not wanting to see Karen's tears.

• • •

Austin headed toward the men's room, head down. He went into the first stall, put the seat down, sat down, pulled up his legs, and let the unmanly tears flow. Whatever humiliation he had endured as a child and young man, he knew it had been worse for Delia.

Being a guy, he had found an outlet for some of his anger. He'd beat up Jon Faldmo in the parking lot after a Cub Scout pack meeting when Jon had made fun of his passed-along Bear book with all the pages coming loose and somebody else's initials on all the achievements. Austin had given him a bloody nose, and their den mother had given an impromptu first aid demonstration. A couple of bruised Bears and whimpering Wolves later, the Cubs had learned not to mess with Austin. After that he had been treated with respect or at least fear.

He sent his thoughts heavenward. *Why did Dee have to go through that?*

Thoughts came quietly into his head that told him there had been reasons his family had been placed in the ward they had. He remembered a picture he had seen of Christ reaching down and helping a girl over some rocks, and he could almost feel that same hand reaching down to help him through his own rocky way. There was no judgment,

160

just a feeling that he was being held in invisible arms in a safe place where no hurts could penetrate. His shoulders shook as he let out some of the pain of his youth.

He sent more thoughts heavenward. *Are you there? Are you really there, God?* Thoughts came again, unbidden, that told him that Dee's sharing from the pulpit and facing her addictions was the beginning of help and healing that had been in the works for some time.

Austin unrolled several squares of toilet paper and wiped his eyes and blew his nose. He tried to let the peace distill on his soul, entering in through the cracks of his broken heart. He took a deep breath, remembering something his mother had said. *Mom says I don't know the answer about a mission because I won't ask the question. I've wasted so much time. I don't see how I can still go. Do you still want me, Heavenly Father? Do you still want me as a missionary?*

It wasn't a bolt of lightning, a voice, or a vision. It was a feeling, like the time he had taken a big swallow of hot chocolate before it had cooled down and he had been able to feel the path of the fluid as it went down his throat and into his stomach. The warmth started in the vicinity of his heart, and he felt it spread through his veins as though they were full of that same hot chocolate. Some of his hurt and anger melted away as the warmth spread. For a brief moment, he had a glimpse of himself a few years back, excited and eager to serve a mission. *I could still go. I think this is what Bishop Parley was talking about. I really still want to go.*

• • •

Brother Doug Morley sat speechless after Dee's diatribe. He knew it was time to end the meeting, but he was unsure what to say after Delia's "testimony." He breathed a sigh of relief when he saw Adrienne Thompson stand up and approach the pulpit. Even though it would run the meeting late, he welcomed anything that might end the meeting on a more uplifting note. Usually, even when people shared difficulties, they ended with an affirmation of their faith or a story of a lesson learned by a hardship. Dee had left everyone on the edge.

Most of the girls her age no longer lived in the ward, though a few parents had hung their heads in shameful recognition of their daughters' actions. The worst of the unkindness had been administered out of sight of a parent who might correct or a teacher who would be motivated to prepare a "special" lesson about being inclusive.

Adrienne tilted the microphone toward herself. "Brothers and sisters, my name is Adrienne Thompson, and I eat too much Jell-O." She paused, hoping the joke had not been in poor taste. She was quick to follow with a serious point. "We all have things we're trying to overcome. I'm proud of Dee for making changes in her life. It's easy for us to judge people with certain challenges, and yet there is one challenge we all face that's been pointed out to us, a need to be more charitable."

Adrienne continued. "I remember when Dee got her new Christmas dress. I realize now that not laughing at the unkind remarks was not enough. Even though Dee may not realize it, at that age all of us suffered from feelings of wanting to fit in, of not daring to speak up."

Adrienne searched the congregation for Dee's face. "I'm sorry, Dee, that I never had the courage to tell the other girls their unkindness needed to stop. To our youth, being young is no excuse for blatant unkindness."

She saw a few heads nodding at that comment. "I know the time is spent. We belong to the restored Church of Jesus Christ of Latter-day Saints. My prayer is that we will all strive more to be worthy to be bearers of His name, our dear elder brother." As she ended her testimony, Adrienne heard an audible sigh of relief from the conducting member of the bishopric.

Brother Morley jumped to his feet. "Brothers and sisters, as my wife, our choir director, might instruct us, hold that high note. The melodies of our lives will have high notes and low notes, sometimes a minor refrain here and there, and sometimes we fall a little flat." He caught his wife's eye. "Anna is giving me the look that says I have used enough musical metaphors. We thank all of you who have shared with us today." He announced the closing song and prayer and took his seat.

• • •

When Dee got home, Karen got up from the sofa and gave her daughter a hug, holding her a few seconds longer than usual. "I made your favorite, fish stick sandwiches, and I got out some Cherry Garcia ice cream."

"Mom, we don't need to eat fish sticks anymore. We're rich."

"But I know you love 'em. I put a little Grey Poupon on mine. And we got the expensive ice cream."

Dee picked up a lone fish stick from the cookie sheet. "I let the ward have it today, huh? That's not what I meant to do, but it's what came out."

"Maybe it was like puss oozin' outta a wound—part of the healin' process. We survived them, and they'll survive us. Let's stitch it up now and don't pick off the scab. I always wondered why you never wore the dress again. Ya told me you spilled something on it."

Karen slammed the plates of food down on the table. Dee could count on one hand the times she had seen her mother angry. "They never knew how much I scrimped and saved to buy you that dress, the one I had seen you lookin' at every single time we went by that store, how for once I wanted you to have sumpthin' nice, sumpthin' new."

"Mom, it was a long time ago."

"You're still hurt and angry. Why shouldn't I be?"

"Because you're the one who always turned the other cheek and figured out how to get along with everybody, no matter what. I'm supposed to be gettin' rid of the anger, not spreading it around."

"Oh, Dee, these smiles have covered many heartaches. I couldn't start feelin' sorry for myself or I mighta sat down one day like a donkey in the road and refused to get back up." She sighed and tried to calm down. "Get Mandee. I don't think Austin's home yet."

Karen said a quick prayer over the food, and the three of them sat down to eat. Mandee piped up, "Mom, I'm gonna buy you a Christmas dress. Gramma said if I picked one out with you, maybe you wouldn't feel so sad about your other Christmas dress."

Dee looked down at her young daughter. *Gosh, I forgot Mandee was listening to all that too.* "You would do that for me?"

"Gramma told me she'd pay me to do some extra chores."

"Overpay you is more like it."

"You can count on it!" Karen said. She hesitated and spoke quietly. "I'm proud you took the first step, Dee."

"Ray said he needed to find meetings here to attend. He asked me to come along to be supportive of him because he said nothing scares him more than public speaking."

"That's true. I ain't never seen him speak in public. Speakin' at AA that first time must have been harder for Ray than admittin' he had a drinkin' problem."

"He didn't get up at AA this time. I did, though. I wasn't planning on talking there or in church today."

"I'm startin' to think Ray is more clever than I ever gave him credit for. He knew if he could get you listenin' to some of the other people, maybe you'd take that first step and realize you had a problem."

"A bunch of people came up to me after church and told me they were proud of me for facing up to things. Maybe I came down too hard on people today, but it wasn't fair the way those girls treated me. It wasn't fair that they had everything and I had the leftovers."

"Is it fair now that we've got all this money? Life ain't fair. How we deal with the unfairness, havin' too much or not enough, is part of the test."

"I don't understand how you survived. Ya must've known how some of the people in the ward looked down on us."

"Sure, I knew. I ain't stupid. When it's grown-ups, ya can't blame it on the ignorance of youth." Her tone softened. "I have that picture in my bedroom of Jesus carryin' a little lamb on His shoulders. When times got tough, I knew He'd carry me through. I always knew I had someone who understood about life not being fair."

She squirted chocolate sauce over her bowl of ice cream. "Whatever unfairness we've experienced, it don't come close to the unfairness of what they did to Jesus. He was perfect, never hurt nobody, spent His whole life helpin' people. He suffered the most unfair thing of all, and that means He always understands whatever unfairness we're going through."

"I know you taught me that, but sometimes . . ."

"When we're hurtin', sometimes the understandin' don't come. You ain't a kid no more either, Dee, so it's time to understand that ya can't fix other people's sins. Everybody's got something they struggle with. There ain't a 'Snobs Anonymous' for people like Alison Arletti, but maybe something humblin' will happen to her someday."

"I hope so!"

"Dee, if you're waitin' for God to smite your enemies, if you're wishin' bad things on 'em, that's something else *you* gotta work on. Let go of the anger and hope that someday Alison has the experiences she needs to become a better person."

Karen looked into Dee's tear-filled eyes. "Shoo them bad feelings, like a big flock of birds. They'll scatter and fly away." She scattered an imaginary flock. "Instead, most folks carry around a big bag of bird seed and keep their bad feelings followin' 'em around. I never in a million years thought Toni Cironni would come over here and crochet with me, laughin' and eatin' cookie dough."

"It don't bother you that she never treated you with any respect until you had money?"

"It ain't that simple, Dee. It just ain't."

"I don't understand how you love people who treat you bad."

"That's the gospel in a nutshell—lovin' people. People can't change if ya don't love 'em. Ain't that what Jesus taught, to love people that ain't nice to us, to turn the other cheek and love your enemies? I believe in the power of love, Dee. I ain't one of them people understands the scriptures backwards and forwards, but I get that part."

"It'd help if they'd apologize or something. You oughta hear some of the things I heard Toni said when you bought this house."

"I don't wanna hear what she said. It don't matter. Dee, we might've been snobs too under different circumstances. It's just a different kind of unfairness. Havin' too much can be more damagin' to the soul than havin' too little. If it ain't pride that gets ya, then it's envy. In the end, we're all stumblin' along together, trippin' over each other and holdin' each other up the best we can."

DOG THERAPY

K aren picked up the bedside phone. "Karen, hello. It's Toni. I'm so sorry to call this early, but I didn't know who else would understand." Toni's voice caught. "We've had a death . . ." Before Karen could jump to any conclusions, Toni took a breath and went on. "It's George, Corina's dog. He died in my arms last night. We want to bury him, but we can't turn the Thompsons' backyard into a dog cemetery. This is presumptuous of me to ask, but do you think . . . ?"

Karen jumped in. "Say no more. I'll get Austin and Ray busy diggin' a hole in the backyard." She looked out the window at the light dusting of snow on the ground. "It might take them awhile, but you bring George on over whenever you're ready."

"I'm letting the children skip school today. We would be honored if you would participate with us in George's funeral."

• • •

Karen looked out the window and saw Ray and Austin digging George's grave, soon joined by a couple of biker brothers who were still hanging around from that morning's detail. Though Austin didn't resemble Ray physically, she noticed their shared mannerisms as they dug the hole with pick and shovel. For the first time since Ray's return, Austin didn't exhibit the negative body language she'd seen any time he was around his father. Perhaps it was the nature of the task.

The Cironni family came over later that morning. Karen watched as several young pallbearers in their winter coats and gloves lifted a large cardboard box out of the back of their van. George was wrapped in a handmade quilt.

Toni followed her children into the backyard. Karen and Toni watched as the children lowered George's cardboard coffin into the hole, with a little help steadying the box from Austin and cousin Victor. "Ya gonna bury that beautiful quilt, Toni?" Karen asked.

"George deserves to be laid to rest in style," she responded, wiping a tear from her eye. "I want to know that I gave him my best because he gave us his best." She smiled through her tears. "And little Alex was worried he wouldn't be warm enough."

After the service, Victor approached the grave and threw in a handful of dirt. "Man's best friend," he said simply. Ray picked up a shovel to fill in the hole. He felt a hand on his back. Alex Cironni spoke. "Let me, Ray. It's a last act of service I can do for George." His voice caught. "He was so good for . . ." He struggled to continue. "He knew somehow. After Corina had been through chemo, he would lie next to her. When her hair fell out, his fur started coming out in clumps. He knew that she'd rescued him from the pound. He loved the other children, but he knew he was Corina's dog."

Ray handed him the shovel. Alex continued. "She's finally responding to the treatment. They won't use the word remission yet, but we're winning. We're winning the fight."

Close to the garage, Toni held a young girl with no hair under her orange and yellow lopsided knit cap, and they cried together. Comforted momentarily, Corina joined her brothers and sisters over at the grave where she put George's favorite chew bone on top of the mounded earth. Karen turned her attention to Victor, who was doing his best not to let his emotions show.

"Lost my dog a month after I lost my dad. I'd really like to see both of them again sometime." He ducked inside the house before anyone else could see his tears.

Karen turned and found Toni standing beside her. She pulled something out of the pocket of her jacket. "I thought I'd show you this, Toni. I didn't know who else would understand. There's a boy that I visit in the hospital—Jeremy. The other day I helped him make a list of all the things he'll avoid if he dies."

Toni took the list and began to read. "Green beans. Mushy broccoli. Stringy squash. Hospital food. Never going to have to do homework.

Never going to get dumped by a girl. Never going to starve to death if there's a famine. Never going to have to watch my parents get a divorce. Never going to get fired from a job."

"Oh, that's so sad. It reminds me of Corina's list of service projects she wanted to do in case she died. That's how we came to get George in the first place."

Toni handed the list back to Karen. "Are his parents having troubles? A child's serious illness can cause problems in a marriage," Toni said quietly. "You have to pull together, but sometimes it tears you apart. Is he . . .?"

"Not much longer," Karen said.

Toni touched Karen's arm and gently changed the subject. "Karen, after I heard Dee's testimony, I thought there were things . . . I mean, I still feel I owe you an apology for so many times that I . . ."

"Toni, ya don't need to go there. You're my friend. That's all I need to know."

● ● ●

After the services, Karen went inside and plopped down on her favorite sofa, now covered with a new tan slipcover. Boomer bounded onto her lap and rolled over for a tummy rub. Karen ran her hand over the dog's belly. "You dogs have got that unconditional love thing down pretty good. Wish us people could figger it out better."

The door opened and Dee came in carrying a small, scrawny puppy. "Mom, I was over at the park. I heard this car pull up. I looked over and they threw this little guy outta the car window like a piece of garbage and drove away."

"Oh, that makes me so sad," Karen said, reaching out for the scrawny little dog. Boomer jostled for position, seeing he was about to be supplanted in his owner's affections.

Dee sat down on the floor and motioned to him. "Here, Boomer." He bounded onto her lap, licking her face enthusiastically.

Karen spoke to the puppy. "We'll get you fattened up and you can stay here with us."

"Mom, what if Bark City becomes a place where people abandon their animals, like those people did at the park today?"

"We can't rescue every animal that's abandoned."

"There's that undeveloped land on the other side of the dog park.

What if we opened a shelter where we adopted animals out and took care of them if no one else wanted 'em?"

"Hmm, that's not a bad idea."

"I haven't had a drink now since I went to AA and the job I have ain't going nowhere."

"Tell me more about your idea."

"Okay, we'd hire people who liked animals, and they could feed them and walk them, and we'd get them to the vet, get them healthy so people would wanna adopt them. Then we could have a dog training program, teach them how to understand a few commands, and then maybe we could start a dog therapy program, taking the most obedient ones to visit nursing homes or detention centers or wherever there might be a need for someone to get a face lick and . . ."

"And a little unconditional love. I love it, Dee! You'd be awesome helpin' run a shelter and a program like that. Let's get Barry on the phone and get the ball rollin'."

GOOD NEWS
AND BAD NEWS

"M om, I've got something I want to tell you." Ray clicked the Pause button on the remote and stopped *Crocodile Dundee* mid-scene when Austin walked in. "Oh, Ray, you're here too. Well, I guess you'll both be interested."

"What's up?" Karen asked.

"I'm meeting with the bishop tonight to turn in my mission papers."

Karen's mouth dropped open. "Hot dang!"

Ray remained silent, but Austin saw something he'd wanted to see all his life—a look that told him his father was proud of him.

● ● ●

Karen's spirits were up when she entered the hospital, encouraged that her prayers about Dee and Austin had finally been answered. She wasn't prepared for the empty bed that greeted Ophelia when she entered Jeremy's room. She approached the nurse's desk, hoping against hope there was another reason for his absence, but realizing immediately that his belongings were gone from the room as well.

"Where's Jeremy?" she asked, her voice barely above a whisper.

The two nurses exchanged a look and she knew. "When a patient is weakened from chemotherapy, their immune system is so compromised that it doesn't take . . ."

Karen fought through her emotions to ask one word. "When?"

"Yesterday."

"Please put me in touch with his family. I need to . . ." She couldn't continue. She headed to the nearest seating area and let the tears flow.

• • •

Later that day Toni Cironni answered the call from a clown in need of some cheering up. "Toni, you're the only person I know that'll really understand."

"I'll be right over."

Soon Toni was seated on the secondhand sofa, holding a crying clown in her arms, without a thought about Karen's garish plastic neon glasses or whether the dogs were shedding on the carpet.

"He was the first kid I visited. I can't take the heartbreak of losin' the kids I grow to love. I don't know if I wanna do the clownin' anymore." Karen wiped her eyes, smearing the clown makeup she hadn't yet removed.

"Oh Karen, you can't quit. Those kids need what you bring to them, a chance to forget that they're sick and just be kids."

"But if laughter's the best medicine, then why ain't he still alive?"

"Only God can answer that one. You brought joy and laughter to Jeremy at a time when there wasn't much to laugh about."

Karen brightened a little. "You should have seen his face when I smuggled in that Big Mac." She paused. "His funeral is day after tomorrow in Nephi." Karen switched gears. "Speakin' of funerals, my cousin Victor told me that the things ya said about George at his funeral touched his heart. He come to me later and told me he was thinkin' about goin' back to church. He ain't been to church since he was a kid."

"So let me get this straight. My eulogy for a dog inspired a Hells Angel to go back to church? Score another one for George."

"God really does work in mysterious ways, don't he?"

"Funerals have a way of stirring people's spirits. So are you going to go to Jeremy's funeral, Karen?"

"Not exactly me." Karen paused. "Ophelia is goin' in my place."

Toni took a good look at her friend, the clown. "Be prepared to redo her makeup."

FREE TO A GOOD HOME

If Mom sees this, she'll think I've sunk to a new level of desperation, trying to meet men online. Dee clicked the mouse and brought up an open game of Solitaire. This was the second time Karen had walked into the office where they kept their computer and had seen the screen immediately change.

Austin had told Karen about some game software that had something called the "boss button" that took you out of your game and into a spreadsheet when the boss walked by. *What's she doing that she don't want me to see? Gosh, Dee, what are ya up to now? Brother Cox taught that class about computers and how to check the places your kids have been visitin'. I'll ask him next time I see him at church.*

Dee waited until her mother left the room and clicked back to the site for LDS singles. *Okay, do I go to church never, sometimes, often or always? Should I look for someone like me and we can be slackers together, or should I look for someone better than me who can drag me along?*

She paused, struck by a moment of insecurity. *Who am I kidding? I'm not gonna find anyone on here. Traffic school, maybe. That time I got the speeding ticket and had to go to that class, there were a lot of guys in there.*

She answered the next question. *I never should have let Austin talk me into this. Okay, Austin. You prayed about whether or not to go on a mission. I took your challenge and exercised my puny little mustard seed of faith. He told me I would know when I had an answer. Well, Austin, sorry but it ain't happening.*

She clicked on another profile and read about a returned missionary who taught early morning seminary in Steamboat Springs, Colorado. *He's not bad looking, but he's not going to be interested in someone like me.*

"Looking for that special someone," read one of the profiles. *Don't want anybody who thinks I'm "special," and besides, he's looking for someone with a temple recommend.*

"Are you my cyber-soulmate?" read another. He was wearing a suit and ugly tie in his picture and looked and sounded a little stuffy for Dee's taste. *I don't care what callings he's had. He even put the dates. These guys are all too churchy. If I don't sign up, Mom will never know I was on here looking, so she won't be disappointed.*

Dee was about to click on the button to close the program when another profile popped to the top of her list. "Free to a good home," the teaser stated. Delia pulled up the full profile, and a funny feeling came over her as she began to read. "I'll always come when you call, loyal and friendly, housebroken, affectionate and playful, enjoys going for rides in cars. If you feed me, scratch my back, and take me for long walks, I'll sit and stay forever. I try to stay out of the doghouse, and I'm gentle with children. Won't chase cars or other women. Willing to at least try and learn new tricks. Pretty good at some old ones. Throw me a bone. Don't make me beg."

On the other hand, who wants someone who gets speeding tickets?

SECRET SANTAS

R ay spread the house plans for the sprawling log house out on the dining room table. "So, is there anything else you wanna add?" he asked.

"We moved the laundry room so it's on the same floor as the bedrooms, right? My favorite part is the courtyard with all the doggie doors leadin' out to it. It's like havin' a yard inside the house," Karen said.

"I can live in a trailer on the property while they're buildin' it." He moved around the table and gave Karen a quick kiss and then another one that wasn't so quick. Austin, unable to stomach their middle-aged display of affection, walked into the family room.

"Whatcha doing, Dee?"

She clicked the button. "Just finishing up this game of Solitaire."

"Been playing Solitaire a lot since you and Zhon called it quits. Do you think we've seen the last of him?"

"What was he gonna do, once he realized I wouldn't go along with his plan? It wouldn't do him any good to hang around."

"Still, I'm glad he stayed away." He hesitated. "We've both been playing Solitaire a lot lately. I have to admit I got my hopes up when Adrienne came back."

"I did too. I would have loved for you to marry Adrienne Thompson."

Karen yelled in from the other room. "You guys ready to go carolin' in the ward?"

"Yeah, Mom. We're coming," Dee answered. She clicked out of

her game and closed another window on the computer. She turned to her brother. "Why are we doing it so early? It's only the first week of December."

"Mom wants to help people in time for them to use the money for Christmas if they need to."

Karen picked up her bag of Santa hats and nose glasses, distributing one of each to the family members. They donned their disguises as the Singing Secret Santas, loaded some treats into the Lucky Duck, and set off to make the rounds of a few select homes in the ward.

"Until the economy tanked, there wasn't nobody in the ward that needed help except us," Karen stated. "We got two more houses to go." She announced their destinations like a bus driver. "Next stop, the Cironnis'. Ray, ya got the music ready? Ya made us stand there too long lookin' like dorks on the porch at the Barnett's before ya pushed the button."

When they were all congregated on the porch, Delia rang the doorbell and Ray pushed the button on the portable CD player. The sound of dogs barking to the tune of *Jingle Bells* filled the air. Ray, Karen, Delia, Austin and little Mandee barked along in sync with the music until the door opened and several Cironni children greeted them with laughter. "Mom, Dad, come look!"

Karen handed them a plate of cookies with a Christmas card in an envelope. "We're the Singing Secret Santas. Merry Christmas!"

Toni looked at the cookies. "Are these cooked, Karen? That must be a first. And they're still warm."

Karen grinned. "Yup! First time I ever bought the dough and actually baked it."

As the Donaldson crew headed to their next stop, Toni set the plate down and the children began devouring the cookies. She opened the card and discovered a document inside. She unfolded it and her hand flew to her mouth. "Alex! Come here, Alex. You're not going to believe this!"

"What?" He rushed to her side. She couldn't speak. She pursed her lips together, trying to control her emotions. She held out the document. "It's, it's . . ."

"What, Toni? Spit it out." He picked up a cookie while he waited for his wife to regain her composure.

She took a deep breath. "It's the deed to our house."

His cookie fell to the floor. "You're kidding!"

"Karen's *giving* us our house back. I can't believe it!"

"Free and clear?"

"She's signed the house back over to us, Alex." Toni sank into a nearby chair. "A bunch of barking dogs in nose glasses and Santa hats gave us our house back." She began to laugh at the absurdity of it all and then suddenly grew serious at the realization of all this would mean to their family.

"At a Relief Society meeting about having your affairs in order, before she got rich, Karen joked that the only way Dee and Austin were going to get an inheritance was if the mortician took out the gold fillings in her teeth." Toni grew quiet. "Their inheritance isn't in her gold fillings, Alex. It's in her heart of gold."

• • •

As the Donaldsons approached, the Arletti family was putting the finishing touches on the artificial tree Olive always adorned to coordinate with her home décor. Alison had come to stay with her parents for the holidays, and her brother, Andrew, would be flying in a few days before Christmas.

With Arthur's recent layoff, they had scaled down on the outside decorations, but Olive's tree was as elegant as ever, decorated with ornaments she had hand picked over the years.

"I heard Adrienne Thompson is engaged," Alison said.

"He seems like a nice boy, very sharp. Of course Adrienne was always very studious and bright, so it stands to reason." Olive readjusted a drooping branch.

"Do you know what's going on with anybody else from my group?"

Olive hesitated. "Delia Donaldson's been coming back to church." She plumped an ivory bow.

"D.I. Dee? I meant anyone I hung around with."

Olive blanched at that comment. "That's not very kind, Alison. Did all the girls call her that?"

Alison shrugged. "I think it was just me and Heidi."

"Heidi was not always the best influence on you, Alison." She hesitated. "Or maybe it was the other way around." Olive left off fussing over her tree and turned her attention to her daughter.

"Oh, come on, Mom. It's not like you didn't complain all the time about Dee's mom. That's too funny about her winning the lottery. I've read some of the news stories. Cow Pie Bingo. That's more her style. It goes to show you can't buy class, no matter how much money you have."

"Alison, maybe I wasn't always the best example to you, but . . ."

"But *what,* Mother?"

"It wouldn't hurt for you to talk to Dee on Sunday, perhaps apologize for some of the things you did when you were younger."

"I'm sure Dee knew we were just having fun, kidding around with her."

Olive grew quiet. "When I was young, my mother used to tell me to say, 'Sticks and stones will break my bones but words will never hurt me' if someone said something unkind to me. That's not true, Alison. Words *do* hurt. Dee told a story in testimony meeting about a new Christmas dress her mother bought her, and I couldn't help but wonder who the girls were, and I hoped that you . . ."

Alison turned away from her mother. "I'm sure I wouldn't remember." *She looked pretty, Mother. We couldn't let her know she was pretty.*

"Since your father lost his job, it's the first time we've had to worry about our finances. He gave all those years to that company, and then they replaced him with a younger man just to save the company money. We're still not sure whether or not his retirement fund is solvent. His loyalty, his years of service—they apparently count for nothing."

"I'm glad I got through the master's program before this happened."

"Yes, Alison, heaven forbid you should have had to work while you were going to school. I hope the day never comes when we have to lean on you and your brother for support."

"You and me both, Mother."

"They knew about your father's diabetes and that it would be difficult for us to get health insurance. It goes without saying that he isn't going to be competitive in the job market at his age. I doubt he'll find anything that will pay like that job did. We can pay to keep the old insurance for a time, but I don't know what we're going to do when that runs out, how we're going to afford our medications. I don't know how long our savings will carry us if he doesn't find work."

"What does any of that possibly have to do with Dee Donaldson?"

Olive sighed. "Everything and nothing, dear."

Her talk with Alison was interrupted by the ringing doorbell. Olive opened the door to find a group that looked suspiciously like the

Donaldsons. "We're the Kris Kringle Karaoke Quintet," Karen stated. "Hit it, Maestro."

Ray pushed the button and they began to sing, affecting an Oriental accent. "Deck the halls with boughs of hah-ree, fa ra ra ra ra ra ra ra ra." As the song ended, they all bowed. Mandee handed her a large Chinese take-out container. "We made you some fortune cookies."

"I learned how to make 'em at one of your Relief Society meetings," Karen stated. "Only I've got a secret ingredient."

Olive opened the take-out container and gasped. Tucked in the side of the container were several gift cards from a nearby drugstore. Inside the fortune cookies were crisp hundred-dollar bills, sticking out both ends.

"That's my secret ingredient. Now those are *true* fortune cookies."

"Oh my goodness, Karen! And Walgreens gift cards? How in the world did you know we . . . ?"

"Santa's got his elves all over, Sister Arletti." *Even in the bathroom at church.*

Austin spoke, swallowing hard, forcing out the words he had been rehearsing as they walked to the door. *I can say this. She meant well. She just went about things awkwardly.* "We are only returning some of the kindness you always showed us over the years. I never thanked you for being willing to help support me on a mission, even though it has taken me awhile to get around to going."

"I heard you're awaiting a mission call. I'm glad you've got it covered, Austin, because we're not in much of a position to help ourselves at the moment, much less anyone else."

Alison had been standing behind her mother, observing from a few feet back. She moved forward. "Austin, it's great that you're going to still go. I always thought you'd be an awesome missionary."

"Thanks, Alison."

She looked at Delia, who was grateful she had the nose glasses to hide behind. "Dee, Mom says you've been going back to church. That's great!" she said, with a little too much enthusiasm. "It must not have been easy because . . ." She took a deep breath and continued. "Because there were people at church who weren't always very nice to you and lots of people would use that as an excuse never to come back."

It was as close as Alison could come to an apology. Alison saw tears fill Dee's eyes behind the nose glasses, and she suddenly had a bright recollection of all the unkind things she had said and done over the years. No matter how hard she fought it, her own eyes filled with tears of remorse, long overdue. The two girls stared at one another through their tears, but no more words were spoken between them.

Sensing emotions had been stirred, Karen bowed. "Merry Christmas. We gotta get down to the auction for the Festival of the Trees. There's a special tree I wanna bid on. Gonna put it up at the vet's office by my dog park."

"Thank you again, all of you." Olive put her open hand over her heart. "You'll never know what this has meant to us."

(42)

. . . .

THE CHOCOLATE LIST

C harles Morris McLelland pushed back the chair from his desk in
the spacious corner office. He reached for his walking stick in the
corner. On the wall across from his desk hung a painting of the Golden
Gate Bridge with the lights of San Francisco in the background.

As the last surviving founding father of Frost, Bringhurst & McLelland, he still came into the office every day for several hours. He read his
newspaper, did a little correspondence, and stayed out of Sylvia's hair so
she was free to putz around their penthouse without him underfoot.

He ventured out into the hall. *Confound it! Which is the way to
Rex's office? These young attorneys change offices so often I can't keep track
of them.* He started down the hall, pausing to peer into each office as he
passed, hoping to find Rex Parley. When passing an occupied office, he
was greeted enthusiastically. "Mr. McLelland! How are you today?"

"I'm eighty-nine years old," he said gruffly. "How do you *think* I
am?"

He never addressed any of them by name. It kept them humble.
"Good afternoon, Mr. McLelland." Ted Simon waited hopefully for
some acknowledgment of his recent achievements.

"Where the devil is Parley?"

"I'll have him paged for you."

"Paged? I don't want him *paged!* Point me in the direction of his
office."

Eventually Mr. McLelland made his way to Rex Parley's office,
which was in the same place it had been for the past three years. He sat

down in one of the wingback chairs across from the desk. "Parley, did you change offices again?"

Rex smiled patiently. "Not recently, Mr. McLelland."

"Recently is a relative term to a man my age, Parley." He tapped his cane against the desk. "I'm working on my chocolate list. What names do I need to add this year?"

Every Christmas, Mr. C. Morris McLelland, senior partner, sent a five-pound box of Ghirardelli chocolates from his City by the Bay to each of the partners in the firm. It was a well-known fact that if an associate got a box of chocolates from Mr. McLelland at Christmas time, he would be a partner in the firm come January.

Rex smiled. He remembered getting his first box of chocolates from Mr. McLelland years ago. Morris had long since turned over the reins to the executive committee in terms of running the firm, but he reserved for himself the pleasure of giving the gift that signaled advance notice of impending partnership. "We have four names to add this year, Mr. McLelland."

"Who are they?" he bellowed impatiently. "Time's precious for a man my age, Parley."

Rex smiled. "Kelly Ward, Lisa Nebeker, David Muecke, and Rod McConkie. Here. I've written them down."

"Where's Camille?"

"She's away from her desk."

"That tells me where she *isn't!* Find her! I'm getting this off later than I usually do. I want to get it out tonight."

He wound his way back through the halls to his office. A group of attorneys chatting near the reception area parted like the Red Sea for Mr. McLelland and his walking staff. He fielded their many greetings like so many mosquitoes, while Rex Parley went in search of their mutual secretary.

As the secretaries compared notes about the approaching holiday season, the break room door opened. Rex Parley stuck his head in.

"Camille, I'm sorry to bother you on your break. Mr. McLelland is looking for you. He's got something for you to type," Rex said.

"Okay, I'll be right there."

Camille picked up her purse and finished drinking the last of her soda.

Lynette spoke. "It must be time for the famous chocolate list."

Camille smiled. "Being new, I wouldn't know about it except that I've already had associates hanging around my desk hoping I'll let slip who is on the list. I've even had a couple of them offer me money, jokingly, of course."

Camille put her purse back in her desk drawer and retrieved a pad of paper before she headed to Mr. McLelland's office. "Mr. Parley said you wanted to see me."

"Yes, I'm ready to send off my chocolate list. Rex has the file for the one from last year. He said he would send it to you to revise. Add these names to it. Look up their addresses from the master list. I'd like to get it out tonight."

"I'll do it right now."

"Are you having a nice holiday season, Camille?"

"Yes, thank you. My little girl is old enough to understand a little, so that makes it fun."

"My children are old, Camille. My grandchildren are middle-aged. Some of my great-grand-children are graduating college." He chuckled. "You know what's best about getting to be my age, Camille?"

"No, what?"

"No peer pressure." He laughed heartily.

"That's a good one, Mr. McLelland."

"You're a lovely girl, Camille. I hope you have a Merry Christmas. Here's a little something to help you with the holidays." He shoved an envelope across the desk to her. She picked it up and looked inside. It was full of twenty-dollar bills.

"Thank you, Mr. McLelland. It's very generous of . . ."

He cut her off, waving his hand. "Buy yourself a nice little bauble. Now skedaddle! Let's get those chocolates on their way. Nobody makes chocolate like Ghirardelli."

"Yes, sir."

• • •

Camille opened the drawer of her desk where she kept her purse and put the envelope full of money in a safe compartment. She pulled up the file Rex had sent her and made the revisions, inputting the names and addresses of the new partners. While it was printing, an idea came to her. *Mr. McLelland gives Ghirardelli chocolates every year because he likes them and it reminds him of his younger years in San Francisco. I've*

*been wondering what to get him. I'll send him a big box of the same choco-
lates. That's a great idea!*

She was in the middle of the letter to place a separate order when
Mr. McLelland stopped by her desk on his way out.

"See you tomorrow, Camille."

"Tomorrow's Saturday, Mr. McLelland. Are you coming by my
house?"

"Oh, that's right. It's Friday. See you Monday, then." He hit the
side of her desk with his cane. "You got me." He chuckled. "Oh, and
Camille, there's someone else I forgot to put on the chocolate list."

*It must be Ted. Ted, the Rainmaker, Ted, the Wonder Boy, Ted, the
Jerk. But Rex said . . .*

"Every year I send out the chocolate I love to the attorneys in this
office, and I never get any for myself. Would you please put me down
for a five-pound box—no make it a ten-pounder. Thank you, Camille,
and have a nice weekend."

There goes that plan. She moved to push the buttons to delete her
half-composed letter, and then she had a wicked thought. *And should
I make it a five-pound box like everybody else? No, let's make it a ten-
pounder.* She looked up one more address, finished the letter, enclosed
payment, and put it in the mail separate from the other order.

That night an order went out for five-pound boxes of chocolates
to be sent to all the partners and soon-to-be partners in the firm. A
separate order printed on plain paper and paid in cash was placed for a
ten-pound box of chocolates to be sent to the home of Ted Simon.

43

FESTIVAL OF THE TREES

Toni and Alex wandered the aisles with their children at the private viewing for the Festival of the Trees. As if reading her mother's mind about their small tree compared to some of the fancier ones, Corina said, "The important thing is that we did it in memory of George."

"How come they put it clear over here in the corner on the last row?" Marcus asked.

"They can't all have the spot by the door as you come in," Toni explained.

"Mom's friend Nancy, who is in charge, didn't like our tree," know-it-all Cecily informed her siblings. "I heard her tell Mom she shouldn't put up the picture of George because he was too ugly with his fur all splotchy and that if she had known, she wouldn't have let us do a tree. Isn't that true, Mom? Tell them."

Toni thought for a moment before she replied. "Nancy was very generous in letting us enter our tree at the last minute, but she hasn't yet learned about inner beauty in dogs, trees, or people. Maybe someday she'll understand."

A pretty young blonde woman standing nearby overheard their conversation. "I think your tree and the story behind it are both beautiful."

"Thank you," Toni replied.

The young woman turned when she heard her name. "Hiya, Camille. What are you doin' here?"

"Oh, hi, Karen. Mr. Parley assigned me to buy a tree for the law firm. I can bid up to five thousand dollars."

"That oughta buy you a nice one." Karen spotted Toni and the children. "Love the tree, Toni. George would be proud!"

Karen soon found herself engulfed in a hug the likes of which she had never experienced in her life. Toni finally let her come up for air. "Karen, I honestly don't know what to say. The house, I can't believe what you did. None of us can."

She grinned. "Merry Christmas! Me and Ray are gonna get married again, and we're gonna build up in Heber by the dog park. Soon as we move in, Bishop Parley said you can file that Quit Claim Deed and you'll have the house back, but I wanted to tell you as a Christmas present." *And I ain't done yet.*

Before Toni could respond further, Karen turned to Camille. "This here is my friend Toni and her kids. Toni, Camille is Bishop Parley's secretary. Camille, I don't think you've met my kids. That's Delia over there by that big gingerbread house, and this here is my son, Austin."

Austin turned and looked into the soft blue eyes of one of the most beautiful girls he had ever seen. Then he noticed the cute little blonde girl holding her hand, a carbon copy of her mother. Without thinking, he blurted out, "Oh, you're married!" It was hard to say which of them turned the reddest.

Austin did his best to recover from the awkward moment while Camille stood tongue-tied, wishing she wasn't so shy and that there was a way to tactfully tell him she was newly single without appearing forward.

"I, um, appreciate all the help you've given my mother," he said.

"Everyone at the office loves Karen," she responded.

I'm off to the mission field, even if she wasn't married, Austin thought.

• • •

Whether or not their tree sold for any appreciable amount of money, Toni consoled herself by remembering they would always have the memories they had made while painting dog biscuits and stringing small Milk-Bone treats on dental floss.

In the final analysis, keeping the design of the tree simple enough that even her youngest had been able to fully participate had been more important to Toni than having a designer tree. In awe of some of the gorgeous trees, Toni still stood proudly in front of their family's creation.

On another easel was the story of a young girl with cancer who had rescued an animal no one else wanted from the pound. Although no one "oohed" and "aahed" over the tree, almost everybody who stopped to read the story walked away wiping their eyes.

Nancy's husband, Miles, was acting as auctioneer. Unwanted feelings rose as Toni watched decorator trees sell for thousands of dollars each. Finally, they projected a picture of their little tree onto the screen. "Folks, we know we can find a home for this tree," he said apologetically.

Alex reached over and touched Toni's arm. "Don't let him get to you."

"We're going to start the bidding at, um, three hundred dollars. Remember, the proceeds go directly to the Primary Children's Hospital." Toni stiffened and then took a deep breath, trying to relax. *Remember what's important. Alex is right. I'm going to take the high road, even if it kills me. I could have decorated a tree that would have blown all these trees out of the water if I had wanted to.*

This was the lowest they had started the bidding for any of the trees. Toni caught Nancy's eye. Again, she fought down the unkind feelings that surfaced, acutely aware that not long ago she would have likely acted the same way.

The room was silent until finally Alex placed the opening bid. Toni squeezed his hand. *Good idea, honey. We'll buy it back. The kids worked so hard on it, they'll enjoy having it around.* A few other sympathy bids were made, raising the amount in small increments.

Seated on the floor, Ray leaned over and whispered to Karen. "It's for the hospital, for the sick kids you visit. Why not make it two?"

"Why don't you do it? That way it won't draw attention to me."

Ray shrugged. "Okay." He stood up. Toni turned at the sound of his voice. "I bid two million dollars." There were gasps from the floor. Miles squinted to get a good look at the nondescript man in the back placing this record-breaking bid. The balding man in the jeans and sweatshirt certainly didn't look like a force to be reckoned with.

"And you *are,* sir?"

Ray grinned, thinking of the new business cards Karen had printed for him to help her in her charitable activities. "Just call me Phil. Phil N. Thropic." He sat down, leaned over and whispered to Karen. "I did it. Public speaking!"

With that, Miles decided it could not possibly be a legitimate bid, but he could use it as an excuse to go on to the next tree. He banged down the gavel. "Going once, going twice, going, going, GONE!"

The Cironni children broke out in squeals and applause and started jumping up and down, game-show style. Little Alex was caught up in the excitement with his brothers and sisters. "Somebody bought aw twee! Somebody bought aw twee!"

She's done it again. Toni hugged her husband tightly, looked into his eyes, and said softly, "Awex, wooks wike somebody wif a wotta money bought aw twee!"

• • •

"That was fun," Ray stated. "That'll teach him to treat a tree like it ain't good enough."

Karen squeezed his hand. "I wanna decorate a tree next year dedicated to Jeremy," she said. "He loved Legos. We could do a tree covered with Legos. It could be his Lego-cy."

"We could make that our family project next Christmas." Ray turned to his son. "Austin, me and you need to go shopping for Legos."

Austin smiled. "It's about time! I love Legos!"

• • •

They weren't home long before Delia was on the computer. Karen sat next to Ray on the sofa and pulled a slip of paper from her purse. "I need your help with this, Ray."

"What is it?"

"It's directions for how to find out what places your kids have been visitin' on the computer. Every time I come into the room, Dee clicks out of whatever she's been lookin' at."

"Whaddya think she's doing?"

"I dunno, but they told us in this class that it ain't just guys goin' to questionable sites. When she goes to bed, we're gonna check it out," she whispered conspiratorially.

• • •

It didn't take long for Ray to pull up the Internet history. Bracing herself for whatever it was Delia hadn't wanted her to see, Karen looked at the sites listed on the screen. To her surprise, the top several listings that popped up appeared to be sites for LDS singles to meet.

"Whaddya know! Another Christmas miracle!"

······························

44

CHOCOLATE, ANYONE?

Ted Simon got off the elevator, ready to share his good news. "Have a chocolate, Lisa? I imagine you got a box too."

"I did," she said quietly, "but I thought I'd wait until January for the official announcement."

"Enough with the false modesty. Everyone knew you would make partner this year. Do you know who else?"

"Everyone is not sharing that information quite so generously as you are, Ted," she said, eying the ten-pound box of chocolates he held out to her. "Don't you think it's meant for a private celebration?"

"Why be miserly?"

Ted made the rounds, sharing his chocolates and their implied good fortune, uncaring that he was flaunting his promotion before other hopeful associates, confirming that they had been passed over, as well as unknowingly lording it over long-time partners who had all received smaller boxes of chocolate than he had.

• • •

Camille retrieved the page of labels as they came off the printer. When she turned around, Ted was there at her desk. "Have a chocolate, Camille?"

"No, thanks."

"Watching your figure?" He looked around quickly and saw that they were alone. "That makes two of us." He set his box of chocolates down on her desk. "So, Cami, is Santa going to be good to you?"

He leaned closer and whispered. "Why not give *me* a chance to make visions of sugar plums dance in your head?"

From under Camille's desk came the sound of rattling tools. Suddenly Ted found himself face-to-face with a young telephone repairman with close-cropped red hair. Ted straightened up, blind-sided by the appearance of someone who could give credence to Camille's allegations against him.

"Wow! Sexual harassment! Just like in the commercials! Actually, you did that *better* than in the television commercials." He turned to Camille. "You gonna let this guy talk to you like that? It's your line next." He put up his hand like a stop sign. In a high voice he said, "Stop! We're talking about sexual harassment, and it's against the law."

He returned to his regular voice. "Those commercials are kind of lame, aren't they?" he asked Camille. He turned to Ted. "The real thing is so much more interesting. It must be real popular here at the law offices. What do I know, but something tells me you're not fantasizing about *'mama in her kerchief.'*"

At a loss for words for once in his life, Ted grabbed his box of chocolates and skulked away to his office. The phone repairman turned to Camille. "You've got that extra line on your phone now, so you can pick up calls for the charitable foundation if Mr. Luskin's secretary is not at her desk."

"Thanks, on both counts, for the line and for getting rid of the office jerk."

He extended his hand. "Timothy Warren, RM, at your service, ma'am. Home from the world's greatest mission five weeks and two days. Telephone technician by day, soon-to-be student by night." She took his hand, and he gave her a vigorous handshake.

"Before my mission I probably would have stayed hidden under the desk, but one thing you learn on a mission is how to talk to people in all kinds of circumstances."

"RM? I'm sorry, but I don't know what that means."

"It means returned missionary." A light went on. "Wait! You're not LDS?"

"No. I've heard a bunch of stuff in the break room, but . . ."

"And would you like to hear more?"

"I do have a few questions. Most of the Mormons that I've met are all really nice. Mr. Parley, especially. I've never worked for anyone like him before. I don't think there is anybody here that I respect more. His wife is such a sweet lady, and he would never . . ."

". . . talk to you the way that other guy did."

"Exactly!"

"Have you ever talked to him about the Church?"

"A little. He's a bishop, so he's explained a few things I might need to know if anyone from church calls."

"How about I bring you some reading material tomorrow, a Book of Mormon, some pamphlets?" He could hardly contain his enthusiasm. Then he was hit with a wave of reality and disappointment. "Sheesh! I'll probably have to turn you over to the *real* missionaries."

"I guess it wouldn't hurt for me to learn a little about the Mormons. After all, you were, kind of . . ." She lowered her voice. ". . . an answer to my prayers. I don't pray that often, but Ted's been bothering me a lot again lately. When I finally complained, it came down to his word against mine, and then a couple of other people weighed in with their opinions."

"I've got an opinion of him already."

"Mr. Parley believes me, but I don't know if anyone else does. They said if I had a witness, my accusations would hold water, but he always waits until no one else is around. I prayed for a way to make it stop, and there you were under the desk when I needed you."

"Glad to be of service. What do you need from me?"

"Could I get your name and phone number? Would you mind sharing what you heard if you were asked to?"

"Here's my card. I'll do whatever I can to help. How about I put it in writing too?" He paused. "Now I need your name and phone number because I would like to send a couple of missionaries over to talk to you."

"I was warned by friends and family before my move that the Mormons would try to enlist me. Of course, they also said they'd be the ones with no makeup, long granny dresses, braided hair, and multiple husbands. I guess it can't hurt to find out a little bit more since Salt Lake City is going to be my home from now on."

• • •

Ted was not far behind Camille as she headed to the parking garage. He followed her to the small gray car in the corner. He looked around and realized they were shielded from view by a large concrete pillar. He moved closer to her car.

She sensed someone behind her and turned to see if she was blocking the access of someone parked next to her. She drew a sharp intake of breath when she found herself face-to-face with Ted Simon. He spoke quietly, but there was no mistaking his threatening tone.

"You may think you have a witness against me, Cami, but you don't want me for an enemy."

She shrunk away from him, pinned against her car. He leaned in until she could feel his breath on her face. "I have a witness of my own, someone in *my* court who saw you and Mr. Parley in a romantic embrace. You bring your witness, and I guarantee I'll drag you and Rex through the mud."

Camille began to tremble as he continued. "Your ex-husband didn't trust you as far as he could throw you, I understand. He'd help me draw a pretty picture, don't you think? How hard do you think it is for someone like me to get hold of documents from your divorce, especially since your hero and defender, Rex Parley, made sure we handled things for you? I know more than you think I know, Cami. Does the name Blaine Goodrich mean anything to you?"

Camille thought back to the day Rex had consoled her with a fatherly hug. She wondered who it was that had seen it and how Ted had found out. Ted continued, glancing around occasionally to see if they were being observed. "I chew up hotshot attorneys and spit them out like used bubble gum. You don't want to go up against me, little girl."

He straightened up and backed off momentarily. "You're probably aware that I'm about to be made partner. After all, you typed up the chocolate list. I'm indispensable to this firm, and they've obviously figured that out. Apparently your previous accusations didn't hold water, did they, Cami? I'd think twice before I made any further accusations, if you get my drift."

• • •

Camille sat in her car, trying to regain her composure after Ted left, wondering what options she had left. She couldn't quit her job. She was a single mother. How could she come forward with her witness and put Rex at risk after all he had done for her?

A COOL RECEPTION

Olive answered the door a few days after Christmas and found Karen standing on her doorstep, this time holding a roll of white paper. "Hiya, Olive. I wanna talk to you and Brother Arletti about my new business idea."

She and Arthur had held a family fast seeking answers to their employment dilemma, but Olive could not even remotely imagine going into business with Karen Donaldson as an answer to her prayers. She pictured Ray's Roadkill Mobile with the ice cream bars still showing through. She gritted her teeth and determined she would hear Karen out and be as polite as possible, in light of the recent service rendered to her family.

Olive invited Karen in. Making herself at home, Karen headed for the dining room and rolled out the drawings on the dining room table. "We bought a great piece of land from a business on Highland Drive that was closing. I wanna build a reception center, and in the wooded area out back, I'm gonna build a little honeymoon cottage."

Karen pointed to the drawings of the tudor-style reception center and cottage. "There'll be a path from the reception center to the little cottage, and a wrought iron fence and a gate with a key so that only the bride and groom can go in and out. After the reception, instead of havin' to drive to a hotel, they'll have their own little honeymoon cottage right there."

Olive tried to stifle her surprise. "Why, Karen, this looks very elegant and tasteful. I love the curved staircase and the arched windows.

And the cottage out back, what a wonderful idea! I can't quite believe it, but I'm truly impressed."

"When I saw the architect's drawings, I knew I'd need somebody with good taste to run it and somebody who was good at business and numbers, like Brother Arletti."

"Oh, Karen, we do not deserve your charity. It seems tailor-made for us. Did you have this business in mind when you purchased the property, or is this a construct purely for the purposes of rescuing the Arletti family?"

"What if it is? It's still a good idea, ain't it?"

"I'll need to talk it over with Arthur, certainly. Would you mind leaving the drawings?"

"Sure! Then he'll know this is for real." She handed Olive the roll of paper. "We gotta get it going 'cause me and Ray are thinkin' about gettin' back together, and we might wanna have a little shindig."

(46)

· ·

PASSED OVER

Ted Simon reread the formal announcement he had pulled from his mail slot. It announced four new partners in the law firm and several new associates, but his name was not one of the four partners. His first thought was how much money had been spent printing the announcements and how expensive it was going to be to reprint them once the mistake was realized.

Why then, he wondered, had they been distributed? Surely if the error had not been caught before they were printed, which in itself was unconscionable, why hadn't someone noticed before they were distributed at the firm, not to mention mailed to all their clients of note.

He strode purposefully to Rex Parley's office, opening the door of his office without knocking. So certain was Ted that this was a mistake, he had not considered any other possibilities. "My name is not on the announcement," he informed Mr. Parley. "Can you explain why?"

Rex looked up from the document he was revising. "Certainly, Ted. It's really quite simple. You did not make partner. You should be able to figure out the reasons why." Rex bowed his head over the document once again, making notations in the margin, ignoring Ted.

"I received a box of chocolates in December," Ted stated definitively, sure that would clear up any confusion.

"The chocolates are something Mr. McLelland does, Ted. They're not an official announcement. Everyone else had the good sense to enjoy their box of chocolates privately, not flaunt them all over the office. We are under no obligation to make you a partner in January because you received a box of Ghirardelli chocolates in December. I have no idea where they came from. Perhaps you ought to demand an explanation from Mr. McLelland, not myself." Rex gave a perfunctory nod of his head. "Now if you'll excuse me, I've got work to do."

GOING UP?

The elevator doors were beginning to close when Camille looked up and realized that it was Ted who had gotten on the elevator. Camille did not want to be alone on an elevator, or anywhere else, with Ted Simon.

"Cami! I've been waiting for a few minutes to chat with you again." As the doors closed, Office Ted morphed seamlessly into Slimy Ted. He moved toward her, blocking her move toward the buttons. His voice took on a threatening tone. His face was menacingly close to hers. "I've tried to be nice, but you want to play hardball. You got me passed over for partner, apparently. I was in."

He leaned one arm against the side of the elevator, forcing her back into the corner. "Only one thing could have messed that up. I guess you came forward with your witness after all. Any day now I'm sure to have a little meeting with the executive committee calling me on the carpet. Don't think I won't make good on my threat, Cami."

Her voice was almost a whisper. "No, I didn't say anything, Ted."

"Don't lie to me, Cami."

"I'm not lying. I didn't say anything to Rex or to anyone."

He thought for a moment. "I would have thought if you had, they would have called me on the carpet immediately, but why else would they have changed their mind? I had the box of . . ." Suddenly a light went on for Ted.

His eyes widened and he gave Camille an appraising look from head to toe. "I've always suspected there was some spirit behind that shy façade. Who is it that types up the chocolate list and would have had easy access to all the information?" He almost spat out the next words. "You knew! You knew I was not going to be made partner, and you made a fool of me in front of the entire firm!"

From somewhere deep within, Camille found an inner strength. She drew herself up, no longer cowering, although her goose bumps remained, and met Ted's eyes, sensing that the balance of power had shifted. "Do you have a witness, Ted?" Her courage was bolstered as she felt the elevator slow down. "Did anyone see me do it? Did I pay with a check so it could be traced? You're the king when it comes to that kind of behavior, aren't you?"

Camille watched the transformation that came over Ted the Chameleon as the elevator door opened. He moved away and smoothed his suit jacket. His countenance changed before her eyes, and the people waiting for the elevator would have thought the two of them had been having a most amiable chat about the weather. "After you, Camille," he said politely. "We'll have to continue this conversation soon."

She turned the opposite direction he did and walked away, trembling from the confrontation, yet not quite feeling as powerless as she had in the past. Back at her desk, she thought of canceling her appointment that evening with the sister missionaries, but she gave up when she couldn't find the slip of paper with their phone number.

HELP ME FIND THE WAY

Though she'd been ready to cancel, Camille felt peaceful after Sister Bennett and Sister Erickson shared their message. She sat quietly after they left, trying to still the voices in her head. *Do I believe it? Would God really appear to a fourteen-year-old boy? Why couldn't this be simple, like signing up for a library card?*

She retrieved a pair of footed pajamas from a nearby laundry basket. *What if I'm trying to convince myself because I want it to be true, because I need something to hold onto while everything else in my life falls apart? What will Jarrod think?* She straightened up and talked back to herself. *And why do I care what Jarrod thinks?*

She dressed Jordan for bed. *This is our first date. I don't have to decide if I want to marry this church. I just have to decide if I want a second date.* She carried Jordan to her bed. "Jordy, want to go to church with me on Sunday?"

* * *

Sister Bennett and Sister Erickson ducked into a classroom after sacrament meeting. "I still think she should attend Gospel Essentials."

"She said she wanted to go with Jordan to nursery," Sister Bennett said.

"But she'll miss out on learning doctrine and . . ."

Sister Erickson started singing a song from one of her favorite Disney movies, her sweet voice carrying out into the hall. "Can you feel the love tonight?"

Sister Bennett shook her head. "Not the gospel according to Walt Disney again."

"Let's pray about it, Sister B. I think . . ." She corrected herself. "I *feel* we should let her go into the nursery and *feel* the love."

The two sister missionaries knelt in the corner, and Sister Bennett said a short prayer. She rose to her feet, humbled. "Okay, the nursery." She glanced sidelong at her companion. "How do you do that, anyway?"

"I don't care how much you know until I know how much you care." She put her arm through that of her junior companion. "A mother can't resist someone who loves her child. Letting Camille feel the spirit of the nursery will help open her heart to the rest of our message."

· · ·

Camille watched as the couple in charge drew her little daughter into the group. At first it didn't seem much different from day care, although there had been a simple opening prayer whispered by the teacher and repeated by one of the older children.

She set her purse against the wall and sat down on the floor in the corner, a silent observer as the children emptied the cabinet full of toys. A few minutes later they sang a little song about cleaning up, and the children willingly put the toys away and gathered to a circle of small chairs for singing time. *Maybe I should join this church that teaches children to put their toys away.*

Camille stopped thinking about toys when she heard the sweet strains of a song she had never heard before. "I am a child of God," the children sang, at least the older ones. "Lead me, guide me, walk beside me, help me find the way." Camille silently repeated the words in her head, and a peaceful feeling came over her. There in the Primary nursery as she watched her daughter trying to sing along to an unfamiliar song, something seemed very familiar to Camille, like she and Jordan were where they were supposed to be. *Yes, I think there will be a second date. In fact, I think this is the beginning of a beautiful relationship.*

(49)

. . . .

GOTCHA!

Sunday after the block of meetings, Karen sat across from the bishop in his office. "Bishop, ya know in two days it's been a year since I sat here and told ya I'd won the lotto."

"So it has. How are plans for the new house coming along?"

"We got most of the bugs worked out."

"So it looks like you and Ray have a future together?"

"Bishop, when we was designin' the house, it was like we both wanted the same things. We're alike, me and Ray. He's even gonna go to clown trainin' so we can do that together."

"I care about you, Karen, and I don't want to see you hurt again."

"Austin wouldn't be goin' on his mission without Ray's help. Dee would never have got herself turned around if it wasn't for him draggin' her off to Alcoholics Anonymous. Ray knew how to cut through the crap and make her face up to that. It was him who got her goin' back to church."

"Don't discount your example, Karen. You are the epitome of the righteous mother who never gave up."

"Yeah, but Ray, see, he took the bad stuff and turned it to something good. He told Dee she didn't wanna be a missing parent like he was, and told Austin he didn't wanna shirk his duty."

"I've still got my reservations about him, Karen."

"I know he's only been comin' back to church regular-like for a few months, but here's the deal, Bishop. I told him this time if he wants to marry me, we're gettin' married in the temple, in *perpetuity*. That's my vocab word of the week. Barry's still tryin' to make me *erudite*."

"I'm glad to see you sticking to your guns." He paused. "The house will be in your name, I presume?"

"Barry said that's how it should be since it's my money buildin' it, but it'll be our house."

"Karen, there are some worthiness issues for Ray concerning the lack of financial support of his children. The guidelines are very clear on paying child support and qualifying for a temple recommend."

"Ya want me to sue him for back child support, all legal like, and then I can loan him the money to pay it off? Then could he get a temple recommend? I'd do it, if that's what it'll take."

"I don't think that will be necessary, no, Karen. I need to counsel with the stake president and with Ray, as well."

"It ain't gonna be a problem that we've slept together, is it?"

"*What?*"

"Gotcha!" Karen grinned. "We *was* married once, ya know, Bishop, and we've got a couple of kids, so I didn't think it'd take ya by surprise like that." She let out a hearty laugh.

He shook his head. "Oh, Karen, isn't it about time you started taking it easy on your poor bishop?"

CALL ME DAD

Bishop Parley sat in President Pearson's office. Robert Pearson spoke. "What's on your mind, Rex?"

Rex inhaled and let his breath out slowly. "You're aware of the situation in our ward with Karen Donaldson?"

"Oh, very much so. What a lady!"

"Her ex-husband, Ray Donaldson, resurfaced shortly after she became wealthy." President Pearson nodded. "He was soon living in our ward. He's a recovering alcoholic, and his desire to make restitution coincidentally coincided with Karen's turn of fortune. I warned Karen to be careful in her dealings with him, but within days, he was living over her garage in a separate apartment and she had started a business and put him to work. I'm sure you've seen the ads and heard the jokes about the Roadkill Mobile."

President Pearson smiled. "Actually I called it once, when there was a dead cat near our driveway."

It figures. Rex shook his head.

"As a judge in Zion, the spirit can dictate to you, Bishop, if you are willing to listen and even perhaps put aside your foregone conclusions about the man."

"He was reluctant to come back into their lives because he knew he owed back support. How can I dismiss that issue, President?"

"For starters, Bishop, let's stop looking at this as a financial problem, which it no longer is at this point. The question then becomes whether he has shown himself to be responsible since his return."

"There's more. They've decided to get back together."

President Pearson nodded. "I would think it is better to reunite a once-intact family than to create a stepfamily situation with a new partner."

"President, you remember the situation with the Goodalls. When I was contacted by the bishop of Brother Goodall's former wife, and I did my due diligence, there was no way I was going to allow him to waltz off to the temple with his new wife when he had totally ignored his financial obligation to his former wife and seven children."

"I supported you in that, Rex."

"Too many men believe that if enough time transpires between the neglect and the present, it is forgotten. They move to a new ward, make friends, perhaps serve in an exemplary way, and somehow history is forgotten or obfuscated. They live like stalwart, respected members of the Church while somewhere the former wife struggles to put food on the table for her children—his children." His voice rose in volume. "I have a zero-tolerance policy for men who do not live up to their responsibilities, President, and under the circumstances, I don't see how Ray can qualify for a temple recommend."

"To the best of your knowledge, would he be able to qualify otherwise?"

"As far as I can tell." Rex sighed. "Karen says that if it is necessary for him to pay the back child support in order to be able to get a temple recommend, she will sue him for it, then loan him the money to pay it."

"That would, I suppose, satisfy the letter of the law. Let's consider the spirit of the law. What you are concerned about is men who totally abandon temporal responsibility for their children."

"Yes. I will not turn a blind eye to men who do not support their families financially."

"Ray is back now. Is he involved in the lives of his children? Where is he now in terms of supporting them, not necessarily financially since they are no longer minors, but emotionally and spiritually?"

"He raised money to pay for Austin's mission, doing yard work around the ward. I'll give him that."

"Even though Karen could write a check for the total amount without blinking an eye?"

"It is a drop in the bucket compared to what he should have been doing all these years."

"True enough, but if I understand, weren't his efforts to raise the money helpful in Austin's decision to serve?"

"It factored in, yes."

"It sounds to me like he is involved with his son in a supportive way now, Bishop, lending financial, spiritual, and emotional support. How is his relationship with his daughter?"

"He has been attending Alcoholics Anonymous meetings with Delia, has been instrumental in helping her admit to and face her drinking problem, largely because he has had one himself in the past."

"Excellent! You know, we're looking for people to work in our addiction recovery program in the stake. It uses the same principles as AA. Perhaps Brother Donaldson would be willing to serve in that capacity."

"Your call, President."

He returned to the previous subject. "So your concern is that in giving him a temple recommend, you are giving him a bye on previous financial support that should have been provided to Karen, Delia, and Austin?"

"Yes, I suppose so."

"Rex, I once served with a bishop who was an accountant by profession, and this man was exceedingly diligent in balancing the books for the ward's funds, so much so that sometimes he let his desire to accumulate an excess in the fast offering fund interfere with helping people who truly needed assistance. I once lovingly counseled him to stop being an accountant and start being a bishop."

President Pearson leaned in close to Bishop Parley. "Bishop Parley, you are a champion of women, and I admire you for the stance you have taken to hold men accountable for their responsibility to their families. The proclamation on the family says, and I quote, 'We warn that individuals who violate covenants of chastity, who abuse spouse or offspring, or who *fail to fulfill family responsibilities* will one day stand accountable before God.' "

President Pearson looked Rex in the eye. "Bishop, you have here the rare opportunity to restore a family. It sounds as if Ray is doing all he can in the present to make up for what he didn't in the past and can't do now. You are worried about letting him off the hook."

"I suppose I am."

"Rex, ultimately, God wants to let all of us off the hook. He would love to have our present behavior show that we have repented of misdeeds of the past. If Ray can answer the questions, Bishop, give the man a temple recommend and let him continue to progress in the gospel. In other words, stop being an attorney and be his bishop."

• • •

"Austin, Bishop Parley said he talked to you about the guidelines for the Sunday we'll talk in church," Karen said. "He probably told you the same stuff he told me. This is supposed to be an upliftin' regular sorta church meeting. It ain't your funeral."

"Do ya think Ray would talk, if I asked him?"

Karen's mouth dropped open. "Ya want Ray to talk?"

"I'm not saying I've completely gotten over things, but Bishop Parley said carrying all that anger into the mission field ain't good. He pointed out how hard Ray has been trying and he said that if I couldn't love him for what he did for me, maybe I could love him for what he's done for Dee. He reminded me that you guys are gonna get married again, and he's gonna be in my life, and said I need to give him more of a chance than I have."

"Wow! *Bishop* said that? I'm glad." She shook her head. "But Ray won't talk in church, Austin. I guaran-dang-tee it."

"I'm gonna ask him if he wants to, just the same. Bishop Parley said that sometimes when you want to have good feelings about someone, you have to act like you already do and the feelings will follow. If he won't do it, he'll know I wanted him, and I can leave on my mission knowing I tried."

• • •

That afternoon Austin tracked Ray down as he was headed out in the Roadkill Mobile for a pickup. "Ray, can I talk to you?"

"I guess that dead raccoon ain't goin' nowhere for a few minutes. Sure. Ya wanna ride along?"

"Yeah, okay. Why not?" Austin climbed into the passenger seat of the old ice cream truck.

"Where we headed?"

"Fruit Heights."

"I guess I should've asked before I climbed aboard."

"Too late now."

They made small talk for a while, and then Austin came to the point. "We're planning my missionary farewell or whatever they call it now. I was wondering if you would like to be one of the speakers."

Ray swallowed hard. *He wants me to speak at his missionary farewell. This is more than I ever dared hope for from him. How can I tell him no?* "Okay, Austin. I'll do it," he blurted out, against his better judgment. Just accepting the assignment caused a feeling like someone was squeezing his innards with a vice grip. "It won't be long, and it probably won't even be good, but I'll try to put together something."

"I've decided to talk on following the Spirit. That's what Mom's gonna talk about too. Maybe you could talk about facing up to responsibilities, like what you told me about that one day."

As they got nearer to Fruit Heights, Ray consulted the notes he'd written down. Finally he spotted a black and white lump of fur up ahead on the highway and slowed down. "This one looks kind of unrecognizable. You wanna spatula or hold the bag?" Ray asked.

Austin jumped out of the vehicle and was immediately overcome by the stench emanating from the black and white animal on the road. He tried to signal Ray to stay in the truck, but it was too late. Ray opened his door. "Whoa! That ain't no raccoon!"

"What do we do now?" Austin asked.

"He's dead. He ain't gonna spray us. We'll just have a little scent after the fact, a little skunk aftershave. Whatever is gonna stick to us is already done. Let's load him up. That's my job."

They drove back home with all the windows on the truck open, but it didn't do much good. Austin turned to his father. "How do you mistake a skunk for a raccoon?"

Ray contemplated for a moment. "By usin' sight instead of smell would be my best guess."

• • •

When they drove up, Karen came out of the house to greet them and immediately began fanning her hand in front of her face. "Boy, Ray, you'll do anything to get out of talkin' in church!"

He turned to his son. "Looks like we're gonna have a little more father/son time together, Austin. Wonder where we're gonna sleep tonight? Do these seats recline?"

• • •

As Karen wrapped up her talk, Ray wiped his palms on his slacks. He could feel his blood pressure rising, could feel each individual hair on his arms standing on end, could feel his intestines tying themselves into a double half hitch. As Karen sat down, he became immobile. He looked over and saw Brother Andrews of the bishopric looking at him expectantly.

Reluctantly Ray forced himself to his feet and approached the pulpit as though he was walking in wet cement. Grasping the podium firmly with both sweaty hands, he looked out over the congregation. *Why'd so many people have to come today? I didn't know Austin had this many friends.* "Brothers and sisters, I . . ."

He looked down at his notes and then back at the intimidating congregation. He felt his fear ratchet up another notch, and his mind seemed to go into slow motion. *There's Sis-ter Ar-let-ti. She has such high ex-pec-ta-tions for ev-e-ry-thing and ev-er-y-bod-y.*

The sea of people before him became blurry. He blinked a couple of times, but they did not get any clearer, nor did his notes. He grasped the pulpit tighter, feeling that his grip on it was the only thing holding him up. Then his knees turned to Jell-O, and Bishop Parley and Brother Andrews caught him on the way down.

Austin rushed over. "Dad, can you hear me? Ya gonna be okay?" Ray's eyes fluttered open, and collectively several people helped him to a seat. *Did Austin call me Dad? Did I imagine it?* The Relief Society president, Sister Pentelute, who was a nurse, rushed up and had him put his head between his legs. Austin came back with a glass of water. The chorister moved to the pulpit and gave the page number for the intermediate hymn.

As Ray came to, he heard snatches of the song "I'll Go Where You Want Me to Go." The one phrase that stuck with him that day was "though dark and rugged the way." He hung his head, not because of nurse's orders, but because he had let Austin down.

After the hymn, Bishop Parley turned the remainder of the time over to Austin. He approached the pulpit and began his talk. "Brothers and sisters, looks like Dad left me a little extra time." A ripple of gentle laughter went through the congregation. "I'm really excited about serving in Buenos Aires."

He looked out over the congregation, surprised to see Adrienne and her new husband there. "I'd like to thank my mother for her talk and her example about following the Spirit. I'd also like to thank my father for facing his fear of public speaking. It means a lot that he was willing to try. Like God did for Abraham, I'm giving him points for willingness. He's faced up to a lot of things, and he's been an example to me of overcoming difficulties."

Ray, fully conscious once more, and comfortably seated away from the toxic effects of the pulpit, raised his head and smiled broadly. His eyes filled with proud tears. *I didn't imagine it. He really called me "Dad."*

• • •

Afterward ward members and friends congregated at the house for an unofficial gathering that was still part of Utah tradition though officially no longer encouraged. Delia stood by the punch bowl with her new boyfriend, Derek. "What do you want me to do, Dee?"

"You hold the glasses and I'll ladle the punch."

"Austin has a lot of friends. Me, I like animals better than people." He reached over and took her hand. "Some people I don't mind being around, though." He hesitated. "Dee, I know your dogs like me, but do you think your mother likes me?"

"I *know* she does."

"How can you tell? We barely said 'hello' before she had to go answer the door."

"Just something she said, but you wouldn't get it, and I don't wanna hafta explain it to you."

"I bet you'll tell me if I do puppy dog eyes." He cocked his head and looked at her soulfully.

"You know I can't resist puppy dog eyes. Okay, I'll tell you, but I won't explain. She said, 'Hot dang! I think I can start eating Jell-O again.' "

POWER TIES

On the first Saturday in March, Bishop Parley dunked and then raised Camille out of the waters of baptism at her ward building. She walked over to the side of the baptismal font where Lydia stood waiting with a towel, which Camille gratefully took, sponging the water out of her long hair. A few minutes later she emerged in a light blue dress, her still-damp hair pulled back in a ponytail.

The next day in fast meeting she would be confirmed a member of the Church by a cherubic red-headed telephone technician, who, although he had reluctantly turned his prize investigator over to the sister missionaries, had kept his finger in the pie all along.

Many of the employees from the law office had attended her baptism. On Monday, others at the law firm stopped by her desk, expressing congratulations.

"Sorry I missed your baptism. Welcome to the fold." Camille looked up to see something she never would have expected in a million years—the outstretched hand of Ted Simon. Ted was a Mormon! Unwanted feelings welled up within her, but she reminded herself that he had left her alone since their encounter in the elevator. Was it possible he had changed? She wanted to live up to the tenets of her new religion. She wanted to be forgiving. She extended her hand.

"Thank you, Ted." She said it as sincerely as she was able, trying to convince herself that from now on perhaps her troubles with Ted were a thing of the past.

Elsewhere in the office an old man looked at the clock and realized his grandson would soon be there to drive him home. Leaving his office, C. Morris McLelland walked quietly and slowly, with the aid of his walking stick, toward the elevators in the back of the office.

Ted looked around quickly. "Like I said, I'm sorry I missed your baptism. At your age, to have your sins washed away. Good plan! What does anyone do before they're eight, after all?" Camille's face turned red at his next suggestive comment. He leaned over her desk. "I'm glad to see you took my advice, Cami, and kept quiet about things. I'm sure to be made partner this year. It should have been last year, but you messed that up for me with your accusations. I've been a good boy for a long time, don't you think? So much for your witness, huh? Some fat little red-headed telephone repairman? And what did *he* get in return, I wonder?"

"How about *this* witness, boy?" a voice boomed behind him. Ted's face went white as he turned to look into the face of C. Morris McLelland, who had just come around the corner. "Just got myself a new-fangled hearing aid, Simon. Amazing the things I can hear now."

Mr. McLelland began talking slowly and distinctly, his voice gravelly but unwavering. *Make him squirm.* "I understand you've been bothering my secretary. I don't still attend the executive committee meetings, but I read the minutes they give me. What do you think I do down here all day? They won't let me practice law anymore."

He held out his tie. "Do you like my tie, Simon?"

"*What?*"

"I asked if you liked my tie. You're wearing a very nice tie today, Simon. Red. That's a powerful color. Isn't that what you fellows call 'a power tie?' "

Mr. McLelland let go of his faded brown tie with the geese flying across it. "I've had this tie for nigh onto thirty years. This, Mr. Simon, is a power tie because it's a tie that's around the neck of the man who has the *power*. I don't have to *report* you to the executive committee. I *am* the executive! You can take your power tie and gather up the rest of your belongings because you are no longer in the employ of Frost, Bringhurst & McLelland."

He wasn't through. "When George Frost and Newell Bringhurst— may they rest in peace—and I founded this firm, it was to provide the protection of the law to those who needed it. What a travesty of justice it is for us to employ someone who purports to uphold the law and surreptitiously breaks it when he thinks no one else is looking. By the time I get through with you, *you'll* be lucky to get a job working as a telephone repairman."

Camille took a deep breath, trying to absorb the implications of what had just transpired. Mr. McLelland stood by her desk, waiting until Ted had wordlessly departed. He took his cane and gave Camille's desk a rap.

"Another good day's work. I knew there must be a reason the Good Lord was still keeping me around." He smiled. "See you tomorrow, Camille, God willing."

• • •

The following morning Camille entered Rex's office and took a seat across from his desk. "You wanted to see me?"

He walked across the room and closed the door. "Mr. McLelland stopped by my office on his way in this morning and told me what happened yesterday. I wanted to let you know that Ted is gone and that the executive committee will be meeting to discuss bringing a legal action against him. I hate to drag you through all this again, especially when you are enjoying such happy events in your life, but rest assured that Ted will not be bothering you again."

"Why didn't you tell me he was a member of the Church?" she asked softly.

"What purpose would that have served, Camille, except to interfere with your good feelings and growing testimony?"

Camille looked down. "All the people I have met at church seem so nice, and they all seem to be what they say they are. How can the Church let . . . I mean, how can a man like Ted go to church on Sunday and then act like . . . ?"

Rex reached down and opened the bottom drawer of his desk and pulled out a small set of scriptures. He held them up. "My office copy. This will not be the last time a member of the Church will offend you or act in an otherwise un-Christlike manner. Let me share a scripture with you, Camille." He began to thumb the pages. "This is one of my favorite scriptures, Helaman five and twelve." He began to read.

"And now, my sons—*and daughters,*" he added, for Camille's benefit, "remember, remember that it us upon the rock of Our Redeemer, who is Christ, the Son of God, that ye must build your foundation; that when the devil shall send forth his mighty winds, yea, his shafts in the whirlwind, yea, when all his hail and his mighty storm shall beat upon you, it shall have no power over you to drag you down to the gulf of misery and endless wo, because of the rock upon which ye are built, which is a sure foundation whereon if men—*and women*—build they cannot fall."

He looked across the desk at her. "Build on the rock, Camille. It doesn't say there won't be storms. In your case, there have already been, certainly, and the weather patterns of our lives can be as changeable as the weather outside. We can never say that we have survived the big storm and it will be fair weather from then on."

He took a breath. "Unfortunately, Ted may not be the last member of the Church to disappoint you."

She nodded her understanding. He began to turn the pages in his scriptures again. "There is another scripture I want to share with you. It's here in Helaman also." He flipped back a couple of pages. "Here it is, chapter three, verse thirty-three: 'And in the fifty and first year of the reign of the judges there was peace also—*much like the peace you are probably feeling now this soon after your baptism*—save it were the pride which began to enter into the church—*now this is the part I want you to listen carefully to*—not into the church of God, but into the hearts of the people who *professed* to belong to the church of God."

"People like Ted."

"Yes, unfortunately. Remember Camille, the Church is true. That doesn't mean that every member will always act as he or she should. Catch yourself anytime you hear yourself holding the Church accountable for the actions of a member. I believe the majority of our members and leaders strive to do their best to live up to the commandments and things they profess to believe."

"I'll try to remember that."

"Camille, no matter what, don't ever let anger and bitterness replace your gentle disposition. Satan would like more than anything to make us all such cantankerous characters that we would be a poor fit for the heaven our Father has planned for those of his children who continue faithful."

He closed the book. "Okay, lecture over. I put on my bishop hat for a minute there."

"I like you in your bishop hat." She looked down. "There's one thing I've been worried about. I did something I shouldn't have, and I don't really know how to go about repenting of it."

"Camille, you have your own bishop now and . . ."

She interrupted him. "I, um, sent someone a box of chocolates."

Rex raised his eyebrows in surprise but brought them back down momentarily as his lips curled into an amused smile. "That doesn't sound like something of which a person needs to repent, Camille. It sounds to me like more of an act of service."

"You don't think . . . ?"

He wielded an imaginary gavel. "Case dismissed." He leaned forward, resting his elbows on his desk. "Now I would like to ask your forgiveness that I did not do a better job of sharing the gospel with you."

"But you did. I looked at you and your family, and I knew that I wanted to have a family like that." She hesitated. "Maybe even someday a husband who treats his wife with love and respect."

He paused as a new thought occurred to him. "Joining the Church a little later in life, you have missed out on some things. I wonder if you might be interested in a missionary pen pal. Missionaries love to get letters."

She smiled. "I'm a little old to be writing to a nineteen-year-old."

"Austin isn't nineteen. He's twenty-three, I believe."

"Karen's son?" She blushed, remembering the handsome young man from the Festival of Trees.

"Oh, you've met Austin?"

She looked down, embarrassed. Then she met his eyes, and he couldn't help but notice how hers had lit up. "If you think it would help my spiritual growth," she said demurely, "sure, give me his address."

Rex picked up his granite paperweight. "I'd like you to have this, Camille, as a reminder of our talk today. It came from the same quarry where they obtained the granite for the Salt Lake Temple. Remember, Camille, build on the rock."

"There is one other thing."

"What's that, Camille?"

"I understand now that the Relief Society isn't like the Red Cross, but would you explain to me about the beehives?"

TAKING A BREAK

Camille headed toward the break room, wondering what Lynette wanted to talk to her about. She opened the door and was surprised to see most of the LDS secretaries from the firm gathered around a small cake. Everyone started clapping. An addition that didn't match the rest of the frosted words had been added so that the cake read "Happy Re-Birthday."

"We wanted to do a little more to congratulate you on your baptism," Barbara explained. "The cake was my idea."

Caroline spoke. "The recording angels have noted your good deed, Barbara. This was *all* of our idea, Camille. And we'd like to thank you for something else."

As they enjoyed their cake, Lynette slipped Camille a Ghirardelli candy bar. "Ted said something to me once that could be taken more than one way. It wasn't until later at home that I realized what he had probably meant. I gave him the benefit of the doubt at the time, but now I realize maybe he did mean it the other way."

Caroline, the source of all breaking news in the office, continued. "Did you hear the rest, Camille? Melinda has been fired too."

"Don't gossip, Caroline," Barbara chastised.

"It isn't gossip. I heard it straight from Melinda." Apparently that was Caroline's guideline for sharing things, Camille realized, something she had learned the hard way.

"She told me all about it while she was clearing out her desk. After what happened with Mr. McLelland and Ted came out, she went and talked to Mr. Parley and said that she had seen him giving you a hug and that she was the one who had told Ted so he could use it to keep you quiet. Go figure. She had evidence of what a jerk he was, and she was helping him get away with it."

"I *knew* something was going on with Melinda," Barbara stated.

"She's been seeing Ted outside the office. She said she got sucked in by his power and charm. That's why she dropped the accusations against him after you reported his comments, Barbara."

Even though Barbara eschewed gossip, she was all ears now. Caroline lowered her voice. "She thought he was going to leave his wife for her. But recently he told her that he would never leave his wife, that it's through her family that he has all his political connections and she was just fun and games. So now Mindy has decided to be a witness against Ted when the firm does whatever they're going to do."

Lynette spoke next. "I'm going to be working for Barry now, and Ted's secretary, Jennifer, will take over my two litigation attorneys." She shook her head. "Ted was such a brilliant man, but look what he flushed down the toilet, all in one fell swoop—his career, probably his marriage."

"His membership in the Church," Barbara added.

"Ted won't be able to treat Melinda like a woman scorned, either. There's too much evidence against him," Lynette said. "I'm going to tell Mr. Parley about what he said to me too in case they need me as a witness."

Caroline raised her glass of soda in the air. "You brought him down, Camille." Several secretaries followed suit. "And the box of chocolates, that was a stroke of genius."

How did they know about that? I just barely told Rex, and he wouldn't say anything to anybody. "What makes you think that I . . . ?" Camille did her best to look sweet and innocent.

"It was the big mystery in the office after he was passed over for partner," Caroline said. "All these smart attorneys around here and we're the ones who figured it out. At least, we had our suspicions. I never knew what kind of things he was saying to you, but one day I realized that every time I'd seen you in tears, Ted was somewhere in the vicinity. Is it true then?"

Camille smiled a shy smile and raised her glass. "It was the best twenty dollars I ever spent."

OUR DAILY BREAD

Karen took her seat by the window for the flight to Raleigh. Barry was beside her in the aisle seat. "Now, Karen, act like you belong in first class. Try not to get too excited about takeoff or the hot towels." He rolled his eyes as a woman boarded with a screaming baby.

"I'll admit I like flyin' first class, but nothing makes us up here better than them folks back there. My mother told me the only reason for lookin' down on somebody is if you're gonna give 'em a hand up."

"Karen, I merely suggested you not send out signals that you think you're out of your league. Now calm down and eat your nuts. See, look. Brazil nuts, cashews. This is the good life."

"Is this another lesson from Barry's finishin' school? I think bein' excited about sumpthin' means you ain't takin' it for granted."

Neither of them spoke to the other for several minutes. She waited until the pilot turned off the "fasten seat belt" button. Barry shook his head awake as Karen climbed in front of him, presumably to take a bathroom break. A few minutes later she came back, followed by the lady with the squalling baby.

"Barry, this is Tammy Morton and little Tyler. Her husband is deployed and she's headed back east to stay with her family. I decided to trade places with her, let her have my seat up here in first class."

Barry rose as mother and baby settled into the window seat beside him. He gave Karen a dirty look as she headed back to Tammy's seat in coach. As far as Barry could see, the baby was oozing out of every orifice, and what wasn't oozing was producing noise sufficient to drown out the sound of the jet engines.

Tammy apologized. "He's teething. I think flying hurts his ears." She reached under the seat to pull a bottle out of her diaper bag and realized she had left it back in coach. "I'm sorry. I need to go get my diaper bag." Barry stood up and let her out into the aisle.

Karen was not long in her new seat before she discovered the diaper bag stashed under the seat. Undoing her seat belt, she began fishing in her pockets and found what she was looking for. As she saw the lady headed down the aisle, Karen picked up the bag and met her halfway.

"Oh, thank you. My life is in that bag."

Karen smiled. *And then some.*

Tammy headed back once more to her new seat. Ever the gentleman, Barry rose and waited for her to settle into the seat. Seated once again, he marveled that the baby seemed able to cry and drink a bottle simultaneously. Suck. Scream. Suck. Scream. It was going to be a long flight. He turned up the volume on the music and adjusted his earphones as snugly as he could. *Karen, I'll get you for this.*

It wasn't long before his nostrils were assaulted by the smell of a dirty diaper so pungent that he fully expected to see the oxygen masks drop down. As Tammy fished in her bag for a clean diaper, she discovered several plastic cards. "How did these get in here?" She held them up. "I wonder if someone accidentally . . . ?"

Barry could see that at least one of them was an airline card and another appeared to be for a restaurant. A third looked like one of the refillable MasterCards Karen carried around.

Barry smiled in spite of the stench. "No, it isn't a mistake. You know how they ask you if anyone has put anything in your luggage while you weren't watching? Those are from the lady who gave you her seat."

"For real?" She began to cry. "My husband's military pay was suspended because of a paperwork mix-up. We'll get it all eventually, but in the meantime, my parents paid my airfare for us to come stay with them." She held the cards as though they were made of solid gold. "Do you have any idea what this means to me? Who is she?"

"An undercover angel, someone who enjoys being good to her fellow man." He took a deep breath. "Speaking of being good to your fellow man, let me get out of your way so you can get that poor baby's diaper changed."

• • •

Barry met up with Karen at the baggage claim carousel. "How was your flight?" Barry inquired.

"Lovely, and yours?"

"I slept like a baby—woke up and cried every few minutes."

Karen laughed. "I guess that wasn't very nice of me."

"I stopped being mad after about ten minutes. Tammy is a lovely young lady. Again you made a difference in someone's life. And you're right that I don't always have as much empathy as I should."

"Good, because where we're goin', you're gonna need lots of it."

• • •

Soon they were in their rental car and on the way to Letherby. Time passed quickly, and before long they pulled off the freeway and into the little town. Karen directed Barry to Our Daily Bread.

Ellie looked up when Karen and Barry came into the bakery. "Hi! Remember me? How about a couple of donuts?"

The reception was unexpectedly cold. "Yes, we remember you." Ellie and Lucy spoke in the plural even if only one of them was present.

"I told ya I'd be back!" Karen said enthusiastically. "I'm glad to see you're still open. I brought my attorney by to meet you and . . ."

Ellie set a plate with several donuts on it on top of the glass. "Yes, we are, but we won't be requiring any more of your assistance," Ellie said icily. "And there is no charge for the donuts."

"We're here to see about renovatin' the factory."

Lucy heard voices and came out from the back. She too seemed distant. "We would like to thank you for your generosity, but we do not need any further help."

Karen was confused. "What'd I do?"

Ellie looked up from her straightening. "If you must know, we don't want your help because you're a Mormon."

Lucy chimed in. "We investigated and found out who you are after you gave us that check."

Ellie continued. "We may be just a couple of small town old maids, but we have the Internet. We know all about your church and . . ."

"Now, let me get this straight," Karen said, picking up a donut. "Ya don't want my help because I'm a Mormon?"

"We saw all those poor teenage brides on the news in their granny dresses with their braids," Ellie informed her.

"We've figured out what you are up to, why you're so interested in our town," Lucy stated.

Ellie furrowed her brow and looked in Barry's direction. "Could be she's one of your wives." Barry looked at Karen, willing her not to say anything about their brief marriage. She continued. "I suppose you think our town is easy pickings right now, but I can tell you right now that even if you buy this whole town, we will never sell out. Our ancestor Jonas Letherby founded this town, and over his dead body will we let you turn it into a polygamous compound." Lucy's folded arms and defiant demeanor communicated that she and Ellie would stand together come hell or high water.

Karen swallowed a bite of donut and laughed out loud. "Is that what you think we are here for? Ya think those people on the news are from my church? Well, let's see. It wasn't this century, and it wasn't last century, but century before that, yup there was polygamy in the early days of our church, crossing the plains. Granny dresses too, I reckon. Probably even braids. For havin' the Internet, you ain't very up-to-date."

Karen looked to Barry for help, but he only nodded for her to continue. "Them people on television call themselves FLDS. That 'F' could stand for 'former' because anybody practicin' polygamy in our Church today finds themselves a former Mormon real fast. Don't get us confused with the Fundamentalists."

Karen continued. "I don't know that much about your religion, either, but if I want to know about it, I'll ask you and give you a chance to tell me. I wish you'd give me that same chance. I've always thought churches oughta get together and do good, not fight with each other and try to nitpick at each other's beliefs. Look at all the religions that get together helping people after a hurricane or an earthquake hits somewhere."

Karen swallowed another bite of donut. "Ya wanna make good use of the Internet. Why dontcha try researching what The Church of Jesus Christ of Latter-day Saints does with their humanitarian service all over the world? By their fruits ye shall know them. It says that in the scriptures. You ladies made some awesome sacrifices to help the people in this town. I thought we had connected because we was all followers of Jesus Christ."

She shoved the remainder of the donut into her mouth, still talking away. "Tune in to our general conference and listen to our prophet sometime, and then tell me he ain't a man of God. We're not here to take over your town. We're here to reopen your factory and give it back to you."

The two Southern Baptist sisters stood quietly behind their glass case of breads and donuts, still not quite willing to believe it could be true.

Karen finished chewing and swallowed hard. She took a deep breath and shifted gears. "I have a song I wanna sing that reminds me of you." She began singing, her voice clear and true. Softly, the gentle words floated through the thick air and did the rest of the convincing the two sisters needed.

Barry recognized the hymn the moment Karen began to sing. In fact, as she sang about sharing the bounty with which she had been blessed by the Lord, about not being able to see a person in need without sharing, he marveled at how the words could have been penned about her. He watched the transformation that came over the countenances of the two sisters as Karen sang of sharing "my glowing fire, my loaf of bread," and he could see that Karen had hit her mark with the owners of Our Daily Bread.

By the time Karen stopped singing, two spinster sisters behind the counter were wiping their eyes on their aprons, and one attorney in the corner had grabbed a nearby napkin.

"Now ya gonna let me help your town?"

Ellie spoke first, through her tears. "Will you come to our town prayer tomorrow and teach everyone that song?"

Lucy held her head high. "I *told* her we shouldn't watch the news late at night." Then she leaned forward, with a sidelong glance toward her sister, and spoke to Karen across the counter. "I didn't think we should get the Internet, either." She lowered her voice a notch. "It's of the devil."

WHAT NOT TO WEAR

Karen had only been back in town a few days when Austin answered the door and found Sister Cironni, Sister Cox, Sister Arletti, and Sister Jensen. He handed them the credit cards he had removed from his mother's vest. "What does she think is going on?" he asked.

Colleen Cox answered. "We told her we're going shopping and out to lunch."

"And we are," Evelyn Jensen added.

"Should I get her?" Austin asked.

"Just announce us, and we'll take it from there."

Karen grabbed her coat. "This is gonna be fun. Where are we goin' shoppin'?"

"Not so fast!" Toni reached into her purse and pulled out a DVD. "First we're going to watch a little television. Have you ever watched the show *What Not to Wear*?"

"Never heard of it," Karen admitted.

"Just as I suspected," Toni said. "First we're going to watch an episode or two, so you'll know what we're doing."

• • •

After they watched the shows on the disc, Toni led the way to Karen's closet. Out of curiosity, Dee followed the four ladies to Karen's bedroom. "Okay, first, Karen. We know you loved working at Smith's and you have . . ." she searched for the word. ". . . an eclectic collection of product T-shirts that you love."

Colleen reached for a stack of sloppily folded tees. "We aren't as brutal as the folks on the show. Well, Toni is. Stacy is her idol. It's the gorgeous long dark hair." She shook out one of the T-shirts. "Cap'n Crunch. Love the man. Ditch the shirt." She flapped open another one. "Orange Crush." She shook her head. "I don't think so." She tossed it to Sister Arletti, followed by a lime green Fruit Loops tee. "Olive is here because of her quilting expertise. Tell her."

Olive cleared her throat. "We're going to do a somewhat unconventional service project for our next quarterly Relief Society meeting. I'll be doing the piecework. We're going to make a memory quilt for you of all your favorite T-shirts from working at the grocery store."

"Really? You'd do that for me?"

"I think it will be a good learning experience for the sisters, certainly, in case any of them want to make a similar quilt someday. And we knew it was likely the only way you'd part with them." She cleared her throat, thinking of the fact that she and her husband had hope for the future now because of Karen. "And where were you last September? You never miss a meeting. Sister Potter's Homemaking Hint was over way too quickly without you there."

Karen hung her head. "I was gamblin' again, up at Swiss Days. I won at . . ."

Toni cut her off. "Don't tell them *that!* We're here to class you up." She picked up a pair of brown loafers. "These shoes look like they were made for going around corners, Karen." Dee, sitting on Karen's bed observing, stifled a giggle at that remark. Toni held the shoes up. "Look how unevenly they're worn."

Toni and Evelyn continued to sort through the rest of Karen's closet, tossing and commenting. "We know you go undercover sometimes, so we're going to leave you two pairs of sweat pants, a couple of T-shirts, two sweatshirts, and one pair of scruffy shoes, not to be worn outside of a soup kitchen," Toni declared.

"Just two of each?" Karen protested.

"You can pick your favorites." Toni sat down next to her on the bed. "Karen, you are the head of a multi-million-dollar charitable foundation. You have a meeting next week where you are trying to convince a national company to buy one of your ideas, one that I believe in wholeheartedly. *Shabby chic* isn't going to cut it."

Evelyn added her observations. "Karen, you spent your whole life raising your kids and sacrificing for them and you have trained yourself not to do anything for yourself. We're here to break you of that habit."

"Yeah, sorta, I guess I did," Karen admitted.

"Evelyn and Olive are going to take the T-shirts and start work on the quilt. Colleen and I are going to take you shopping. We've got a handful of those cards you give out, the prepaid credit cards, thanks to the cooperation of your kids. We're going to go out and get you some new clothes, new shoes, a haircut, some makeup tips, and maybe even a little jewelry."

Colleen spoke up. "Toni's here because of her sense of style. I'm along to help you find fashionable clothes that look good on a woman of substance."

"When are ya gonna unveil me?" Karen asked.

"Your debut will be at the meeting with the Create-a-Critter people," Toni said. "We've already warned Ray that he might have to get a few more Hell's Angels on duty to keep the next batch of suitors away."

COMFORT CREATURES

A few days later, Karen saw Dee coming out of her bedroom with a box of clothes. "What ya got there, Dee?"

Dee shrugged. "I decided to make a donation to the Deseret Industries instead of shopping there."

"Stuff that don't fit no more?"

"I guess ya could say that." Dee still wasn't sure she was buying that whole "modest is hottest" stuff, but after watching the ladies make over Karen's wardrobe, she had decided she had a few things she might as well part with. "A lot of this stuff reminds me of Zhon," Dee explained. "And I guess I oughta, you know, be a better example, for Mandee."

Karen reached into the box, and pulled out a yellow and pink dress, accidentally knocking a denim mini-skirt to the ground. "Retirin' Little Bo Peep? I'm not sure the D.I. is gonna know what to do with this either."

Dee smiled sheepishly. "I decided to do my own *What Not to Wear.*"

Karen reached over and gave her daughter a hug. "I'm proud of ya, Dee."

"Really? Because I was hoping you'd get out some of those credit cards you carry around and take me clothes shopping and maybe to Toni's hairstylist."

• • •

Along with Toni and Corina, Karen waited for Barry outside the conference room. She wore black pants with a maroon top and a tunic-length black jacket. On her feet were new black flats. A comb festooned with maroon and silver crystals held a section of her newly styled hair away from her face. He walked past, not recognizing her, and then he did a double take. "Karen, is that you? You look, you look . . . Words escape me!"

Karen raised a newly shaped eyebrow. "Comin' from the man with a dictionary on a stand, that is high praise. My Relief Society friends did an intervention. They said *shabby chic* wasn't gonna cut it for this meeting. I got a new hair guy, Pierre." Karen flipped a strand of hair. "I got highlights. Wearin' makeup too. If I lost fifty pounds, maybe I could be a plus-size model, huh?"

• • •

The lights went down, and the presentation began. "Comfort Creatures" read the colorful headline. The music began—soft, soothing, emotionally manipulative music. Patrick Lawson had not come cheap, but he had been worth every penny they'd spent on the presentation.

First came the story of a young girl for whom Karen had doctored a stuffed animal, followed by the story of that same girl and her dog, George, and how much it had meant to her to have a creature who went through the same thing she did. Toni and Corina stood up and were introduced after that portion. Corina held up the original Kimo Kat.

The next frame showed a little girl in a hospital bed, clinging to a stuffed cat wearing a hat that matched hers. In the next frame, both of the hats were off, revealing two hairless heads. "Kimo Kat brings an empathetic friend to children suffering from cancer and enduring the effects of chemotherapy," spoke the narrator. Karen looked on approvingly. *He's just like I wanted. He's got attitude, like Chester Cheetah, only Hawaiian.*

Another slide showed an adorable dark-haired little boy standing in front of the remains of his demolished home, clutching Windblown Walrus with his tusks and hair both blown to the side. "While truckloads of supplies are on their way to hurricane disaster sites, a shipment of Comfort Creatures can also be on the way within hours."

"A Brokenhearted Bunny may be the only friend a child in foster care has." The little blonde girl clutched the bunny as if he truly were her only friend. The camera zoomed in on the crystal tear in the bunny's eye and on the Band-aid over its heart. *Where'd he get these kids? This is perfect!*

"A Battered Bear can comfort a child with a broken leg or a broken spirit." Two more pictures—one of a boy in a baseball cap with his leg in a cast, and a bear with a matching cast. Another showed a little boy with his mother in front of a women's shelter, clutching a teddy with its arm in a sling, matching the one on his arm.

As a doctor approached a tiny little girl in a hospital bed with a needle, she wielded "Poked Porcupine" and pushed a button to activate the sound. "No more pokes or I poke back." The doctor and the little girl then both burst out laughing.

Amputee Aardvark had all his body pieces attached by Velcro, including his long snout. Chicken Pox was covered in red spots. Feverish Frog had an ice bag on his head, and Stitched-up Snake had stitches that ran the entire length of his underside.

Next came the marketing sales pitch. "Comfort Creatures is a one-size-fits-all fund-raiser. From Cub Scouts to corporations, church groups to charities. Perfect for individuals wanting to make a difference to just one child or organizations able to give in larger measure. Perfect for hospital gift shops, paramedics and police officers, clergymen, clowns, and counselors."

Next came pictures of the factory in Letherby, boarded up businesses, and the little bakery that had stayed open against all odds. "Comfort Creatures will not only bring hope and joy to children all over the world, but will bring hope back to a little town when the factory upon which the people depended for their livelihood is reopened."

Barry looked around at the faces, at least the ones he could see in the darkened room. "We've got 'em!"

• • •

Karen looked at the architectural drawings spread out on the table in the conference room, wondering where Barry was, when she heard the door open.

"Took ya long enough."

"Sorry I'm late. I just came from a doctor's appointment. Seems working with you is good for my heart."

"Maybe it ain't me. Maybe it's that you ain't arguin' in court no more."

"No, it's you."

"So can ya believe it? The Create-a-Critter people are really gonna manufacture the Comfort Creatures! They're even gonna open up Create-a-Critter shops at a couple of big children's hospitals. The shops will be like the kind they have at the mall where you come in and pick the animal and have it stuffed and pick the accessories."

"That is wonderful news, isn't it? I thought Patrick did such a nice job with the presentation," Barry said. "I gave him the prototypes and stories and told him what we wanted."

"He came through, all right. Looks like he went all over to get them pictures," Karen observed.

"Karen, all those shots were done with special effects, like in the movies."

"That little kid wasn't really standing in front of his demolished house? He looked so sad."

"That was an actor standing in front of a green screen. Everything else was added in."

"The kid's a good actor, then. He was twanging my heart strings. However it works, he done an awesome job."

"This should provide as many or more jobs for Letherby than the furniture factory did. For now, even having construction crews get started will bring revenue into the town."

"I called Lucy and Ellie and told them the good news. They're already planning a town picnic to celebrate. Lucy was goin' on about persimmon pudding, fried chicken, okra—whatever that is."

"You'd best fly down and find out. You're a hero down there, you know."

"The heroes are them people that never gave up hope for their little town and never gave up faith that God would find a way to help. I think I was more of a hero when I stood on my feet eight hours a day and checked out groceries so I could feed my babies. Lucy and Ellie, they're my heroes."

DIAMOND IN THE ROUGH

Rex spotted Ben waiting just inside the door at the restaurant. It was time to collect on their "bet."

"I hope you don't mind, Ben, but I invited Barry to join us for dinner."

Ben smiled. "What's one more? I am nothing if not a good sport. This will be on my expense account, you understand, as a business expense, since we are discussing a client, are we not?"

The waitress handed them their menus. "Let me know when you are ready to order." Rex nodded.

"So what is the good word, gentlemen?" asked Ben.

"The phones are ringing off the hooks at the Foundation offices," Barry informed him. "Every television station and newspaper wants to do a story about Karen bringing Letherby back to life. Oprah wants to do a special about her. Can you imagine Karen on an Oprah special? You know what a loose cannon she can be."

"Better than just about anyone, yes," Rex answered.

Ben turned to Barry. "What are you going to do to minimize the publicity surrounding this latest endeavor?"

"Nothing, my friend." Barry smiled. "Absolutely nothing."

The waitress returned with a basket of fresh rolls and took their orders. After their orders had been placed, Rex instructed the waitress further. "Please ask them not to cut my prime rib until their steaks are done, because rare will no longer be rare if you leave it on a warming tray while you wait for someone else's shoe leather to be sufficiently

228

shriveled and dried out." Rex glanced pointedly in Barry's direction, since he had ordered a steak, well done.

Over their entrees, the conversation turned back to Karen. "I remember vividly the night she came to confess that she had bought a lottery ticket. She was so obtuse, I thought she was confessing something else entirely." Rex fought his emotions. "She's changed our ward, humbled some of the proudest people I know, and she did it with love, pure unadulterated love. I'm still not even sure how."

Barry wiped his eyes. "Now you've got me started. My doctor said something miraculous has happened to my heart health, as if I was under the influence of a 'steady stream of healing hormones.' "

"She has a bunch of Southern Baptists singing our hymns in North Carolina, and she's got at least one Hells Angel going back to church," Rex added. "But the thing I'm most happy about, for Karen's sake, is that she's got both her children headed in a positive direction. She never gave up on them."

"And she's back with the love of her life," Barry added, "however convoluted the path might have been." He sighed. "It's lonely going through life alone."

"Perhaps you and Karen should never have had your Vegas wedding annulled." Ben laughed.

"You laugh, Mr. Gardner," Barry said. "but I've grown fonder of the lady than I ever thought possible. The attorney/client complication aside, it wouldn't have worked, not without one of us giving up who we truly were, but she filled more of the empty spaces than anyone will ever know."

After the final bite of chocolate mousse, Bishop Parley wiped his mouth with his napkin. "Years ago, our ward was invaded by a woman who had just moved into the Thompsons' basement. She used poor grammar, and she obviously wasn't educated. She didn't fit in with the sophisticated, stylish women in our ward, but it turns out she wasn't the one who needed polishing." He laid his napkin over his plate. "She was the diamond used to polish the rest of us."

Ben Gardner sighed. "It looks like I'm buying dinner."

"Ya think?" Barry and Rex said, simultaneously.

Ben signaled the waitress. "Check, please."

ABOUT THE AUTHOR

    Susan Law Corpany grew up in Salt Lake City, part of the Mormon community for which she writes. She currently lives on the Big Island of Hawaii. She is the mother/stepmother of six children scattered across the western United States. She is an avid reader, as most writers are, and enjoys doing anything creative. She loves making people laugh, spoiling her grandbabies, and traveling the world with her husband, Thom. She believes in lifelong learning and therefore has attended Utah State University and the University of Utah and is currently enrolled at the University of Hawaii in Hilo. Her goal is to inspire her grandchildren by being the oldest graduate of the class of 20?? When not working on a new novel, she manages the family vacation rental home, where she has honed the fine art of towel origami and has finally developed a green thumb.

    Contact the author at susancorpany@aol.com. Also check out her blog at http://paradisepromotions.blogspot.com/.

0 26575 53924 0